FAR STARS, NEW TRADE

Andrew van Aardvark

Table of Contents

1: Surprises in the Dark	1
2: Status Quo in Peril	19
3: Movement	33
4: Sitting Down to Drink	63
5: Mind Games	77
6: Indigestion	97
7: News	123
8: The Shadows Gather	133
9: Plan Meet Enemy	155
10: For a Job Well Done	169
11: Trying	191
12: Some Confrontation	203
13: A Fleet In Being	209
14: Pushing It Home	221
15: Death Ground	229
16: A Battle Fought	237
17: Amidst the Debris	243

Copyright ©2020 Napoleonsims Publishing

www.Napoleonsims..com

Cover Image: Silhouette of Woman(c) Majivecka | Dreamstime.com, Sunrise over Earth (c) Johannes Gerhardus Swanepoel|Dreamstime.com, Spaceship (c) Abidal | Dreamstime.com

All rights reserved.

ISBN-13: 979-8-67030-710-9

1: Surprises in the Dark

Jack dismissed his guards and walked into his private chambers. They were dark.

He always kept the lighting and other controls on manual, but he didn't remember turning the lights off. He reached to turn them on.

"Don't," came a voice out of the gloom. "Don't move."

Jack froze and listened. Looked around as much of the room as he could without moving his head. He picked out a dark patch at the edge of his sight in an armchair in the corner. A dark silhouette, a man likely, as the voice had suggested.

"In particular, don't reach for either of those pistols hidden on your left and right sides," the mystery man's voice said. "If I meant you harm, you'd be dead now."

"Okay," Jack replied. The man was correct. It was a little scary, very annoying, and quite impressive.

There'd been many attempts on Jack's life over the past couple of years. None of those had succeeded. Obviously, he snickered to himself.

"Not your quick thinking that's kept you alive this long, is it?" the voice asked a little impatiently.

"My security chief is very good," Jack said.

"Jackson is one of the best," the voice agreed. "Not going to get much privacy once you report this, are you?"

Jack grimaced. It was true, high security was intrusive as well as awkward. They'd just relaxed it. As well as being uncomfortable for Jack, it put people off.

"Thanks for that," Jack said. "I assume you don't want me to see your face. You do want to talk. I've had a long night. I'd like to be more comfortable than frozen practically mid-step."

The voice chuckled. "There's that famed resilience. You can, moving slowly mind, sit facing the other way on the edge of your bed."

"You have a name?" Jack asked. It never hurt to ask.

Another chuckle. Bastard was enjoying this.

"You can call me 'Bonaparte'," the voice said. "Doesn't entirely fit, but it's unique and memorable."

"Ambitious too," Jack replied. "Moving now," he warned Bonaparte before slowly walking to his bed and sitting on its edge, his back to Bonaparte. Physically, if not psychologically, more comfortable. Seemed Bonaparte was not one to give up an advantage.

"Our time is limited," Bonaparte said. "Imagine you're wondering what this is about?"

"Yes," Jack said. He wanted nothing more than to get to bed and after reporting this to Jackson he was going to be up another couple of hours. Ex-Sergeant Jackson of the Federation marines might technically be his employee, but on matters of security Jack took his direction.

"You're newly powerful, Jack," Bonaparte said. "You know that. Everybody knows that. Bears repeating, though, because it puts you in place to distort the plans of even more powerful interests in an already delicate situation."

"Simply trying to operate a business," Jack said. "A big important business, but just a business. Ad Astra exists to carry cargo from one star to the next and make a profit from it. Getting involved in other people's quarrels isn't profitable."

Bonaparte chuckled again. It was a hollow sound. "I bet you wish that was true," he said. "I think you know it isn't."

Jack sighed. It was true, establishing Ad Astra had involved a lot more politics than he'd ever hope to see, and it had been politics of the violent kind. "Aspirational perhaps at this point," he admitted, "but seriously it's our goal. As a business that deals with many different governments and other parties, we have to be seen to be neutral, not taking sides, or we'll start losing customers."

"Hmmm, an admirable sentiment," Bonaparte said. "How do your Newtonian friends and Captain Taylor feel about that?"

"They may not like it, but I believe they understand the necessity," Jack said.

"Really?" Bonaparte asked.

"Really. You seem well informed. Surely you understand we're walking on the edge of a precipice?"

"Federation has kept too tight of a grip on FTL technology and security in general. If it crumbles or withdraws from the sector interstellar civilization here goes with it."

Jack nodded. "So I've been told," he said. "I believe it. More importantly I think they do. They're not going to jostle me and send us all over the edge."

"Neutral is acceptable to the interests I represent," Bonaparte said. "Watch that you are, Jack."

With that, he shot him.

**

Jack woke with a splitting headache. He was in his quarters, sprawled sideways across the bed. The main in-suite screen was on showing local news, the audio a low mutter.

He took a few seconds to register his surroundings and to remember. With that, his anger spiked. It exacerbated the pain in his head. He sat up and fumbled for the pain killers he'd started keeping in his nightstand.

He was fed up even more than he was angry. Felt like everybody in the sector had been taking turns pushing him around. He'd been reacting too long. Going from one desperate expedient to another. Time for that to change.

First some water to swallow with his pill. Mustn't disturb the scene too much. Jackson, his security chief, would want to go over it with a fine-toothed comb. Right, contact Jackson.

He walked over to his in-suite restroom, popped his pill, took a swallow of water, pulled out his comms unit and stabbed a button.

"Jackson here," a voice responded just seconds later. Jack knew he must have raised Jackson from a sound sleep. Marines and ex-marines always seemed able to sleep soundly, anywhere at anytime. Jackson's voice gave no hint of that to Jack.

"Jack here. We need to talk. My quarters. Now."

"Roger," Jackson replied before hanging up.

Jack had a few minutes to think.

First thing, let's admit it, he was richer, more powerful, and more important than he'd ever imagined he'd be.

If truth be told more than he'd even wanted to be.

He wasn't living on the cheapest rations available, constantly worried about bankruptcy, and vulnerable to the whims of minor functionaries anymore.

That had been the state of his affairs a couple of years ago. His prospects had been that he could expect to die near broke and alone, an unmissed loser, and the only real question was if it would happen sooner or later.

He could eat what he liked now and live in the best hotels too. While traveling he had the owner's cabin on the ships his company owned.

His life expectancy was still uncertain. He'd felt like the duck in a shooting gallery more than once over the last few years. His death would not go unnoticed anymore. Quite the contrary.

He'd been too busy to notice if any of the many flirtatious women he'd met during the social events he was repeatedly required to attend were serious, but there was at least one woman who interested him. She might be moving from the realm of the unattainable to possible.

All in all, if he allowed himself to be honest his life had improved immeasurably.

Also truth be told he didn't mind the danger or hard work involved. He was no stranger to either.

No, it wasn't that that angered him.

It was the feeling that he'd mortgaged his soul. Sold it bit by bit to a dozen different parties. In desperation, he'd made at least implicit promises to hundreds of people in dozens of star systems. He had no idea how he could keep them all. He had at least a third mortgage on his soul.

He owed the Newtonians the most. Dr. Ted Smith had recruited him more than two years ago when he was still a struggling merchant captain, a free trader as the romantics like to call them. Recruited him as an agent of the CHSG, the Current History Studies Group, Newton's external intelligence agency. As far as Jack knew spies didn't get to retire. Not really.

More than that, he'd developed a bond of sorts working in the field with a more conventional CHSG agent. She went by the name of Dr. Cynthia Dallemagne. Young and beautiful, as well as educated and intelligent, she was a deadly combination.

Those were strong ties. The Federation in the form of its naval arm, the SDF, as represented by a Commander James Taylor, had managed to get hooks into him that were as strong.

Jack had been an NCO in the Solarian Defense Force, the SDF. It'd been no picnic, but he'd retired with honor after a long career. His savings plus cashing in his not ungenerous pension had paid for his first small trading ship. He understood and sympathized with the SDF and its goals.

Taylor had provided Jack and Cynthia critical, life saving, support in their mission to expose and bring down the crooked smuggler who'd previously dominated the sector's shipping through a seemingly legitimate front company.

Taylor also sat on the board of directors of the successor company to that one, Ad Astra Ventures. The same company that Jack was both CEO and Chief Operating Officer of.

Even worse Taylor had arranged for Jack to be called back into service with a commission to act as a representative to certain interests on (or arguably beyond) the Frontier.

Jack had multiple employers. Literally.

That was fine as along as their interests mostly coincided and they saw him as a bridge to allies. If it ever changed Jack would be torn in multiple directions.

That was before considering the many promises he'd made to various interests in multiple systems.

The El Doradians on the Frontier with their traditions of blood feud against those they believed to have betrayed them were only the scariest of them.

He'd promised producers on both Jefferson and New Lustania he'd sell their hides and meat. He'd promised to bring back light manufactures in return.

The Hanshanians expected him to sell their tea and mid-tech manufactures. They wanted fuel, food, luxuries, and high tech in return.

The Al-Alhadeenians expected him to sell their coffee, and he'd somehow ended up operating a sort of rescue service for young women of compromised virtue there.

The Heinleinians had bailed him out when he was desperate for extra investment at the cost of an agreement that would let them swoop in and take control of Ad Astra if he stumbled. An agreement that had not pleased his original sponsors back on Newton.

Worse than that, from an SDF or Federation point of view, he'd reached an accommodation with the ideological fanatics of the Marx system.

In exchange for vital, legally strings free, assistance at a critical junction and some generous shipping agreements he'd basically signed on to help paper over the deficiencies of their rather rigid command economy. A command economy the Federation had been hoping would fail for centuries, but somehow never quite had.

Worst of all the SDF likely suspected the Marxians wanted to use him as a conduit to get access to Newton's FTL technology. The outstanding strategic fact of space faring humanity being that only Terra and Newton knew how to manufacture FTL drives.

It meant all of humanity was vulnerable, but neither Earth nor Newton were eager to share their valuable secrets. Though currently allies under the aegis of the Federation, in fact, neither would mind if the other ceased to be a competitor.

It went on and on, he'd promised all sorts of things to get investment and cargoes both.

It was an unholy mess. Once he'd talked to Jackson and got some sleep Jack was going to make it his top priority to figure it out.

He had to stop just reacting.

***

The food served by the Faculty Club of the University of Newton at New Cambridge was superb.

Dr. Edward "Ted" Smith had come to dread his meals there.

It wasn't the company. True, Dr. Michael Blake, Newton's Chief Archivist, was his de facto boss, but he was also a friend. He was reasonable as well as pleasant company.

Unfortunately, the problems they faced were not so pleasant. They were a murky tangle of intractable competing interests.

"You should be happy," Blake was saying. "The Ad Astra operation was brilliantly conceived and has succeeded beyond any reasonable expectation."

"Yes, relative to what could have happened it was way out on the tail end of best cases," Ted admitted. "In fact, it was not much short of a miracle."

Blake smiled. A thin, saturnine expression.

"I have faith in you, Ted," he said. "I think you can learn from your successes as well as your mistakes."

From the Chief Archivist it was an extraordinary compliment. His position and temperament were both semi-judicial. He gathered and resolved information. He rarely expressed opinions. His censures were infrequent and always moderate in tone. His praises were rare to the point of non-existence. What he'd just said was his equivalent of shouting Ted's praises from the rooftops.

"Thank you," Ted said. He meant it. "That means a lot coming from you, Michael."

"It's true and has context," Blake said. "I'm not just expressing a sentiment."

"Right," Ted said. This was a debriefing more than a pleasant meal between friends. The Chief Archivist wanted his summary of what had happened. He wanted Ted's assessment of what had gone right and what had gone wrong. He wanted some indicators, solid action points, and goals would be better, but he wanted some indicators of what that meant for their future plans. "First, we didn't do this alone. Jack Black was key and a surprise to the upside."

"Granted," Blake said. "Where do his loyalties really lie?"

"I doubt he's completely sure of that himself," Ted replied. "In neither of his past careers did he have any reason to distinguish between different governments. As far as the old Jack Black was concerned they were all 'The Authorities' to be placated as needed and avoided as much as possible."

"He was an NCO in the SDF," Blake said. "He swore an oath to the Federation."

"As has every significant formal official throughout human settled space," Ted replied. "You and me, and those like us, we've always been aware of the political fissures in the Federation and thought about where we stand in respect to them. The common folk see the Federation as a monolith. It's just a fact of life they have to deal with."

"Surely the SDF is more concerned about the loyalty of its members than that," Blake said.

"Here's something we can do better in the future," Ted replied. "In the past, I've always focused on briefing you about questions we've been specifically directed to investigate."

"Yes, it's too easy to get lost in a deluge of complicated information," Blake said. "It's important to stay focused."

"I believe filtered and focused might have become tunnel vision," Ted said. "I think our reports need to be more broad spectrum and to promote more situational awareness. I think they should include more purely background facts."

Blake pursed his lips slightly and briefly stared at a distant point beyond the wood-paneled walls of the room they were in. He was giving the matter genuine thought. "Agreed," he finally said. "Modify your reports to have a wider scope and to proactively answer questions not asked."

"Thank you," Ted said. "Case in point, to get back to our original discussion, the SDF is greatly concerned with the loyalty of its officer corps. Most of them go to the Academy on Earth where they are assimilated to the Terran elite if they weren't already part of it."

"Most of them?" Blake asked.

"Oddly enough," Ted said, "people from Earth or people who've become comfortable there don't like spending years on the Frontier or on one of the middle worlds. The SDF recruits officers from the ranks and by direct entry there, but only in sufficient numbers to fill lower local slots that might otherwise go unoccupied. Those officers never get promoted beyond Commander. They rarely get beyond Lieutenant Commander."

"Hmmm, interesting," Blake said. "You'd expect that to raise resentment."

"Surprisingly little," Ted replied. "In practice it's almost like there are two organizations that only interact in a limited, very formal way. The SDF beyond the Core is mostly small units with commanders of local origin. The few senior officers of Core origin either don't stay long or when they do stay long tend to become assimilated to the local cultures."

"A key point in the event they decide to pull back to the Core," Blake observed. "I'd not been aware of this. It appears to validate your earlier point."

"I believe so," Ted said rather smugly. "Have to stay somewhat focused. They pay little to no attention to what their enlisted personnel think. The men and women in the ranks are expected to be competent and follow orders."

"Seems unexpectedly rigid," Blake said. "Oddly enough on thing your man Black does not seem to be is rigid. Stubborn, yes, but adaptable."

"True, likely less fixed in his ways than most of his colleagues," Ted said, "but in general the SDF's NCOs appear to carry greater responsibility than they get credit for."

"If true a fact worth further investigation," Blake said.

"I'll follow up," Ted said. "You shouldn't think, however, that it implies any widespread disloyalty. The NCO corps might be disgruntled at not being recognized for their efforts, but doubtless very few have ever considered active disloyalty to the Federation. Like the common folk in general the Federation is just a fact of life that they take for granted."

"So they're all perfectly loyal to the Federation?"

"The odd one has been bribed by local authority, pirates, or crooks to supply information. A lot of them seem to have scams of varying legality on the side, but an active desire to undermine the Federation or loyalties to other actors, I've found no indication of those."

"So loyal, but in an unquestioning, untested passive way," Blake said.

"Just so," Ted confirmed.

"How much of this do you have from Black himself?" Blake asked quizzically while spearing a small piece of meat.

"I started investigating it because of conversations with him but followed up through other channels," Ted replied. "Turns out many rankers will talk your ear off for the price of a drink. There was even a thesis on the composition of the SDF. It was from a generation ago and had been gathering dust on the shelf."

"Black, does he retain this unquestioning loyalty to the Federation?" Blake asked.

"Jack has been forced to start thinking for himself," Ted said.

"Could be dangerous," Blake said with a smirk.

"It's a different psychological world, Michael," Ted said flatly. "Having looked into it, I'm surprised it doesn't entirely grind the ability to think out of the people in it."

"My apologies, Ted," Blake said. "I take the point seriously. Are we going to have to start a special division to investigate and document the worldview of various groups? Something along the lines of the system cultural studies you've been doing for me the last few years."

"It's a good idea, but it'll require additional resources," Ted said with resignation. His superiors frequently assured him of the importance of the work he did, but seemed determined to keep him working on a relative shoestring.

"Cheer up," Blake said. "Recent events have the board spooked and a bit antsy."

"That's not good," Ted said.

"Hence the grilling," Blake said. "They want reassuring answers. On the other hand, they're willing to throw some money at you if you promise it'll ward the bogeyman off."

"I'm not feeling reassured myself," Ted said.

"The Ad Astra operation was a huge departure for us," Blake said. "I think maybe you're too close to the trees to see the forest. What might have seemed a series of field expedients to you was a huge strategic break viewed from further away."

"It'll be a welcome change to step away from immediate operations and take a wider view for a period," Ted agreed.

"Good, please do that, Ted," Blake said. "While doing so consider that while success can cover over indiscretions such as being less than candid with one's colleagues, it doesn't mean they went unnoticed."

Ted swallowed. He'd gone out on a limb to allow Jack Black the freedom to make the decisions he needed to. He'd not lied to any of his colleagues on Newton, neither had he failed to inform them of any pertinent facts he was aware of. He had been careful not to inquire after facts he didn't want to know. "It doesn't work to micromanage over interstellar distances," he said, looking Blake straight in the eye. He had to stand his ground on this.

"Trivially true on the face of it," Blake replied.

"But?" Ted asked after the implied qualification.

"But," Blake answered, "even if we accept the need to appoint potentates with wide ranging powers and discretion to represent our interests in other systems we're going to want to be very sure of them. Sure of their competence. Sure of their loyalty."

"You can count on Jack Black to be Jack Black," Ted said. "He believes in order achieved with as little violence and as much consensus as possible. He'll be loyal to his friends. He'll be true to his word. He will not be corrupted by wealth, women, or power."

Blake raised his eyebrows at Ted. Newtonian academics were as a habit measured and nuanced. Passionate absolutes were not usually part of their vocabulary. "A ringing endorsement," he said.

"True," Ted agreed, "but deserved. Also not just of Captain Black himself. It speaks well of the system that produced him. The Federation for all its imperfections and despite the crippling problems it now faces has done an immense amount of good for humanity."

"Yes, the Federation," Blake acknowledged. "One of the most disturbing revelations to come out of this mess was that a Federation faction exists that's willing to send an assassination team into the middle worlds, apparently with the aim of promulgating chaos."

"Couldn't agree more," Ted said. "Might I point out having a Federation spec ops team taking a shot at killing him undoubtedly cured Black of any unthinking loyalty to the Federation bureaucracy."

"He was saved by only nominally retired Federation marines, and you've already said he still believes in the Federation's values."

"Yes, and he can see that some high officers in its institutions have betrayed those ideals. They crossed a line with this. Furthermore, it's an action that only makes sense if they see the Federation as bound to fail. That attack might make sense for Terran partisans, but it doesn't for Federation officers working for all of humanity. The only plausible outcome of Black's death and Ad Astra's failure was chaos in the sector."

"My turn to agree," Blake said, smiling thinly. "Yet another blank check for you. You must develop sources of information on what's going on in the Federation bureaucracy on Earth."

"Wish I could cash it," Ted said. "I'm afraid it's going to take time and care to build up sources. It's a tough problem. The personnel flow tends to be all one way from the Core to the outer worlds. There aren't many candidates for potential sources."

"I trust you'll do what you can," Blake said.

"Of course," Ted said. "You realize that we'll likely be losing Taylor as an ally in the sector?"

"But they'll assign him to the Core, won't they?" Blake asked.

"Yes, but he is an ally not an asset and having independent command he is important locally, but will be a small fish in a big pond back in the Solar System."

"I see," Blake said. "You've heard rumors of SDF redeployments?"

"Yes," Ted said. "Nothing solid but personnel analysis suggests some sort of surge to this sector."

"You seem strangely calm," Blake observed. "Isn't our FTL engine production the Federation's most important strategic asset in the sector?"

"Indeed," Ted agreed. "The concentration of FTL production here and in the Solar System is the overwhelming strategic fact of our era. But to be clear, Michael, we're utterly defenseless against the SDF and Federation. The smallest of their corvettes could hang in orbit and destroy our production capability completely or sterilize the planet at will."

"Ouch," Blake said. "That bad? I mean, it's so unthinkable that I'm afraid I've never given the issue any consideration."

"Bottom line, the SDF doesn't need to redeploy to take care of Newton," Ted said. "Pirates of which there are none I know of, or the Beyonders are the only logical targets."

"The Beyonders?" Blake asked. "Why?"

"A preliminary to bringing us all under control and making us pay taxes to keep the Federation going."

Dr. Blake stared at Ted. "Strictly speaking that's logical," he said slowly. "It's also unimaginable. They must know no local system government would stand for it."

"And with every local source of military power suppressed what could we do about it?" Ted asked.

"As is, not much," Blake conceded reluctantly.

"It's a whole Brave New World," Ted said.

* * *

Jack was shopping. Shopping for bric-a-brac.

He was not a people person. He'd never had much time for stuff. Impediments. Things that didn't serve a clear and immediate purpose.

But here he was, shopping in an upscale station mall for high end mementos for some of the many people he'd somehow acquired in his life.

With some effort, he could make a convincing business case for it.

Sure he could.

Jack looked around at the bright glittering concourse, only moderately crowded with well dressed and well behaved shoppers. He could see a stationery store, "Pleasing Paper" and the usual computer store "Good Bytes". Chain stores, branches of which you could find anywhere there were people with a little extra money. Most of the store fronts had purely local names though.

"Revere's Silverware", for instance, what was that about?

"Revere" was no doubt some old American of note, this being the Jefferson system, references to the old United States of America and its mythology were everywhere.

Jack wandered that way.

His guards trailed behind him. At least with them along he shouldn't be mistaken for a vagrant and end up being hassled by the concourse's security. Didn't happen these days, but Jack still had unpleasant memories of how he'd been treated by minor functionaries when he'd been less prosperous.

He assumed "silverware" was made from the metal. Ought to be less fragile than fine china, which was another sort of gift he was thinking of getting for his friend and associate, Mary Waldgreen, back on Slovo Station.

His guards, although large, were admittedly anything but clumsy, but still Jack mentally cringed at the idea of the little group of them meandering through a shop packed with china and glassware.

Just as he did at the idea of finding a tasteful gift for Mary. She ran a shop that sold high end unique and very tasteful curiosities.

It was largely on her advice that he was looking for small gifts from other systems for his various friends and contacts. "It shows that you're thinking of them outside of your immediate business dealings," she'd said.

He'd been thankful for that advice at the time.

He had the navigation and operation parts of being an

interstellar trader down pat. He understood ships and space, and even spacers pretty well. He'd also learned the financial mechanics of being in business, through hard work and some sharp learning experiences. The people part of business, managing employees, and building up useful associations with other business people, that part of the business was still a work in progress. He was grateful for all the help he could get.

"You going to go in, sir?" one his guards, Miller, asked. He'd been through a lot with Miller. The "sir" was simple professionalism. Despite his apparently deferential tone, the man was chiding him for being a wimp.

"Just getting the lay of the ground," Jack said. Marines, his were technically ex-marines, rarely saw combat on a planetary surface but still like to hark back to their roots in pre-history.

"Don't think silverware bites, sir," Miller replied. "Never heard it shoots at you or blows up either."

"You know how to make shopping exciting, Miller," Jack said. The other guard snorted. "You want to pick out a gift for Miss Waldgreen?"

"No, sir. Not my job."

"Maybe you'd do better finding something for Dr. Dallemagne?"

"No, sir." Miller retorted with feeling. "No offense, sir, but that woman is like a good fighting knife. Pretty to look at, but nothing you want to idly play with."

Jack tried to choke back a snort. Unsuccessfully. "I should tell her you said so," he said.

"Please, sir, no." Miller replied.

"You owe me," Jack said.

"Yes, sir."

"Okay," Jack said. "Let's do this." With that, he moved into the silverware shop.

It wasn't unpleasant inside.

Calm, tasteful, quiet except for the fading low tinkle of the bells that had been triggered by their entry.

It was a lot less cluttered than most of the curiosity shops Jack had been in too.

As expected a wide variety of items made of silver were on display. Most of them seemed to have some utilitarian value as forks, knives, spoons, platters, or tea services, but they were being presented as if they were works of art. Given some of the elegant curves and fancy etching to be seen Jack figured that was fair.

The most prominent display, almost a chapel in tone, was set against the back wall.

Museum quality glass cases held a variety of tea services, candlesticks, and even belt buckles, all made of silver. The wall behind them held a variety of prints, behind non-shiny glass. Jack had recently learned it was called "matte glass". Generally it was used in framing expensive art.

The prints didn't look like expensive art. They looked kind of crude really, but old showing people in old fashioned, pre-space age costumes. That and the carefully arranged but subdued lighting suggested the prints were valuable and therefore of historical value. Which was odd.

Jack had seen displays like this before, but only in videos made about museums back on Earth.

"Yes, this all belongs in a museum, not in my humble shop," came a voice from just behind him.

Damn, it startled him. What had happened to his situational awareness? Woolgathering like this at the wrong time could get him killed. He turned to the voice.

A short, but very erect woman in late middle age stood there, primly dressed in some sort of period costume. Wide skirts billowed around her. Her hair was tightly held back in a bun. It was black with streaks of gray. Her appearance politely screamed defiance of modern mores.

"I'm Jack Black. What's the story then?"

"Anne Hitchborn," the woman replied. "Paul Revere was a revolutionary. These prints in particular document that. Back when Jefferson was first being colonized the authorities on Earth weren't interested in preserving anything that suggested revolution was possible, let alone desirable."

Jack was no born politician, but he'd managed to pick up a few clues in the last couple of years. He made a noncommittal noise of interest.

"Revere was a hero of the American Revolution as well as a talented silversmith," Anne continued.

"So these are valuable museum pieces and not for sale?" Jack asked. "That's too bad I know a young woman back on Newton with a doctorate in history who'd love to own anything here."

"Your reputation proceeds you, Captain Black," Anne replied. "You're right, normally none of these articles would be for sale."

"But?" Jack asked hopefully.

"I'm willing to believe that I can trust you, and if the lady in question is who I think it is, her, to properly care for artifacts like these," Anne said.

"Dr. Dallemagne?"

"Indeed," Anne confirmed. "The young lady has acquired quite the reputation in certain circles."

"There's something you're not saying," Jack observed.

"There's much I'm not saying," Anne said. "Most immediately we haven't discussed price. I won't part with even the least valuable of the items here for anything less than a not so small fortune. There would also be expensive conditions on how the items are stored and displayed."

Jack winced.

"We both know you can afford it," Anne went on. "If you want to. If it's important to you."

"And you think it ought to be?" Jack asked.

"Yes, I do," Anne replied with a little lift of her chin. "I'll be more forward than is my normal wont. You're new. You need to show who you are and what you want. The right purchases here for the right people will send several important signals."

"Including, I guess, that I'm willing to spend large sums of money on sending signals," Jack grumbled.

Anne stared coldly at Jack for a second before responding. "Yes."

Jack grunted.

"You're dealing with a different class of people now, Captain Black," Anne said primly. "You have to show you know that and that you're willing to act like it. You have to show you're not just a spacer who lucked into a lot of money, and temporarily, power."

Jack wasn't about to say he wasn't sure at all himself that wasn't the case.

Anne seeing his hesitation might have smiled. A very small, thin smile. "Sadly one way of demonstrating one's power and wealth is by wasting both wealth and time."

"Time is one thing I don't have a lot of," Jack said.

"And yet here you are spending time finding expensive items of no immediately obvious utility to spend money on," Anne replied. Her smile, and amusement, were obvious now.

"I like to think I'm a reasonable man," Jack said. He wished the woman would get to the point.

"Reason only goes so far," Anne replied with a hint of sympathy. "First things first. Dr. Dallemagne. Doubtless you wish you could spend more of your precious time with her but you can't. So you must demonstrate your commitment by spending money, in a way that moves you out of your comfort zone and shows your willingness to accommodate her sensibilities and interests."

Jack had thought he was well past being romantically embarrassed and blushing. Apparently not. He hoped it didn't show. "Sounds good," he said.

Anne gave a little nod and shifted her gaze to one of the prints on the wall. "There are very few copies of this print remaining. It's a unique historical artifact that will make her the envy of her colleagues. I believe she will also enjoy it for itself."

Jack peered at the crude drawing of red-coated soldiers firing on a crowd of civilians. "Bloody mess. You really think so?" he said.

"Yes, and if she displays it publicly it'll send an important signal," Anne said somewhat grimly.

"A signal?" Jack asked. "What sort of signal?"

"The Newtonians were never revolutionaries," Anne answered. "To be frank they've always been elitists. Ivory Tower types at best. Here in Jefferson we've never forgotten our roots. Our forefathers were willing to fight for their liberty when they needed to. If they're willing to display this print publicly it will hint they understand that."

Jack was glad he trusted his guards. It bothered him not a little that this Anne Hitchborn did too. It felt too much like she'd been waiting for him. He wondered who she truly represented. He knew too that it'd do no good to ask.

"Okay," he said. "How much are you asking?"

She smiled widely. "Does it matter?"

"No," Jack sighed.

"You have other people you'd like buy gifts for? Our tea sets are very popular with discerning individuals."

He bought a couple of them. He bargained with her for them, but couldn't shake the feeling she was just humoring him.

For all that he couldn't help feeling pleased that he'd found such suitable gifts.

He had friends now. He wanted them to know he appreciated them.

2: Status Quo in Peril

Newton had based the organization of its intelligence agencies on the model of the liberal democracies as they existed just prior to and after the beginning of the space age.

Idealistically speaking the colony had been consciously set up to embody the best of what those entities represented. Thinking practically those ancient nations had spent centuries in long, often close, struggles with their rivals and they'd largely triumphed.

It was an open question whether the formation of the Federation had been another success on their part, but it had certainly incorporated many of their institutions and paid fulsome lip service to their ideals.

The question was not one Dr. Ted Smith had given much consideration since his undergraduate years.

As he sat in his calm and comfortable home office and mulled over the matter it was a question that acquired a new importance. A matter that acquired a new and very practical urgency in fact.

One of the key principles those states had followed was a stringent separation between domestic and foreign intelligence organizations.

It was a principle Ted Smith was currently having a great deal of difficulty with.

It was bad enough that Newton was technically a part of the Federation he'd just been asked to spy on. Gathering information on co-equal competitors within the Federal system that was one thing. Actually penetrating the institutions that he was as a Federation citizen supposed to be loyal to. Now that was another thing.

It looked like at least some members of those institutions were betraying the ideals the Federation was supposed to stand for. Somehow that didn't help Ted feel better.

Ted ran a finger across the wood of his desk. It was real wood. The desk was an heirloom of genuine solid wood. It'd come to Newton from Earth with the first colonists and been in the family ever since. His grandmother had given it to him as a graduation gift.

"Keep this as a reminder of the importance of quality and tradition," she'd said at the time. "Pass it on when you've done your bit."

He'd been comfortable with the advice. Then. Back then at the beginning of his career he'd had no doubts about either her standards or his ability to live up to them.

Back then his desk had been a comforting link to the homeworld and a welcome reminder of the importance of a family that had always been good to him.

Earth would always be humanity's homeworld and although he recognized that sooner or later her children would have to leave the nest, he regretted it was coming so soon and in his time. The oldest trees on Newton in the few locations they could grow on the mostly desert planet were only now reaching the size of the one the wood in his desk had come from. It seemed too soon.

He could live with that though, sad as the impending break was.

No, the source of most of his angst was much closer to home.

Quite literally.

Earlier that evening, before the onset of the nighttime hours in which he did most of his real work, he'd been at one of the regular family dinners. Dinners, however inconvenient they might be for a man with a busy schedule, that he usually ended up enjoying.

The wife of one of his older brothers had let something slip.

He might not have noticed it if Michael hadn't been at such

pains to get her to change the topic and then to minimize its importance. Michael wasn't naturally easy-going but at these dinners he was usually relaxed and indulgent.

Michael, the family's fair-haired boy, educated as a physicist which was to say a "real scientist", was also the CEO of Stardrives Inc.. The firm manufactured the FTL drives that ensured Newton's place in the universe. There wasn't a more important or more prestigious job on the entire planet. Truthfully in the sector.

Usually Ted managed not to be jealous. He was resigned to his family's perception of him as a scribbler, a mere scholar, not a scientist, with his head in the past who spent his time sorting through dry old records. He could hardly tell them what his real job was.

Be all that as it may, Michael generally wore his importance pretty lightly. "Place runs like a well-oiled machine. There really isn't much for me to do," he'd once said.

So when Maria his wife had off handedly remarked that it was good he was getting a little time to relax from work, it'd caught the attention of his mother who'd asked when that had started.

"Been about a year now," Maria had said. "He won't talk about it."

Ted had been talking to another brother, Fred, about designing scientific instruments for the export market. "You can't assume they know anything," Fred had been saying. He only noticed the conversation between Maria and his mother in passing with a small corner of his mind.

The tense but quiet "Maria!" his brother had directed at his wife had startled him.

So much so he'd failed to completely hide the fact.

"Sorry, if I'm boring you," Fred had said.

"No, no," Ted had replied. "Just made me think. You know my group is studying current changes in trade patterns. Lots of moving parts, and it reminded me of something else."

In fact, what he'd noticed was that his older brother, the head of Newton's FTL production, had suddenly become busy at just the same time Jack Black had discovered a warehouse full of purloined FTL drives being smuggled out to a pirate base.

Ted had always assumed they'd been diverted after being turned over to the Navy. The mandate of his organization, the Current History Studies Group, the CHSG, was an external one.

He wasn't supposed to worry about or interfere in matters internal to Newton.

The tradition he was from held that allowing externally focused intelligence agencies to become interested in internal matters always ended up distorting their operations. Even if they did not end up interfering in internal issues in an inappropriate fashion it weakened the external efforts that they were supposed to focus on.

He'd never questioned that tradition before.

But if there were factions on Newton, in his own family in fact, that were co-operating with outside interests to undermine the status quo and against the wishes of the rest of Newton's leadership, he clearly couldn't ignore that.

It wasn't clear what he could do though.

It wasn't even clear who he could trust.

Ted's world was crumbling around him. He was not happy.

Didn't mean he'd shirk his duties. Either his formal ones or the ones that might lie a little outside of his formal job description.

He'd be damned careful, he'd just try to gather information in a low key deniable way, and he'd gather the resources to act if it became necessary.

He'd not hurry it more than he had to.

Unfortunately, he wasn't sure how much time they had. Not as much as he'd like.

**

One of the perks of being the owner of a shipping company was you got your own cabin and office aboard your ships.

Jack felt guilty that he'd didn't appreciate it more. For all that he'd got used to his space aboard *The Bird of Profit* he missed his cozy niche in the tiny multi-purpose mess on his personal ship, the *Meal Ticket*. Sadly, the *Meal Ticket* was laid up and not really paying her way anymore. He really didn't want to think about that too much right now. And to be sure a private office of his own was more a necessity he needed to do his job than it was some sort of personal luxury.

He was wool gathering. It was easy to do when you were trying to avoid a thorny issue that required decisions you didn't want to make.

They were outbound from Slovo Station for Newton. They

hadn't done much more than pause there to quickly offload some cargo and take on some more. Under other circumstances Jack would have been impressed by the efficiency of his people both on board ship and at the station. In fact, he'd have to remember to commend them somehow. At least mention he was pleased.

He'd gotten a data dump from Newton at Slovo Station. To all external appearances it was nothing but the necessary but boring paperwork required by the running of any large widely spread out company.

Appearances can be deceiving. Buried in the reams of spreadsheets dealing with the prices of spices, farm tools, and teas, and the various FYI personal memos was a message. A message important enough to be carefully obfuscated as well as hidden, and then one pad encrypted with the most random key the geniuses of Newton's Math department could devise.

A message from Dr. Edward "Ted" Smith. Maybe his boss, maybe a colleague, certainly an ally he couldn't ignore.

You would have thought given the extreme security of the channel he was using that "Ted" could have been a bit less vague or even have given Jack some clear orders, or at least suggestions.

No such luck.

Most of the communication was pointers to other pieces of information in the public domain. Things already part of the information dumps Jack got as a matter of routine. None of the little stories pointed to was of any significance or importance on their own.

A destroyer canceled leave on New Shetland. A party of junior officers just graduated from the Academy were interviewed at Tau Ceti on their way out to assume posts on the Frontier as part of a new program to give graduates more exposure to the Frontier. Prices of dried food had spiked on Newton, apparently because of purchasing by SDF victualers. A young socialite on Earth was complaining about the Federation bureaucracy failing to accommodate her wedding plans. All the stories related to the SDF, the Federation's navy.

Jack as a veteran could read between the lines. The SDF was planning a major operation in the sector. Something very unusual, something that had not happened since the anti-pirate campaigns of almost a decade before.

And how did that affect Jack Black and his company, Ad

Astra? Dr. Smith was less than clear about that.

He'd been clear about not being clear. "These rumors that the SDF will be making a major push in the sector might be wrong," Dr. Smith had written. "But I don't think so," he'd gone on. "I think the push is coming, and it's going to be one unprecedented in size likely aimed at extending the Federation's territory into what is now Beyonder space."

Jack reread that. It was like something out of a bad speculative fiction video. The head of the Current History Studies Group, probably one of humanity's best informed individuals and not one given to sick jokes, was completely serious. He'd underlined the point. "I know this is hard to believe, Jack, but please take me seriously. It's urgent that you do."

Not just "important" or "serious" or "necessary" rather "urgent". The good doctor wanted Jack to do something, and soon. What?

And that's where the equivocation began. Jack reviewed the next part as calmly and attentively as he could.

"The government of Newton, and the University as part of that government, will, of course, support the Federation to the full extent that they are able," Smith wrote.

"*Sure,*" Jack thought, "*like the government of Newton wasn't a sock puppet for the University and it didn't have a distinct agenda of its own.*"

Still, that part was pretty clear, however obliquely stated. Newton was going to keep its head down and didn't intend to give the Federation and the SDF any hint that it wasn't fully supportive of whatever it was they thought they were doing.

Reasonable, if cowardly. It wasn't like they had a navy of their own that could defy the Federation. Worse, they had families and other civilians living in large numbers on a planetary surface. Planets were great for living life as people were meant to. Unfortunately, they were also completely naked to attack from even the smallest force in local space.

Nobody had ever actually attacked a planetary surface from space, not even during the worse of the Troubles back on Earth. The Federation had been formed to prevent that, and so far it'd been successful. It was the reason it enjoyed as much support as it did.

God help them all if the Federation broke down.

Too bad it looked like it was doing just that, and that some genocidal fools back on Earth seemed to have decided that the way to protect themselves from that part of humanity that lived outside of the Solar System was a preemptive strike to drive them back to the dark ages before space travel.

Good Lord, thinking about the multiple different ways this could go wrong was giving Jack a headache.

The bunch that had organized this rumored push against the Beyonders looked like yet another faction. One that thought strengthening the Federation's hold outside the Solar System, not withdrawing, was the way to go.

Jack could sympathize with that. Too bad he didn't think the idea had a snowball's chance in hell of succeeding, and that it was likely to fail in a horrific and costly manner.

Jack tried not to sigh yet again. He was doing too much of that. It didn't project the image of a confident leader who knew what to do.

It was going to take some outstanding leadership to rescue something from this dog's breakfast.

There was no way the SDF had the logistics train to support an operation like this.

Transport ships just aren't sexy. Officers looked upon them as career death. Politicians preferred to allocate funds for destroyers, cruisers, and even bigger ships they could hold receptions for their allies on.

The large units and fleets of the SDF were all based back in the Core and rarely left it. The units based elsewhere were small, generally fighter squadrons for local defense and patrol craft to maintain a somewhat greater presence. There were few of them in the middle worlds, even on the Frontier given how big it was they were thinly spread. In most places it wasn't hard for them t maintain themselves off of the local economy.

Some of the more distant Frontier bases had purpose-built dedicated support facilities, but those were extraordinarily expensive, and therefore rare. They were also very limited in their capacity.

Any major SDF push was going to require obtaining transport ships from the local economy. In this case that meant Jack' ships.

Jack didn't think so.

Hard to tell the only navy around straight up "no" though. Particularly since they had the full legal authority to requisition what they needed, and he had to have their good will to operate anyway.

Somehow he was going to regretfully just not have the ships available.

Nice to have a clear goal.

Not that the idea of trying to defy the SDF and Federation didn't make him sick to his stomach. Not that it wasn't going to be very tricky indeed to execute on that goal.

***

Jack wanted to take another pill. His head was killing him.

He'd thought he'd had a goal and a plan for achieving it.

He was beginning to have serious doubts regards both points.

None of his associates here on Newton wanted to be seen talking to him. Unfortunate given what a lovely day it was in New Cambridge's university district. It would have pleasant to have been sharing his tea with any of them. The mid-morning sun penetrated into the open-air patio where Jack was sitting with enough force to warm him without being unduly harsh. The sounds of traffic beyond the pedestrian mall were subdued. The sounds of birds singing and people moving about a quiet counterpoint to them.

And nobody wanted to be there. Nobody wanted to be seen talking to him. Not encouraging.

Jack took a deep breath, relaxed, and tried to enjoy his pleasant surroundings. Surroundings so different from the narrow metal corridors and small compartments full of overused air he'd spent most of his life in.

It wasn't personal, he told himself. In any case, being emotional didn't make for good decisions in a complicated situation. He had to think, and he had to think dispassionately.

Once Jack had started on a course of action he didn't like to give up. He really didn't like to give up. He was no quitter. Never had been.

That stubborn determination had served him well.

Didn't mean it was always appropriate.

Worse, he wasn't the only one who'd suffer if the chances he took now didn't pan out. A lot of other people stood to suffer too.

A dozen or so who he knew as individuals, and many, many more he didn't, but who were real people despite that.

As far as Jack could tell he no longer had any good choices. It looked like all his options resulted in someone's ox getting gored.

The strong hint Ted Smith had left him that the SDF was likely to try and press all or some of his shipping fleet into service annoyed him to no end.

Jack didn't like the idea of all he had worked for being taken over by officious bureaucrats. He was less than impressed by the unwillingness of any of his supposed allies and friends to stand by his side.

Still, wasn't there some old saying about anger giving bad advice? If there wasn't there ought to be. And the heavens knew he was angry.

Best tamp that down and try to think about it from another point of view. What were the arguments for not being stubborn and bucking the SDF and by extension the Federation?

Well for one he didn't own a crystal ball. He didn't know for sure what the SDF was going to be doing. He knew even less about how it might work out. It might be best if they succeeded in whatever it was they were trying to do. He didn't know. He couldn't know could he? Additionally, even if the SDF operation failed, it might still be better for Jack, Ad Astra, Newton, and the rest of the trading network if he went along with the SDF's efforts.

Again he had no way of knowing for sure, and there was no doubt at all that the SDF and the Federation would be powerful enemies to have.

Witness his current de facto persona non grata status. Nobody in their right minds had any doubt of that particular fact.

So maybe the best thing Jack could do regards Dr. Smith's unwelcome news was nothing at all.

Maybe he should wait on events and if the SDF asked to take over his ships to support some operation to give his whole hearted help as cheerfully as possible.

Certainly that was the conventional thing for any loyal Federation citizen to do. Nobody could fault him for that.

So why not?

What could go wrong?

Well, there was the fact that he had contracts to supply various parties goods that required he have those ships available. But if the Federation requisitioned the ships, could he be legally held to those contracts?

How much time and money would end up tied up in court in that event? How much help could he expect from the Federation for the trouble they'd caused him?

Could he expect them to compensate him for the lost profits he'd forfeit?

Likely couldn't expect any compensation for the trust lost and the relationships destroyed. With the best will in the many worlds, some of his clients would have their own businesses devastated by a failure on his part to ship their goods to market. They were taking risks based on his promises he'd deliver those goods. If he failed they might lose more than they could afford. They'd be less willing to take the same risks again even if they didn't.

Jack didn't like the idea of breaking his promises.

There was a time he'd sworn to support the Federation by serving in the SDF, even at the risk of his own life.

Well that was a while ago and there was more than just his own life at stake now.

Guess that was it. Guess that was his decision there.

There were just too many people depending on the promises he'd made on Ad Astra's behalf. He was going to have to do whatever he could to make sure he could fulfill those promises.

Somehow he was going to have to keep his ships out of the SDF's hands.

* * *

The happiest day of John Malcolm's life was the day he graduated from the Academy. He'd been a newly minted ensign in the SDF. He had anticipated a long, productive career in that organization. It wasn't to be.

John Malcolm was a sleeper agent.

A Federation sleeper agent, and so as far the public, all his associates, and friends knew he'd resigned his commission over a decade before. He'd spent that decade in the Jefferson system pretending to be disillusioned with the Federation and especially the way Earth ran it.

Nothing could have been further from the truth he felt deep in his heart, which was that the Federation was the best thing that had ever happened to the human race.

Moreover he firmly believed that Earth had been if anything far too lax, lazy in fact, in its control of the Federation. He was convinced malcontents like the founders and current inhabitants of Jefferson system had been allowed far too much free rein. That discontent and wrong headed political theories had been allowed to fester like an infection of humanity's political body.

John Malcolm believed it was past time someone administered the antibodies to that infection. He intended to be part of the course of treatment. He intended to be that despite what it had, and likely would, cost him personally.

He'd left more than a bright career behind on Earth. He'd left behind the girl, the woman now, who he'd hoped to spend his life with.

He turned over and looked at his actual wife. Another woman, and one he'd come to love. One who loved the man she thought she knew, but who would be appalled by who he really was.

She stirred. "What's wrong, dear?" she said sleepily.

"Can't sleep, Louise," he replied. "I think I might as well get a little work done. Go back to sleep."

"Need your sleep," Louise slurred, burying her head in her pillow.

"Yes, dear. You're right," John replied. "I'll be back shortly. Just need to get some ideas out of my system."

"Kay, promise?"

"Promise," he answered. "Half hour, forty minutes at most."

He wasn't sure she'd heard him. A few minutes later she started to snore lightly.

He slipped out of bed carefully so as to not disturb her rest and made his way to the little room that served as his home office.

It contained nothing obviously incriminating, but it was where he would let his thoughts depart from those appropriate to the role he was playing.

He sat down, leaned his chin on his hand, took a deep breath, and sighed. It was like he was surfacing after a deep dive.

He let his mind relax, and his thoughts drift for a few minutes.

It was a little ritual he performed periodically in the privacy of his own mind.

It was necessary to making the transition from thinking like who he pretended to be, to thinking like who he really was. At least making it without too much psychological pain.

He sighed. He'd known the job wouldn't be easy when he took it on.

So far on this decade long mission, he'd done nothing to betray those he was embedded among. Nothing more than pretending to be someone he wasn't and sending regular reports back to Earth.

That and recruiting a set of contacts and agents.

It looked like that was about to change. He couldn't be sure. His masters back in the Solar System weren't sharing more about their plans than they had to. Good tradecraft that was, and professionally John approved. Still, he couldn't help but worry that they no longer fully trusted him after his having been out in the cold so long.

He knew he was being silly. They knew their business. They'd been doing this sort of thing for centuries.

He had his doubts about himself, but his bosses must be sure of him or they'd not have given him this job. If he couldn't believe in himself he had to have faith in them. He had to trust that when the time came, he'd be able to do what was necessary no matter how emotionally painful it might be.

Still, he'd known the job might require betrayal, extortion, murder, and the sabotage of Jeffersonian economic interests when he'd taken it on, but his most recent orders had suggested actions even more extreme than those.

He hoped he was wrong. He hoped his suspicions were ill founded. Ideally, he was being excessively paranoid. Paranoia was a natural hazard in his situation. It really was not part of his job to speculate on the reasons for the things he was asked to do.

It was hard not to though. It'd take a blind man not to see the nature of some of the requests that had come his way.

He was being asked for ways to destroy whole habitats and parts of the entire sector's economy. Parts of the economy not just essential to the profit of local bigwigs, but the continued sustenance of many millions of people.

It was unthinkable, but he couldn't help thinking it.

His bosses were asking about who was essential to the running of local financial institutions and businesses. They were asking what technical personal were required to keep local industries going. They were also asking about how to blow entire docks and how to sabotage freighters so they were lost in transit. Worse, they were inquiring after weak spots in the life support of entire stations. They'd even asked about orbital threats to planetary surfaces.

He'd have liked to think the only reason to inquire after threats to planetary systems would be so one could figure out ways to thwart them. The Federation and its naval arm the SDF existed, after all, to protect humanity, not to threaten parts of it with annihilation.

In context, it was uncomfortably hard to do that.

3: Movement

"Captain Black, I'm sorry but the problem is we've been running Ad Astra from here on Newton," Moe Libreman, Jack's accountant, said.

Well technically he was Ad Astra's Chief Financial Officer, but as far as Jack was concerned that translated to "Jack's accountant".

In Jack's experience accountants were rather gray non-entities who quietly did what the people paying them asked them to, thereby somehow magically keeping the authorities, especially the ones with the right to tax one, happy.

Moe was not living up to this billing.

"For less than a year," Jack said. "Surely you're not telling me you can't replicate the setup work somewhere else further from the main Federation route to the Frontier and also closer to the middle of our own trade routes?"

Moe nibbled on his lip. Jack looked around at the spaceport "consultation room" they were meeting in. It had a set of large windows taking up an entire wall. They faced out onto the spaceport's tarmac. A freighter was in the process of taking off. It was a pretty sight. Jack wished he was on board.

"There are problems, Jack," Moe finally said. His face twisted in a thin, tired, and cynical smile. "Please, hear me out," he continued.

"Okay," Jack replied looking at the man. He'd come to respect him. Moe had been Cynthia's choice for CFO and Jack had at first been pleased with his performance, but not that taken by the man himself. A lot of trouble and several outright crises later, he'd come to a more generous appreciation of him.

Moe worried a lot, but he had a lot to worry about. Jack thought Moe knew too much and saw too much that could go wrong. He managed to deal. He'd stuck it out like a good soldier and pulled Ad Astra, and Jack's butt along with it, through some tricky times. He didn't let his worries get the best of him. He was worth listening to.

"The organization of Ad Astra's home office is, shall we say, thin to nonexistent," Moe said with another thin grimace that approximated a smile.

"Okay," Jack replied. "Afraid I haven't been paying it much attention. Been very busy. I've got good excuses, but that doesn't change the fact I've been completely ignoring the issue."

"Yeah, I understand," Moe answered with a looking down at the table they were sprawled around and nodding. He frowned. "You were leaving that to me. Frankly, our finances were a horror show until recently and I was busy myself juggling all our various investors and creditors. I handled things ad hoc as best as I could. The bank was understanding, but that was about it. Still, our 'home office' doesn't amount to much more than me, Cynthia, our receptionist, Stephanie and our back office data analyst, Terry."

"Haven't met Stephanie or Terry, but I'm guessing they don't amount to a whole proper home office on their own," Jack said. "But doesn't that make it easier to move? Heck, we could give both of them very generous relocation packages."

Moe frowned. Then he let out a deep breath and sighed. "You're serious about this, aren't you?" he said.

"I am," said Jack. "We're right on the Federation's main route to the Frontier here, and though that's convenient in some ways, it makes us a big fat target for SDF intervention."

"What?" Moe exclaimed. He sounded more startled than outraged. "That sort of thing is unheard of. What ever else you can say about the Federation they've always tip toed around local governments and institutions."

It was Jack's turn to sigh and look grim. "I know," he said. "Spacers in the SDF were always complaining about how they spent their careers out in the dark voids in between the places where people lived and things happened."

"Not enough girls for them is what you mean," Moe said, smirking.

"Young men like to see some young women at least occasionally," Jack replied. "SDF has never been the most gender balanced of institutions. I always suspected it was because young women had more sense."

Moe snorted.

"Human nature," Jack said. "Sort of think it's kind of a relief people are the same where ever and whenever you find them. Gives me a fragile sort of hope."

"Something predictable in an uncertain world."

"Exactly," Jack agreed. "Anyhow that's all beside the point. Yes, the SDF by policy always avoided the heavily populated middle worlds for whatever reason. And, yes, the Federation civilian bureaucracy has been deliberately discreet and low profile from what I've been told."

"Cynthia?" Moe asked.

"Dr. Dallemagne has taken it upon herself to fill some of the gaps in my education," Jack admitted.

"Worse teachers," Moe opined.

"She knows her stuff," Jack said. "She's pleasant. Never took liberties with her."

Moe chuckled. "Yeah, I wouldn't want to cross that woman," he said. "Or her family either," he said in a more solemn tone. "You know about them?"

"I've heard enough," Jack replied. "Back to the point. It might be unprecedented, and it might be unpleasant to think about but I've been given reason to believe that policy is about to change."

"Dr. Ted Smith?" Moe asked.

"You don't want to know," Jack said.

"Great. It's like that is it?"

"It is," Jack replied. "Welcome to the wonderful world of being a mushroom."

"Fed crap and kept in the dark."

"Precisely."

"For my own good, no doubt."

"At least in part."

"Should I be thinking about moving my own butt to someplace more out of the way?" Moe asked.

"Well, if our HQ moves you'll have to go to what ever place we chose to help set it up, won't you?"

"Help, he says," Moe replied. "Like I won't be doing most of the work."

"I appreciate your understanding of the situation," Jack answered with mock formality. If Moe was openly grumbling, he was already at least half convinced.

"No way that's not going to be disruptive," Moe said. "I've been acting as the clearing house for the messages between our trading posts and ships. Not going to be modest. I've been the glue holding this mess together. All the orders and schedules you and Cynthia have been dreaming up, I've been the one making sure they get to the people who needed to make them happen."

"So leave a forwarding address," Jack said.

"Delays, some missed messages," Moe replied. "Like we're not already running on the thin edge of a knife."

"We're up and running. We can afford a few glitches in communications. Our people can make good decisions without hand holding." Jack sat back and gave Moe a calm, assessing look. Moe was just dragging his feet now, not making solid arguments. Shortly, he'd realize it himself.

"Me, Cynthia, and Dr. Smith all have positions and commitments here on Newton," Moe ventured. "Going to look strange to anyone asking questions later if we all of a sudden take off for places beyond easy reach. Going to look very conspiratorial."

"Okay, right. I guess Dr. Smith is stuck here, but Dr. Dallemagne has always traveled a lot. I don't think it'll be hard to find an excuse for you to make a trip to check out how your new responsibilities are going. There's no need for either of you to put it out you're moving for good. In fact, whatever is happening I'd be surprised if it's not over in under a year. One way or the other."

Moe gave Jack a hard look. "That quick?"

"SDF and Federation both are both slow moving under normal circumstances," Jack replied. "Usually their main concern is to not rock any boats. Policy is, and always has been, if they need to intervene to keep things on an even keel outside the Core they act quickly and decisively, and then they go back to the Core and the status quo. They don't want to get assets bogged down in the middle worlds, let alone on the Frontier."

"You sure?" Moe asked. "In my experience organizations are creatures of habit and not so rational."

"People running the Federation and SDF might have a different point of view than we do, but they're not stupid, Moe," Jack answered. He sat up.

"Smart people can do stupid things," Moe said bleakly.

"They know what they're doing. When it's necessary they can act decisively. Do you remember, Moe, the last anti-pirate operation in the sector?"

"Vaguely," Moe replied. "It was a long time ago. I was young. It was in the news but not for long."

"Just so," Jack said. "It wasn't in the news long. They deployed, finished the pirate threat off, and went home. Bang, just like that. It's the way they've operated for the last two centuries. It's a pattern. You can bet on it."

"I'd rather not bet so much," Moe muttered.

"That's the thing about life, it's a game you don't get a choice about playing," Jack said. "Just be glad our cards are as good as they are."

"Okay, you know I'm all in, Jack."

"I know," Jack said. "You want to make sure we're playing the game as best we can. I think we are. I don't think we can leave Ad Astra's nerve center vulnerable here in Newton during the next round." He gave Moe a few seconds to mull that over.

"Okay," Moe finally said. "Taking that as given, it's still going to be pretty obvious if we move Stephanie and Terry off planet, or even just start a new office elsewhere."

"I think we can sell it as an administrative move," Jack said. "Newton is at the end of our trade routes. Having our message clearing center somewhere closer to the middle of them makes a lot of sense."

"So don't even try to obfuscate it," Moe said with a contemplative tone. "Just openly do it. Announce a perfectly plausible reason and carry on."

"Yep," Jack affirmed.

"Okay," Moe replied. "I'm not saying I'm convinced yet, but let's game out how we'd do this."

"Sure."

"First thing, you're right Newton is at the far end of the trade routes we've set up," Moe said. "Not unimportant, but at the far end of our territory. Also the one place all our trade routes go through. Except El Dorado that is."

"And El Dorado is hardly even in the Federation, at the other end of everything, and would, aah, disturb the Federation bureaucracy," Jack finished for him.

"Be the next best thing to running up the Jolly Rodger as far the Feds and SDF are concerned," Moe confirmed. "And what about the SDF's seat on the board? Heard Commander Taylor is about to be posted back to the Solar System."

"Rumor is correct this time," Jack admitted. "Position was never formally the Navy's. Taylor was appointed on his merits as an individual." That was what Smith had suggested Jack say if asked.

"Right, pull the other one," Moe replied. "You don't know what you're going to do, do you?"

"Let's figure out where we want to go to and then figure out how we're going to sell it," Jack suggested. "El Dorado and Newton are both out. Figure New Lustania and Slovo are too close to Newton. What does that leave us?"

"Local governments a bit too proactive in Marx and Hanshan for my taste," Moe said.

Jack snorted. "That's putting it mildly," he said. "Agreed. Too many sharks, big and hungry, in the Heinlein pool too."

"Somewhere lawful enough to be safe and comfortable without authorities so overbearing they keep nosing into our business is what want," elaborated Moe.

"Right," Jack agreed. "Al-Alhadeen system belt station might be tempting but not sure how stable their current hands off kaffir business policy really is. Cultural issues too."

Moe shuddered. "A pit of snakes with a garnish of religious nuts, if you ask me," he said.

Jack smiled. "An unkind characterization, Mr. Libreman."

"Not inaccurate though, Captain, is it?" Moe retorted. "How many gun fights do you want to fight in the corridors of your Head Offices?"

"A one-time thing," Jack replied. "Still, I guess there is a terrorist problem."

"A general political stability problem," Moe said. "Al-Alhadeen is out."

"So what does that leave us?" Jack asked. "Nova Britannia, Alta Iberia, and Jefferson systems? Can't say any of them thrill me. Locals weren't very helpful when we needed them and they're all pretty much firmly in the Federation's pocket."

"To say nothing of the pirates based on Jefferson who tried to take you out and blew the crap out the place when it didn't work," Moe added.

"That's all the big inhabited systems with planets that we're trading with," Jack said solemnly. "Is there no good place at all? What about one of the trading clan stations?"

"Now you're grasping at straws," Moe said dryly. "Stations are small by planetary standards. They're firmly under the control of one clan or another, and most of them are almost as far out on the Frontier as El Dorado. The Feds and Navy will react to us basing ourselves out of one of them almost as badly."

"Going to have to reach out to them sooner or later," Jack said.

"True, but not right away and that's not the same as basing ourselves out of one of their strongholds," Moe retorted.

"Okay, so we're back to settled systems with planets again. Ones we're already trading with," Jack said. "Nova Britannia, Alta Iberia, and Jefferson right?"

"Right," Moe agreed. "Our trade volume is the least with Alta Iberia and the local language is Spanish. I don't know about the local politics. More trade with Nova Britannia, but not huge yet and think they're pretty much Federation loyalists. No language issues."

"You're thinking Jefferson right?"

"I am," Moe admitted. "Trade prospects are good there and they've always been skeptical towards the Federation bureaucracy. Local politics are in turmoil though."

"Jeffersonians don't like any government very much," Jack said. "There were some very hostile actors based there. Still not sure how deep it went or exactly who they were, but I think they've been burned out. I think the people there would welcome help putting matters back on an even keel. They're still rebuilding, so that might be an opening we don't have anywhere else."

"I think me, Stephanie and Terry all need to go on a fact finding mission to Jefferson," Moe said.

"I think that's a good idea," Jack said.

* * *

Ted Smith had long feared what the outside world might mean for his home, and his family. It had never occurred to him to expect problems within the family. He'd always thought Newton and her people were sane, solid, and they were always going to be on the same side, the right side, of any issue.

He'd believed it so deeply he'd not even thought of it as a belief. It'd been solid fact, as real as the wooden table he was sitting at. No more subject to question than the fact that if he was to knock that table with his hand that his hand would fail to pass through it. There'd be a knocking sound, and he'd have sore knuckles.

Ted felt sick.

Somehow he'd ended on the other side of a struggle from one of his brothers. It was a struggle no one even acknowledged publicly. It didn't make the fact any less bitter.

Being completely dispassionate, or at least as much as he could manage, it was no small thing. His brother was neither an incompetent nor a raving fanatic. He'd had the same upbringing as Ted himself. He was a good man. A rational, decent man dedicated to the greater good.

A man that he was going to have to dissemble to and work against unless he changed course and betrayed other perfectly good decent and rational people. It was a hell of a choice for anyone to have to make.

The Faculty Club had a few private rooms for intimate get-togethers among friends or colleagues when they didn't want to share their conversation or their perhaps excessive cheer with a wider audience. Right now Ted had one all to himself. He was waiting for both Cynthia Dallemagne and Moe Libreman to arrive. It shouldn't be long.

It was a very low profile meeting with a quorum of Ad Astra Venture's board. Practically secret and plausibly deniable. At least it would be for a time. Ted didn't believe that what they decided here wouldn't eventually come out. He didn't believe they'd be able to evade the responsibility for and the consequences of the decisions they were about to make.

He couldn't see the right or wrong of it. Seemed to him that he just had a choice of bad decisions. Uncertain bad decisions. That either his brother and some part of Federation bureaucracy would feel betrayed or the people who'd trusted him and gone out on a limb to build Ad Astra would.

They ought to all be on the same side.

They weren't.

They were all supposed to be loyal to the Federation, and the Federation was supposed to protect all of humanity. It was supposed to be concerned with protecting the lives, safety, freedom, and prosperity of people everywhere, on Earth, in the Core, in middle worlds Newton, on the Frontier, and even beyond it despite that being formally out of its jurisdiction. It clearly said so in its founding charter.

And somehow various people in various places, like him, his brother and some homicidal group back on Earth had come to the conclusion that wasn't true any longer and had begun to work in the interests of smaller groups within the greater whole. Work in those interests at the expense of others in the larger whole. At least Ted had never ordered an assassination or deliberately broken laws he was pledged to uphold.

Somebody high up in the Federation back on Earth had done the first. The attempted killing of Jack Black proved that.

His own brother, he hoped it wasn't true but feared it was, seemed to have done the second. Once he allowed himself to think about it Ted found it impossible to believe that the FTL parts Black had found in a nearby warehouse had gone missing without his brother's knowledge. It was damning.

It was heart breaking.

It made Ted angry. Yet another inconvenient emotion he couldn't afford to indulge.

"Dr. Smith, you okay?"

Ted looked up. Moe Libreman had come into the room and Ted had been so lost in his thoughts he'd not even noticed.

"We have some difficult decisions to make," Dr. Ted Smith said, not directly answering Moe's question.

"Excrement about to meet the air impeller?" Moe said.

Ted snorted. "Indeed."

"So what options do we have?" Moe asked.

Ted smiled up at Moe grimly. "We have the poor one, the ugly one, and the very bad one," Ted replied. "There might be some other nasty, unlikely, but not so bad ones I haven't thought of.

Please don't hesitate to suggest any you can think of."

Moe sighed as he sat down. "Well, that's a very colorful palette of choices, but details?" he said. "Cold facts laid out clearly are best for making good decisions."

"The cold facts are the ugliest part of it, Moe," Ted said. It was an unusual degree of informality for him, but they were all in the same boat together and it behooved them to get comfortable with each other. "I think we've been living in a dream world and reality is about come crashing down on us hard."

"Jack was coy. It was odd coming from him," Moe started tentatively. He looked at Ted hard.

Ted nodded. "Go on."

"He suggested it might be prudent to move some of the co-ordinating of our operations to somewhere else other than Newton," Moe went on.

"He did?"

"Yes, he did," Moe said with a certain exasperation. "And although he wasn't entirely clear about why and less clear about where he was getting his information, I think it was likely you. I think you need to bring me into the loop because I'm the guy who's going to have to execute on whatever we decide."

"Okay, but don't think you're going to thank me for it," Ted said. "Also we should wait for Cynthia. She shouldn't be long."

Moe fidgeted in his seat. "I'd like to just rip the bandage off, but it makes sense. Any chance you can give me some of her time to help?"

Ted smiled. He'd been afraid he might have his work set for him to persuade Moe about their best chance of success. Either Jack Black or Moe's own logic seemed to have him resigned to the necessary course of action.

"Some maybe," Ted said. "But not much and she'll have other priorities. She's our main troubleshooter, something unexpected comes up and off she'll have to go."

"Better than nothing," Moe said in listlessly monotonic tone. He looked around blankly before his gaze settled mid-table on a carafe filled with amber liquid. Several empty glasses were arrayed around it.

"Port," Ted explained. "Best quality straight from Earth itself."

Moe queried Ted with raised eyebrows.

Ted leaned over and poured a glass. "Help yourself, can't hurt, might help. This is going to be long often uncomfortable journey we might as well take our pleasures while we can," he said.

And so they were sipping port, relaxing, when Cynthia Dallemagne strode into the room.

"Cynthia!" Moe exclaimed with excessively hearty cheer. "You have to try this. It's good. It's port from the old home, mudball itself."

"Isn't a little early to start drinking?" she asked Moe skeptically.

"A little lubrication mightn't go amiss for what we need to discuss," Ted said.

Cynthia looked at Ted, eyebrows arched. "So okay," she said, leaning over to fill a glass with some port before sitting herself. She took a sip, glanced at Moe, and then straight at Ted. "You've got bad news."

"Not much solid," Ted replied. "Straws in the wind, rumor, and nasty suspicions."

"Dr. Smith that I know likes to get all his ducks in a row before coming to a conclusion," she said.

Ted gave a slight nod. "He likes to," he agreed.

"He doesn't spook easy either," Cynthia said.

"I'd like to think that's also true," Ted allowed. He took a deep breath and admiring the color of his port went on. "The state of my understanding of current affairs has recently undergone what our physicist friends like to call a phase change."

"So a change of plans then?" Cynthia asked.

"Exactly," Ted confirmed.

"Ted hasn't shared the details yet," Moe said. "We were waiting for you, but long story short SDF is going to be increasing its local presence substantially and it looks like it might be a good idea to remove Ad Astra's ships and center of operations beyond their control. Which might not look good."

"You're kidding," Cynthia said to him before looking to Ted for confirmation.

"He's not," Ted confirmed. "Hard to believe, I'll admit."

Cynthia gave him a slight nod of confirmation while Moe stared glumly into his drink his early heartiness forgotten.

"Which if we were looking for excuses might be a good one for having missed this for so long," Ted said in an even resigned tone looking her directly in the eye. Moe looked and caught his eye too.

Ted was about to get down to business.

"If we act at all it looks like we'll have to do it quickly then, won't we?" Moe said.

"Yes we will," Ted agreed. "We're getting ahead of ourselves though. Like Cynthia mentioned, I think it's best to get all your facts laid out, analyzed, and understood before setting a course of action."

"Actually, as an intelligence agency we don't normally act at all beyond writing reports," Cynthia said.

"True," Ted said. "A policy you've had issues with in the past."

"Yes, I know," Cynthia said. "We've let some bad shit happen because it wasn't formally our job to do anything. That's frustrating. I always understood why the policy made sense though."

"And it still does," Ted said. "Direct action compromises our intelligence gathering, and it imperils us politically as formally Newton isn't even supposed to have its own information gathering organization let along one that takes direct political action in places off of Newton. Every time we take direct action we risk both the Federation and our superiors here on Newton coming down on us hard."

"Particularly if we don't have some plausible deniability or it doesn't work out," Cynthia elaborated.

"Remind me why I let you drag me into this," Moe asked Cynthia with a crooked smile.

"You've got an old crush on me, you were bored, and you understood you could contribute to making the world a better place," Cynthia replied.

"Right," Moe agreed. "I was a delusional fool. Also was worried about the planet and the sector going down the drain more than creating paradise."

"Things looked pretty bad a year ago," Cynthia said. "Mightn't be widely known, but we put down some bad people and prevented sector wide catastrophe. You can be proud of that."

"Thank you," Moe said thoughtfully. He seemed a little mollified.

"Do they really look worse now?" Cynthia asked, turning to Ted.

"The situation certainly looks worse," Ted answered. "I'm not certain if that's because it really is or simply that the problems are more obvious now."

"That's vague," Cynthia said. "You're having trouble with this, aren't you?" Her tone was blunt and not overly respectful.

Ted was startled. He was used to thinking of himself as Cynthia's mentor and boss. His mistake in this context at least. "Yes, I am," he admitted. "And for a number of reasons, not all of which I can discuss."

"That's awkward," Moe interjected.

"Yes, I am well aware of that," Ted said dryly. "I'm sorry."

"But?" Moe asked.

"I am sorry, Moe. I do regret the necessities of the dilemma we find ourselves in," Ted said, leaning forward and looking at his colleagues intently. "Some of this is both personal and conjectural. A lot is need to know. Trust me, I'll share everything pertinent to the decisions we need to make today. I'll give you everything you need to do what's required."

Moe just gave a sharp nod. It was Cynthia who really reacted. "Dr. Smith," she said much more than usually formal. "Am I right to think I need to be brought up to speed here. More than Moe." She hesitated, also not a natural behavior from her. "This sounds unusually serious."

Moe snorted. "That's an understatement."

Ted couldn't help giving him an annoyed glance. This was hard enough already. "To put it short and simply," he said, "the Federation is fracturing and we need to start deciding where our loyalties lie."

"Just like that?" Cynthia asked. "Does this have to do with that assassination attempt on Jack? Why would anyone in the Federation do that?"

"The attack on Jack," Ted answered, "which by the way we've since confirmed was an SDF special forces operation directed from Earth itself, is only one puzzle piece in the picture."

"Okay, so what are the other pieces and what decisions do we have to make. What is that we have to do?" Cynthia asked. "I know you like to just sit on the sidelines and interfere as little as possible, but it sounds like you don't think that's going to work this time."

"Well, as regards your assertions regards my preferences, you're right," Ted acknowledged sitting back and giving a sadly amused if thin smile. "I'd love to just sit back and analyze this until I properly understood it. I don't think we have that luxury. Some faction in the Federation appears to have prodded the larger beast into action. Action sometime soon that's going to force us all to react. They're launching a major SDF operation through Newton, apparently against the Beyonders."

Cynthia sat back herself, trying to keep a stunned look off of her face and not completely succeeding.

"Yeah, that was my reaction too," Moe said with some sympathy.

"It is hard to believe," Cynthia said slowly.

"Not if you think about it logically," Ted responded coolly. "It's unheard of and unthinkable, but if you look at the facts of the geo-political situation and what the Federation can logically do to respond to them it makes a lot of sense."

"Haven't had time to carefully run the numbers," Moe put in, "but talk of trade and civilization collapsing in the entire sector tends to catch my attention."

"It does that," Ted agreed with a small smile. Moe's small joke managed to relax him some.

"Yes, it does," Moe went on, "And unfortunately the idea that our FTL fleet has been kept too small and that trade though vital in the long term is unprofitable in the short term is very plausible."

"That's only half of it," Cynthia said.

"The other half," Ted said, "being that the Federation as constituted, being paid for mainly by the Core worlds but having to provide safety to almost the entirety of human settled space, is simply unsustainable. A fact that's been kicked into the future for generations, but which is starting to bite. We're running out of time."

"Without the SDF's protection trade is instantly more expensive, ships are lost, and trade collapses quite suddenly," Moe said. "I did find time to run some quick simulations."

"So we're all reading from the same hymn book here then?" Ted asked.

Cynthia looked at Moe. "Up to a point," she said. "Moe?"

"So we're agreed we're facing a sector wide crisis, probably in our lifetimes," Moe replied. "I believe we're agreed on the broad outlines of what form it'll take. It's that crisis that Ad Astra was set up to avoid. I'd thought we'd at least managed to buy some time."

Cynthia looked at Ted. "So did I," she said. "Breathing room at least."

"We did. We solved the immediate problem of Foxall participating the inevitable crisis early and setting up a pirate kingdom in the ruins," Ted answered. "We might even be slowing down the decline process with Ad Astra. We haven't addressed the underlying problems though. Also we underestimated the Federation. At least somebody with some influence back in the Core has managed to see what's happening and to prod the SDF into action."

"By attacking the Beyonders?" Cynthia asked.

"And why do we have to get involved, let alone take sides?" Moe asked. "I mean there are lots of reactions to this situation that don't require conflict. More in which that conflict doesn't include us, Ad Astra, Newton, you, Cynthia or me, or even Jack Black."

"If the Federation has to pull out it's not likely to want to leave a viable source of FTL drives behind on Newton," Cynthia said partly answering Moe's question to Ted. "Still, Moe's got a good question there, Ted. If the Federation does need to take actions we don't like that still doesn't mean we need to be involved, does it? If we do need to be involved aren't the Federation and the SDF the good guys?"

"That tried to have Jack assassinated," Moe grumbled. Cynthia gave him a hard look.

"I know you've been shot at and I haven't," Moe said apologetically to her. "But high-powered rifles aren't my idea of the proper tools for trade negotiations."

Cynthia managed something between a snort and sniff, a soft, harsh and bitterly amused sound. "Mine neither, but sometimes the other guy sets the terms."

"Which is exactly our problem," Ted said, trying to bring the conversation back around to the point.

Once again Cynthia looked to Moe.

"How is that?" Moe asked obediently.

"Whatever this rumored, but almost certainly happening, SDF deployment is, it isn't a parade we can just watch pass by," Ted answered. "Two pieces of information have come to my notice. One, the SDF doesn't have means to support a large deployment out of its own resources. It's going to need to requisition resources from the local economy."

"They're going to take our ships from us," Moe interjected with a hint of anger.

"Yes, almost certainly," Ted affirmed. "And, two, it they've been making surreptitious preparations locally. Not sure how deep it goes, or how long they've been doing it, or if it's just Newton, but they've been running secret operations here in Newton."

"Is that legal?" Cynthia asked.

"They haven't gone through official channels or even traditional informal ones," Ted answered. "Whatever they're doing, they didn't bother getting permission from local authorities. Since I've clear evidence some of what they've been doing is highly illegal under both Federation and Newtonian law, that's not so surprising."

Cynthia cursed softly under her breath. It earned her a surprised glance from Moe. Cynthia was normally very self possessed.

"By the book we should simply report them to the responsible authorities," Moe said. Ted looked at him. Moe raised his eyebrows.

"As I imagine you can guess," Ted said, "I believe that would amount to starting the conflict early and picking a side all in one. On terms not of our choosing. Not likely to be effective either. If you two have trouble believing this is happening just think how any neutral person in a position of responsibility is going to deal with it. The authorities are likely to be already hostile or disbelieving."

"It's like a bad dream," Moe said.

"I've seen things like this other places," Cynthia said. "Never thought I'd see it here at home."

"So a murky mess with no good choices," Moe said. "What are our options?" he asked Ted.

"Murky as the future might be I think sometime in the near future, not a few weeks likely, more likely in a few months a large SDF task force is going to turn up here," Ted said.

"Distillery and brewery stocks likely to go up," Moe said.

Ted lent him a quelling glance. "About the same time as notice of a major operation against the largest Beyonder groups across the Frontier reaches us," he went on.

"Do we have a good census of just how big the Beyonders are?" Cynthia asked.

"We have estimates of the size of their FTL fleet based how many drives we think they could manage to procure on the black market," Ted said. "System ship numbers, stations, their populations, and planets we have only guesses on. We don't think they've got much in the way of habitable planets."

Cynthia sucked in her breath. "Anyone redo those estimates based on what we've learned in the last year or so?" she asked.

Ted grimaced. "No"

"So they're all likely to be wildly off and to the downside?" Cynthia summed up.

Moe looked to Cynthia and then blandly at Ted. Ted nodded back. It was an immense failure on the part of Newton's intelligence. One that he was responsible for. That he'd been very busy and hadn't been tasked with obtaining the information as a priority didn't change that. Ted was grateful for Moe's forbearance in not stating that plainly.

"Do the Feds have better intelligence?" Moe did ask.

"Probably given that they've obviously been planning this operation for a while," Ted answered. "However, their sources here aren't much better than ours and I suspect they've significantly underestimated what they're biting off."

"Is that material to us?" Cynthia asked.

"It is," Ted replied. "Win or lose the SDF is likely to get a nasty surprise and have to scramble."

"So they'll try to hit us up to make good the costs of their mistakes, and they won't be delicate about it or give us a lot of warning," Cynthia extrapolated.

"I expect," Ted said.

"You think they'll try to press Ad Astra ships into service and then lose them," Moe said.

"I've got analysts working on what the logistical requirements of a large SDF deployment from the Core through Newton to the Frontier would be," Ted said.

"Could be in hopes of anticipating their needs," Cynthia noted. "Plausibly deniable."

"Yes," Ted admitted. "Haven't got formal results yet."

"But we can all guess what they're going to be," Moe said.

"You're right, Moe," Ted said. "They're going to need to hire ships in sector especially if they're trying to retain an element of surprise."

"And despite the fact all our shipping is already committed, legally committed in most cases, they'll offer us overriding deals we can't refuse," Moe said.

"I've checked," Ted said. "Turns out that, although the laws allowing it are rarely invoked, the SDF can requisition ships at need. Their needs override all prior contracts in the event of an emergency."

"Which they'll doubtless declare if they have to," Cynthia said.

"We're just building our business, that would set us back years and might put us out of business," Moe said.

"Without assuming they lose some of our ships?" Cynthia asked.

"Yes, that's even assuming we don't lose ships outright," Moe confirmed. "Even if we assume we're fairly compensated...," he looked at Ted questioningly.

"I wouldn't assume that," Ted said. "But continue with your analysis."

"Even if we're made good financially and we can somehow quickly replace any missing ships our business will be wrecked," Moe said. "The Heinleiners and the Marxians will pick up what pieces are left. Neither of them give a damn for the Federation or even the sector as a whole."

"Cynthia, do you concur with Moe's analysis?" Ted asked nonchalantly before taking a sip of his port.

Cynthia smiled. Ted doubted she was in the least fooled by his act. "I do. I think it's one of the better case scenarios. There are many worse case scenarios that are as likely."

"I was hoping," Moe said bleakly, "that you'd tell me I was a delusional fool and jumping at shadows."

"No, sorry," Cynthia said. "You're a smart man who understands our predicament all too well."

"Well," Moe said sipping his port contemplatively, "I was afraid of that. Ted?"

"I've reached similar conclusions," Ted said. "I also hoped one or both of you might be able to make good arguments I was wrong."

"You didn't really expect that?" Moe said.

"No, I didn't," Ted admitted.

"So the safest and most comfortable course of action for us," Moe said, "which would be to wait on events then co-operate fully with the Federation authorities when they made requests of us, is not viable."

"That's my assessment," Ted said.

"And our other option is to get ourselves, our people and our ships out of Dodge pronto?" Moe asked.

Cynthia sighed. "Maybe you watch too many old Westerns," she said.

"Perhaps an appropriate cultural context given our current circumstances," Ted commented.

"Glad someone is getting some amusement out of it," Cynthia retorted tartly.

"But in essence Moe is right," Ted said, "however quaint you find his phrasing."

"In essence?" Cynthia said with an edge of exaggerated patience.

"You, Moe, our key people without too many local ties, and our ships need to relocate," Ted said. "Moe's been studying it. Jefferson looks like our best bet. I can't go. I have to stay here and ride it out. My position as the head of the Current History Studies Group is too key and too high profile."

Cynthia stared at him blankly. It was apparent she didn't know what to say.

Moe sitting up filled the gap. "You'll be lucky if they merely try you for treason. Legal formalities won't matter, the SDF and Feds will be in charge and they'll be looking for scapegoats."

"I have considered the likely outcomes," Ted said dryly while placidly sipping yet more port. "We don't how this will work out in detail. We don't even know what personalities will be involved. It's possible the SDF officers involved will be too busy to worry about a bit player like me."

"That's a big high stakes bet," Cynthia said flatly.

"I've been risking other people's lives elsewhere for years," Ted said contemplating her. He'd put her in harm's way all too often. It'd prayed on his conscience. "Taking some risks myself here, it does not seem so unfair."

Cynthia replied with a rude sound and by taking a gulp of her fine port.

"We're decided then?" Moe asked. "We're done?"

"Imagine it's best we record a formal meeting for the sake of posterity and covering our butts in case we should by some fluke end up facing a fair trial," Cynthia said looking a query at Ted.

"It's an unlikely outcome but one we can prepare for at low cost," Ted answered. "No point getting sloppy."

Moe grunted. "While we're all candid and touchy feely, Ted, don't hold on too long. Don't be a martyr." Moe paused. "And good luck."

Cynthia filled another glass of port and silently pushed it Ted's way.

* * *

Jack looked at a little business card. It was for a dentist's and gave the address he was currently at. He still had a few minutes before the appointment time given on the card.

It wasn't an appointment he'd made. He'd been enjoying the sun drinking tea on a nearby patio when a passer-by had dropped the card on his table and bustled off.

There was a short note on the card. It said: *"I've made you an appointment. Ted."*

Jack could guess this was a direction from Dr. Edward "Ted" Smith but the card was all sorts of vague, need to know, and deniable.

It was a still a nice sunny warm day. The building Jack stood before was pleasant enough in a nondescript professional medical clinic way, but somehow Jack didn't feel very cheerful about finding himself there.

He gathered his nerve and walked in regardless. A directory in the lobby located his "dentist" on the top floor. He jogged up a flight of stairs and followed the signage there. Entering the appropriate door he found himself in what from his childhood memories appeared to be a typical dentist's office.

Generally with oral disease largely preventable only children and old people saw dentists on a regular basis. The SDF had its members submit to check ups every few years, but a ship's sickbay didn't resemble a civilian professional's office much. The place was reassuring and disconcerting all at once.

There was a thin dark complected woman sitting behind a counter. A name plate attached to the light sweater she was wearing identified her as "Christine Laplace". Christine looked up at him.

"Hi, I have an appointment with Dr. Caligari," Jack said.

"Right. You're just on time," Christine replied in a clipped professional tone. "Through that door," she said pointing, "and to your right and then through the door at the very end of the corridor."

"Thank you," Jack said before proceeding to do as directed.

The corridor was basically featureless except for a variety of doors. Taking the one at the end Jack found himself in a second small waiting room. Ted Smith was seated in it reading a hardcopy magazine with a lot of glossy pictures. He looked up and waved at a chair.

"What's up?" Jack asked as he seated himself.

"You've broken a molar sampling one of those off world foods you're importing," Ted said.

"Ouch," Jack replied dryly. "That's too bad."

"Yes, it's also unfortunate that we've both been so busy and you didn't get to see me this on this trip to Newton," Ted said blandly. "I'm not here."

"Yeah," Jack agreed. "We'll have to make a point of getting together next time. Good thing Moe knows what needs to be done."

"Indeed," Ted said. "Ad Astra seems to be up and running fine. However, we'd still miss you if something unhealthy was to happen to you during one of these many scrapes you keep getting into."

"I'm touched," Jack said.

"Dr. Caligari is going to help increase your survivability in the event of any future incidents," Ted said.

"I seem to be on a lot of lists for special treatment," Jack commented sourly.

"Exactly," Ted said. "I'm afraid I'm going to be out of touch for most of the duration, but this one last parting gift should help."

"Okay," Jack said. "Anything more to share?"

"Not a lot," Ted said. "We expect an SDF deployment that's going to disrupt business on a line from the Core through Newton to the Frontier. The political and therefore business climate will be volatile and unpredictable. Best center Ad Astra's operations elsewhere, but I have to stay here and it'll be hard staying in touch."

"So I'm on my own?" Jack asked.

"You have Ad Astra including Libreman, as well as a call on Cynthia," Ted answered. "I trust your judgment."

"Thanks," Jack said.

"It's warranted," Ted said. "Regards your personal safety, which I'm afraid is likely at stake, you have Sergeant Jackson and his marines of course, but I also expect Dr. Caligari's work to help. He's going to give you the equivalent of a card up your sleeve in a poker game in the event of further violence directed your way."

"So who is Caligari and what is this place?" Jack said. "What are you having done to my perfectly fine teeth?"

"Dr. Caligari is a dentist but not just a dentist," Ted answered. "We don't have time for a long history lesson but he's also the head of a secret research institute, archive really, that dates back to Newton's founding."

"Secret research institute?" Jack repeated. "I'm getting some spy gadgets?" Jack had seen various old vids about spies where they always had some fantastical gadgets that saved their skin in their moments of greatest peril. The vids were fun but Jack had never taken them seriously.

"The doctor will explain," Ted answered. He waved at a second door into the little room. It was dark brown with a brass door knob and completely unlabeled. "Right through there. It's open. Go on."

"On the other side," Jack said and did as directed. The door knob turned easily.

It led into a room that was larger and much more brightly lit. It was all shades of gleaming white and shiny metal. A harsh white tiled mad scientist's lab minus the glasswork, but with a dentist's chair from hell right in the middle of it.

A chuckle sounded from Jack's right. "Impressive isn't it," an oily dark voice said. "It's amazing what you can do with a government budget even if you don't really exist."

Jack looked at the source of the voice. The man's appearance matched it. He was dark complected but not African, in fact, with a big hooked nose and bushy black hair he was a parody of the stock Arab trader from an old Middle Eastern themed romance vid. Only in modern medical scrubs not flowing robes.

"Dr. Caligari, I presume," Jack said.

Caligari chuckled again. His big white teeth flashed, he seemed amused but somehow not jolly. "Fond of the classics myself," he said. He sighed dramatically. "Some times I think I was born in the wrong time and place."

"Yet you seem to take a certain delight in your work," Jack said.

"Take a seat my boy," Caligari answered pointing at the massive contraption that resembled the bastard cross of a couch and a lazy chair amidst a forest of equipment. Jack didn't recognize most of it though some had to be scanning devices of some sort and there was at least one dentist's drill there.

Jack navigated past them all and inserted himself onto the chair. He felt strangely helpless.

"To answer your question," Dr. Caligari said leaning over Jack and peering at his eyes. "I haven't had this much fun in years."

"You don't say," Jack said. "How is that?"

"Need to know. Need to know, my boy," Dr. Caligari replied. "But I guess it won't hurt to unload a little. Federation dumped all its most interesting research projects here on Newton about the time it was being formed."

"That's interesting," Jack said quite sincerely.

"Yes the usual story that Newton was founded as a center for undistracted academic research is so much hooey. Forgive my language," Dr. Caligari replied. "Who ever heard of politicians valuing knowledge for its own sake?"

"So what sort of research was it formed for?" Jack asked.

"Dangerous research. Research too secret to be carried on back in the Solar System where there were so many nosy people," Dr. Caligari answered.

"Well," Jack opined carefully while looking up at the blank white ceiling. "Doesn't sound boring at least."

Dr. Caligari grunted. "It wouldn't have been if they'd ever allowed us to do any research," he said. "They chickened out. Didn't have the courage to continue any of the work and didn't have the nerve to destroy it either."

"So what did they do?" Jack said. He was curious although he wasn't sure what this had to with him.

"They archived it," Dr. Caligari said while fiddling with something out of Jack's line of sight. "And for generations me and my predecessors have been little more than glorified caretakers."

"It's honest work," Jack ventured.

"Ha!" Dr. Caligari exclaimed. "The smartest best educated people in each generation forced to keep secrets that could change life for all of humanity. Not allowed to do anything with that knowledge or even admit they have it. Forced to pretend to be doing the most mundane of professional work for a living."

"You don't like being a dentist?" Jack asked for the lack of anything better to say. He regretted the words as soon they left his mouth.

"Nothing wrong with it," Dr. Caligari said much more mildly than Jack had feared. "It's useful, but boring after the first few years, and a complete waste of my talents."

"Sorry to hear that," Jack said trying to sound sympathetic. He'd had his own dreams and been lucky enough to largely achieve them, but most people he knew just worked to live and didn't worry much about achieving self-fulfillment.

"Ah, but you shouldn't be," Dr. Caligari said with excessive glee. "You're giving me the chance to do some truly interesting work."

"Um, glad to help," Jack said despite feeling alarmed. The idea of being the subject of dangerous research somehow lacked appeal.

Caligari laughed. "Don't worry this is a win-win situation," he said. "Won't pretend it doesn't have some risks of its own, but if you're smart about it, it'll get you out of some tough jams."

"Great," Jack said. He didn't manage to sound enthusiastic.

Caligari paused in what he was doing and turning leaned over Jack. Peering at him he said, "Ted told me you tend to get into tough jams. That you were lucky to survive a number of them."

Jack sighed. "It's true. Never planned to make a habit of it.

Caligari smiled down at Jack. The smile managed to be both amused and grim. "There you go, life doesn't always turn out how we'd like," he said. "I'm going to give you an edge that might save your life next time someone springs a little, intended to be fatal, surprise on you."

"Okay," Jack said. "Admit that sounds good."

"You should be more appreciative," Dr. Caligari said. "This is some unique work I'm going to do for you. Like I said potentially life saving work."

"Thank you, Doctor," Jack said.

"You're welcome," Dr. Caligari said moving back out of Jack's line of sight. The blank white ceiling was beginning to look better. "Must say one thing being a dentist has done for me is that I've learned that people don't appreciate what you're doing for them unless you're relieving immediate significant pain."

"People are short sighted and focused on the moment," Jack agreed. "Not pretty but it makes sense, Doc. You never really know what's going to happen, might as well make the best of the here and now."

Caligari's face reappeared above Jack. "Most people might have that luxury," he said. "Me and you we don't. Anyhow I've got my initial scans done."

"So what's next?" Jack asked.

"In layman's terms I stick something in behind an eye and something else into a tooth," Dr. Caligari said.

"Sounds uncomfortable," Jack said.

"Sissy," Dr. Caligari said. "Yes, uncomfortable but not painful. I'll knock you out for it in any case. We don't have time to fiddle about. First there are some things you need to know."

"I'm listening, Doc," Jack replied.

"I hope so. This is important," Dr. Caligari said. "I'm inserting two packages, both contain an interface component and an active one. The active part consists of microscopic machines called nanos. When activated they'll change both your brain function and the function of your overall nervous system and muscles."

"For the better I trust," Jack said.

"For a time, at a cost," Dr. Caligari said. "Time will slow down. You'll think faster, move faster, see more, and have greater strength. For a time."

"How long?" Jack asked.

"Depends on how hard you push yourself," Dr. Caligari answered. "Ten minutes at least with minimal side effects, fifteen is reasonable and twenty likely wouldn't kill you though you'd feel it. Half hour at most and you'll probably fall over when you come down."

"Ouch, that's not long, and sounds like I'll be out of it afterward," Jack said.

"Enough to get you out of immediate danger from what Ted has told me," Dr. Caligari answered. "If you're well fed and rested and stay in shape and carry a little extra fat, you'll get a few more minutes."

"Stay in shape?" Jack asked.

Caligari inspected Jack then referred to something out of Jack's line sight again. That was getting annoying. "Yes, you're not in bad shape," he said, "but wouldn't hurt for you to start running a few miles a day and some muscle building is indicated too."

Jack thought about it. The military had had physical fitness standards, but they weren't too stringent for spacers, not like for marines, and he'd let his fitness slide the last couple of years. Been busy, but that was only an excuse. "Right, Doc," Jack said. "I'll get a routine set up. Sounds like this thing is risky. That it's a desperate last option in a dire emergency."

The doctor nodded. "That's fair," he said. "Pretty safe for a short period, but you don't want to try it more than once every couple of days. You should be able to tell how you can handle from how you feel."

"Okay, Doc," Jack said. "I've got it."

"Good," Dr. Caligari said. "Sadly I'm not going to walk you through a trial run of any sort. In fact I won't even be here when you come out of the procedure. Appearances require I be somewhere else shortly."

"That's not good," Jack said.

"It is what it is," Dr. Caligari said. "Briefly there are two ways of activating your supercharged state and two modes. Visualizing my face and thinking supper should bring up an overlay menu in your vision which you can pick options from by just concentrating on them."

"Your gadgets read minds?" Jack asked.

"No, they pick up certain patterns in your brain activity and on your optic nerve."

"Okay." It sounded like high-tech mind reading to Jack.

"Anyhow that's how it's supposed to work but my personal testing of the feature has been limited. As a backup you will be able to directly activate supercharged mode by physically crushing your back right molar. Twice. First to initialize. Second to fully activate. Ideally you'll space out initialization over five or ten minutes, but you can crash activate. Crash activation means it'll hurt a bit more, you'll be a bit weaker and slower at first, and the side effects afterward will be more severe."

"So no cracking nuts with my back teeth then?" Jack asked.

Seemed like that there were a lot of caveats and gotchas with this procedure but he had to trust Ted Smith and therefore Caligari.

"Obviously, at least on your right side," Dr. Caligari said somewhat testily. "A bit of common sense and care is called for."

"Right, Doc," Jack said. "Just wanted to get that straight."

"Good. Now when you come out of supercharged mode you'll be tired, hungry and thirsty," Dr. Caligari said. "Rest, plenty of food high in fat and protein, and fluid, the more sugar in it the better are called for."

"Right got that, Doc. Pig out, drink a lot, and then flake out," Jack replied.

Dr. Caligari grunted again. Seemed he didn't entirely shar Jack's sense of humor. "Time to get to it. Lie back stare straight up at the ceiling. Don't move," he said. He rubbed some ointment around Jack's left eye. "Okay, open wide," he said and then pried Jack's mouth open to do the same to the gums on the back right side of Jack's mouth. At some point he had put plastic surgical gloves on. Much to Jack's relief. "How's that feel?"

"Tingly think I'm going numb where you spread that gunk," Jack replied.

"Good. Now I'm putting you under," Dr. Caligari said placing a breathing mask over Jack's face. His bedside manner was lacking in Jack's opinion. "Take a deep breath," Caligari said. Jack did that. "Now shortly I'm going to put this big needle in your eye," Dr. Caligari continued. The tone of sadistic amusement was unmistakable now. He showed Jack the needle, but it was very blurry.

That was all Jack remembered before waking up with a headache and a mostly numb but still rather sore jaw. He was all alone.

He struggled up out of the dentist's chair. He checked the time. It was over an hour later. Well that'd been interesting, but he had things to do.

He looked around and saw a second door to the room. It had a piece of paper attached. It said *"This way out."* He took the hint and left via the door.

Down a flight of stairs and out an unmarked door left him in an alley. The alley connected to a street that wasn't the one he'd entered by.

Jack shrugged and went on his way.

***

John Malcolm walked past a gutted store front.

He'd been down on the planet, Lincoln, taking care of some business in Franklin City when the explosions had ripped through the shopping concourse of Washington Station. It'd been like a blow to his stomach.

His wife and kids had still been on station. It'd been hours before he was sure they were safe. He'd warned his superiors back in SDFHQ intelligence about organized crime infiltrating Jefferson system and they'd done nothing. Scary and frustrating all in one package.

He stopped and surveyed the damage. Much of it had already been cleaned up in the months since.

"Shocking isn't it?" a nearby older man sitting on a bench said to him. The old fellow had a cane and by the way he was leaning on it with both hands needed it. His eyes were bright though and his look sharp like some predatory bird's.

John turned and looked back. He was at a temporary loss. "It was," he finally replied. "Wish somebody could have prevented it."

The old man looked away and made a disgusted sound. It turned into a hacking cough. "Pirates!" he spit out at length. "Lay down with dogs and you get fleas," he went on. In a sudden spasm of energy he waved his cane at John. "People here don't want the Federation nosing around in their business, but they do want it to keep them safe," the old geezer declaimed. "Idiots!" he snorted before subsiding.

John could hardly admit just how much he agreed with the old man. "Well, it's human to want to have your cake and eat too," he said. He looked around and sighed. "Maybe this'll be a wake up call for us."

The old man folded over his cane again snorted. "Maybe," he wheezed. "Guess you have to hope. Forgive me, young man, I'm just so tired. Tired of people always making the same stupid mistakes over and over. Get to my age and you start to lose faith. Still the world goes on."

"Guess it does," John said stepping over and patting the old guy on the shoulder. "We'll get this sorted out don't worry. It was good talking to you, but I've got business. Bye now." With that he walked off not looking back.

He wished he could have told the old fellow that the Federation was in Jefferson and working to fix the situation. He wished he could have told he himself was working to make everyone safe and not have basically blown him off with empty words.

He wished he was certain of it himself.

He was a Federation agent. He was taking action. He wasn't sure what his bosses back on Earth intended to achieve.

Hopefully once his current errand was done, he'd have a better idea.

John worked for Jefferson's main in-system shipping company. At first he'd been a pilot, but he worked himself up to dispatcher, then Chief of Operations. Despite its importance the company wasn't a big one, and it wasn't odd that he should be personally dealing with the receipt of a high value shipment from out system.

Good thing. If it had been, he'd have to have made other arrangements for communicating with his bosses back in SDFHQ.

His last set of instructions hard on the heels of the attacks on Jefferson system had emphasized the need to keep a close eye on the operations of the new interstellar trading company Ad Astra Ventures. He'd wondered about that in the light of attacks by what was obviously organized crime on an interstellar scale but had followed his instructions.

"Your elevator is here," a light female voice said. A petite woman in young middle age was looking at him in bemusement. "Lost in heavy thoughts?" she asked.

He'd made his way to the end of the concourse and to the elevator bank that connected the station's different levels without consciously noticing it. Apparently pushed the button to the warehouse level without noticing it too.

"Thanks. Sorry," he said to the woman while backing into the elevator. "In shipping. The attacks messed us all up." He could see her nodding sympathetically as the elevator doors closed behind him.

It was one thing he liked about Jefferson. The people were all friendly and helpful. He'd heard there were rural areas and small towns like that back in the Solar System, but in his experience in the larger cities and stations people minded their own business to a fault.

He dearly hoped his impending instructions wouldn't put him at odds with his fellow Jeffersonians. He was glad the report he was sending the other way was going to indicate Ad Astra hadn't been involved with the criminal elements that had attacked the system.

He didn't know what to think of the fact it looked like Ad Astra was about to significantly expand its offices in-system and even apparently planned to direct at least some of its operations from Jefferson. Jefferson was more central than Newton, but the company's principals were all from Newton, and central control barely worked for system level shipping let alone interstellar operations.

Maybe it'd make more sense to his bosses back on Earth.

4: Sitting Down to Drink

Sergeant Jackson, technically ex-sergeant Jackson, also technically an ex-SDF marine, strode down the deckplates of a Slovo Station shopping district.

A mixed entertainment and shopping district to be precise. One that was not anywhere as nice or fancy as the one he'd just left after checking on Jack Black and the security team guarding him. Looking around, Jackson saw a lot less fake marble and bright lighting, fewer fashionable boutiques and more clothing stores selling practical work clothes. Instead of restaurants featuring foreign cuisine, he saw fast food kiosks and diners.

He rounded a corner featuring a burger shop on one side and walked past the entrance to discount store stocking an eclectic mixture of necessities and small cheap fripperies and luxuries. He doubted most of the people who frequented the tony upper deck shopping concourse would have been seen dead in such a place.

He smiled. Poor Jack Black, he'd have been much more comfortable down here. Now, however, he had to pretend to share the snobbery of his former betters, the better to hob-nob and politic with them. For all the significant perks that Black's new found wealth had, Jackson wouldn't have changed places with him for anything.

Jackson was happy with who he was and good at what he did. That being a tough, no-nonsense bad ass who fought bad guys and won.

Black could keep his wine bars, balls, and soiree's. Black was stuck playing the wealthy businessman and swimming in murky political waters.

Jackson got to go to honest Irish pubs like the one just coming into sight.

It was called "O'Keefes". It had the stereotypical corridor facing front of fake dark wood and opaque colored glass windows typical of such places. Anyone seeing it would know it for it was. An important feature down here near the docks.

Local regulars might come close to covering the regular fixed costs of such a place, but it was high spending visitors from passing ships that provided a profit margin.

High spending being relative, they were mostly older men, the odd woman, veteran civilian spacers, SDF NCOs both spacer and marine. The place was a known haunt for them. They fit in with the local regulars, mostly veteran security and police, some small business, and trades people.

The clientele and ownership were both second generation. The date in discreet discolored bronze that Jackson saw as he reached the door of the place was from some sixty years prior. Charlie had retired from the SDF to start the place. Paddy, his son, who'd retired some thirty years later, ran it now.

His eyes adjusting to the interior gloom, Jackson saw Paddy himself behind the bar.

The bar was quiet if not silent. A ballad played in the background, not quite loud enough for its words to be discernible. The few patrons were scattered about alone or in small groups. The loudest of them was the party of men in the back, his men, that Jackson was about to join. Even their conversation, animated as it was, wasn't actually loud.

Jackson bellied up to the bar. Paddy seeing him poured him a dark hued draft without asking. Jackson admired the efficiency. Nodding to the bartender, he took his mug and made his way back past the dart boards not currently in use to his men who surrounded a table in a lighted raised alcove in the back. It was one of the largest tables in the moderately sized place.

"Hey, Sarge," one of the men, Miller, greeted him as he sat

himself down.

"Evening all," Jackson said once seated. He looked around at his men. "Imagine you've all got your papers by now."

"Yep, discharge, or reup, health plan election, pension election, and relocation on final discharge election," Miller said. A chorus of "Yep, me too,", "Same here," and a couple of nods from the other men answered Jackson's question.

"Just like promised when Taylor asked us to do this," Miller said.

Jackson grunted. He looked around again, making certain he had each man's attention. "I did too," he said. "Taylor sent a little note along with my papers."

"We staying then, Sarge?" Miller said. Apparently he'd set himself up as the men's spokesman.

"Taylor won't be," Jackson said. "They're sending him back to the Core."

Miller grunted. The rest of them waited expectantly, a few took silent sips of their brew. The mood was resigned, if glum. "He's one of the best," Miller said. "We'll miss him. Here's to Captain Taylor!"

Jackson and the rest raised glasses in a toast. "Here's to," they muttered a chorus before drinking deep.

The toast done, he looked around at the circle of expectant faces. "So that much was in the clear," Jackson said. "The rest was between the lines. We did agree on some phrases ahead of time."

"Spit it out, Sarge," Miller asked impatiently. "Stay or go?"

"Stay," Jackson replied to Miller with an annoyed stare. "I'm taking a final discharge and electing for lump sum payouts across the board."

A quiet, emphatic "Geez" from ex-corporal Juan Lopez was the sole response.

"I haven't got a better crystal ball than any of the rest of you," Jackson said. "I don't think Captain Taylor does either. Still, he's better situated to see what's happening than we are."

"Captain was always a straight shooter," Miller said. "But sharp too. No flies on that man."

"Smart man," Jackson agreed. "So no details and no guarantees of anything but he thinks if we stick with Black and Ad Astra we're on our own."

"Kind of a shock," Miller admitted, "but really we were always more or less on our own here weren't we?"

"We were," Jackson agreed. "But now it looks like the Federation might stop even pretending. You all have to decide on your own, but Taylor thinks, and I do too, that we're best off sticking with Black."

"And not just retiring for real, but cutting all ties?" Miller asked. "No pension, no health plan?"

"When the crap hits the fan, do you really want to put your faith in a politician's promises?" Jackson asked.

His men's faces looked grim. Some just gazed into their beer. They could have pointed out that the Federation's promises had been as good or better than gold for over two centuries. None of them did.

"No," Miller replied harshly. "Looks sunny from Earth, but we've all seen too much out here."

"So who's staying and who's going," Jackson asked. "I've got duty rosters to make up."

"I'm in. I'm staying," Miller led off. One by one, each and every one of the men around the table responded the same.

Jackson kept his relief to himself. He raised his mug. "One for all and all for one," he toasted.

With that, the drinking got serious.

* * *

Cynthia Dallemagne was a young woman, but right now she was feeling a lot older.

A little over a day out of Newton in jump to New Lustania and Slovo Station and she had some planning to do.

She sighed, fiddled with her coffee cup, and committed to taking a sip.

"So what's bothering you, lass?" the gnomish old man sharing a table with her asked. His name was Ebenezar Greyfield, he was captain of the *Frontier Falcon*. It was the *Falcon*'s main mess they were currently sitting in.

"It's sensitive," Cynthia said.

"Of course it is," Ebenezar replied. "No one close by though. Besides, there isn't a person on this ship we can't trust."

Cynthia grimaced and bought time with another sip of coffee. It was strong and bitter and half creamy milk but she'd got used to it. She couldn't help thinking both her cabin and Ebenezar's had private tables they could be talking at. However, Ebenezar

Greyfield didn't use his cabin for meals or breaks or even most meetings, he used the same mess all the rest of the crew did.

"And, take note," Ebenezar went on in answer to Cynthia's silence, "I like to show my crew that I trust them. You have to give trust to get trust."

It was unusual for him to give advice so directly. Cynthia nodded in acknowledgment. She'd come to appreciate the man's patience and was taking advantage of it. It was another thing that distinguished his style from both Captain Taylor's and Dr. Smith's. They always gave the impression their time was precious, and they'd definitely would have been holding this meeting in their private quarters. She frowned.

She wasn't sure about Jack Black. He was new to being in charge of things and didn't really have a command style, but she had a feeling it'd be more like Ebenezar Greyfield's than Captain Taylor's for all that he was ex-SDF. At least ex-SDF in theory. She had no doubt Taylor was using whatever leverage he could on Black.

"I'll keep it in mind," she finally said. "I'm used to working independently."

"So your boss, let's you figure out how to do things on your own," Ebenezar said. "With little or no help, I'd guess."

"That's right," Cynthia said.

"But he sets the goals," Ebenezar continued. "And I'm guessing again you've worked mostly alone and haven't had to spend much time herding others in the right direction."

Cynthia smiled at Ebenezar's phrasing. "Well, sometimes Jack felt like a whole herd on his own."

"Don't kid yourself, lassie," Ebenezar replied firmly. "That man would follow you to hell and thank you for the favor."

Cynthia was tempted to retort that men's infatuation with women often didn't amount to solid commitment, but thought better of it. Jack's attraction to her was obvious. At first she hadn't minded trading on it.

Later a lot of time together and much of that in extreme danger had created much temptation. Jack had been a gentleman. A relief to be practical. As the daughter of an old Newtonian family and a rising young academic, any relationship with Jack was wholly inappropriate. In very bad taste, in fact. As the undercover agent she'd been in reality most of her adult life, all relationships had been temporary expedients.

Who she really was and whatever relationship she had with Jack didn't feel like it fit into either category. It was a puzzle.

"You'll be needing to figure that out," Ebenezar said once again, apparently reading her mind. "But that's not your immediate problem, is it?"

"I believe you're right on both counts, Captain," Cynthia said. Despite herself, she couldn't help liking the old pirate and even trusting him to a degree. She only hoped he wasn't literally an old pirate, the law being on the thin side out on the Frontier.

"So?"

"My problem, Captain, is I'm not sure what my problems are or how I should prioritize them," Cynthia replied looking directly at Ebenezar. It was an effort. She was embarrassed by her confusion. "Dr. Smith was damned vague while verbally wandering all over the map in the discussions we had before I left."

"Is that normal for him?" Ebenezar asked innocently.

"No it's not," Cynthia replied.

"So it was deliberate," Ebenezar said.

Cynthia squinted at the man. Good heavens, for the life of her he looked all the world like a jolly elf. He looked back at her with a blandly quizzical expression. "I guess it must have been," she allowed. She took another sip of coffee to hide her confusion at the realization.

"Seems to me," Ebenezar said a slow calm voice, "that Dr. Smith wanted you to figure out your own objectives. He did have a reason for sending you away from Newton, right?"

Cynthia took a deep breath. What she chose to say next was a critical decision in its own right. "He thinks the SDF is going to attack the Beyonders and stage through Newton to do it," she said. She was surprised she sounded so calm and matter of fact about it. "Sometime in the next few months."

"Wanted you and our ships out the reach of Federation officers claiming what's not theirs, did he?" Ebenezar asked.

"Our back office staff too," Cynthia added. Might as well be hung for a sheep as for a lamb.

"Perfectly within your legal rights aren't you?" Ebenezar said, leaning back with his hands on his belly and a beatific expression.

Cynthia snorted. Captain Ebenezar Greyfield was no innocent.

"Right we're all within our rights aren't we?" she said. The Captain had clarified the issue beautifully. "But the SDF commanders and the Federation aren't going to care, are they?"

"Time will tell," Ebenezar said. "Best not to be too hasty, but I think we'd both bet that way."

"I feel like an idiot," Cynthia said. It wasn't a good feeling.

"You know," Ebenezar went on in a quiet contemplative tone, "the captains and watch crew of FTL ships are all required to be certified. We get a certain amount of education on standing watches and handling emergencies."

Cynthia looked at him blankly. She knew he was leading up to a piece of advice. Probably advice it'd be good to listen to. "Yes," she said.

"They've been studying how people act in a crisis for hundreds of years," he said. "Do you know how people usually go wrong?"

"They panic?" she ventured.

"You'd think," he answered. "But no. Maybe it's fear of seeming to panic, or looking silly, or of putting themselves and others to pointless effort, or just mental inertia, but people's main mistake is not reacting at all until it's too late."

She looked at him. The twinkle in his eye was still there, but it was tinged with a certain sadness. This was as serious as Ebenezar Greyfield got. "That's odd," she said quietly. "How do you know when action is needed?" She felt silly as soon as the words left her mouth.

Ebenezar smiled sympathetically. "You have to be willing to be mistaken for someone who overreacts. Someone who's too by the book," he said. "You can't worry too much about false alarms. On the other hand, you don't abandon ship because of one, but for damned sure you rouse the crew and have everybody closed up at their emergency stations."

"You drill and you have clear criteria for what to do," Cynthia supplied. Of course you did. Even passengers on a cruise liner were required to be familiar with the routines.

"That's right," Ebenezar said, beaming at her. For all the world, he seemed like a proud parent whose child had just got a good mark in school.

"So the watch crew has sounded the alarm and we're all going to emergency stations," she said, drawing out the simile.

"Climb into your escape capsule and when the order to

abandon ship comes don't hesitate to hit the big red button," Ebenezar said continuing the thought.

"Better figure out where that big red button is," Cynthia said.

"Good idea," Ebenezar agreed.

***

Jack had been warned to remain neutral in no uncertain terms.

What had been uncertain, vague indeed, was neutral between who and how.

"A penny for your thoughts," Mary Waldgreen asked him.

Jack startled. He looked around the open-air patio they were sitting on along with the rest of their large party. It'd be dark soon. The sun was approaching the horizon over the ocean. They'd just enjoyed a good steak dinner at the "Ocean's Bluff" one of the finest restaurants New Chicago boasted.

"I was thinking about conflicts, and sides, and friends and allies," Jack said rather more honestly than he'd intended. Could lack of clarity be a saving grace?

Mary smiled. A sphinx-like smile. She stirred some milk into her tea. She took the opportunity to make sure there was no one close who could hear their conversation. Most of their company had wandered off or were busy with their own conversations. The dinner was winding down. "Should I be worried that you're trying to figure who you can trust and who you can't?" she asked.

"No," Jack said. "You're a friend."

"I'm flattered," Mary said. "An ally too?"

"That too," Jack said. He looked up into the darkening sky and saw a bright dot. It was Slovo Station if he wasn't mistaken. A familiar place, if not his favorite. He'd been shot at too many times up there. "World's a big place and I don't think I'll ever figure much of it out."

"But you sense trouble coming," Mary said.

"I do," Jack said. "I think it's better if I don't go into details. It'd be betraying people who trusted me to mention some of it."

Mary nodded. Lifting her tea to her lips, she sipped it while giving Jack a cool look over the rim of her cup.

"Sorry," Jack said.

Mary put her cup down daintily in its saucer and looked at Jack forthrightly. "I thought it was both generous and a little over complicated," she said, "that you had us form our own trading co-op to deal with Ad Astra here in New Lustania."

"We are stretched rather thin," Jack said. "If we set up a wholly owned and controlled trading company here with folks on salary, we get better control and margins for sure, but we don't have a lot of people we know we can trust. Short on working capital, too."

"Yes, your reasons for outsourcing to a local organization are plausible," she agreed. "You could have organized it differently though."

"True," Jack agreed. He'd never really expected to fool her. He'd just hoped she'd trust him and let it go.

"You think there's some reason we here in New Lustania might not want to be too closely associated with the Ad Astra name in the near future," Mary declared. "You don't have to say why."

Jack colored. He hadn't been completely open with her and he wasn't going to start being so now despite being caught out. Just associating with him placed her in some danger, and he'd not warned her of that. He still wasn't going to share the nature of threat. "I'm not certain, but I think Ad Astra might be unpopular in some quarters in the coming months," he said. "Really, I'm sorry but I can't go into details about why I think that."

"I understand," Mary said with a sad smile. Her eyes twinkled. "You should know there are some things you can't hide," she added. "Ship movements and people suddenly taking long trips for instance."

"Ouch," Jack said. "Good thing most people aren't as smart or observant as you are." What really worried him was smart, but maybe too imaginative and paranoid, people reading things into sensible precautions that weren't there. Jack had had his share of fights. He didn't want more. Unfortunately people were watching him and inclined to interpret anything he or Ad Astra did as picking a side when the ka-ka finally hit the fan.

Mary grinned at him. Almost despite herself, it seemed. She dipped her head to hide her expression. "You wish you weren't being watched," she said with amusement. "You'd like to just run your business, have everyone make a steady profit and not to make any big fuss about it."

"It doesn't seem like that much to ask," Jack replied.

"I'm sorry, Jack," Mary said. "I'm used to people who are ambitious, pompous or more usually both. It's rather amusing that you've succeeded beyond most of their wildest dreams and not only don't want them, but actively dislike the fame and power."

"I think you exaggerate," Jack said. Her assertions made him distinctly uncomfortable. He was just a guy doing his best who'd had a lot of luck. Plenty of help too, not a little from Mary herself.

She looked at him sternly. "No, I do not," she said. "It's vital you understand this. You have power and you have influence and you have to accept that." She fiddled with the handle of her fragile looking teacup. "In a different time and place and maybe your dream of being a small trader of only moderate importance with limited responsibility might have been possible. This is not that time or place. You're important. You're prominent. You accept that and prosper or you don't and fail. Failure means at best misery. Likely it means the end of you. You understand that much?"

"I get that much in theory," Jack admitted sadly. He took a sip of his own coffee to buy a few seconds of time. "I'm having a hard time feeling it in my guts. Honestly, I've been busy, but I think I've done as much as anyone could expect. You've got more to say don't you?"

Mary gave Jack a sharp nod. "You've done well, Jack," she said, "but all that means is that you're going to have to do better in the future. A lot of people like me are depending on you. Like it or not, you've got my future and a lot of other futures as well as your own in your hands."

"So buck up and face my responsibilities, is that it?" Jack asked.

"That's it," Mary confirmed. "It's going to mean making choices, and it's going to mean making mistakes. There's no avoiding that."

"Maybe not," Jack replied solemnly, "but the choices don't seem as clear to me as the seem to you and some other people. I'm on unfamiliar ground and I'm not at all sure some of my friends aren't reading more into little things than's really justified."

"So you're trying to hedge your bets and not make any irretrievable commitments," Mary amplified. "That makes sense just as soon as it doesn't paralyze you come the time you have to act." She snorted.

Sitting Down to Drink

"What's so funny?" Jack asked.

"Just listen to me, the shopkeeper trained as an historian lecturing you," Mary replied.

"Sometimes a little distance helps you see the forest, not the trees," Jack said. "I don't mind. I value your advice. It bothers me I might be leaving you and my other friends here in New Lustania to fend for yourselves."

Mary reached over and touched the back of Jack's hand. "Well don't worry about that," she said. "We're all big girls and boys. That's not all though, is it?"

"No, it isn't," Jack said. "Even if my assessment of the strategic situation is right." He squirmed slightly in his seat. He sounded pompous to his own ears, but "strategic assessment" was in fact part of his job now. "Even if my feelings about the situation and those of my not to be mentioned friends..."

"The ones on Newton, no doubt," Mary muttered acerbically.

"My friends who I can't honorably identify," Jack said, plowing on. "Even if we've accurately figured out what's happening, I'm not sure trying to fight it or evade it are the right things to do."

"Why not?" Mary asked.

"Because even if not everyone in the Federation has the best interest of everyone else in it in mind, that doesn't mean the Federation isn't itself the best we can all hope for," Jack said. "It might not be perfect and it might be getting a lot less perfect, but that doesn't mean there are any better alternatives."

"The very fact that you were worried about discussing the issue suggests it's already got pretty bad," Mary said. She grimaced. "You have to have faith that people can build a good future for themselves without direction from hundreds of light years away."

"Hundreds of light years," Jack repeated. "That's the other issue. There's no space travel without the FTL engines from either Luna or Newton. I don't know why anybody thinks the Federation would abandon the sector and leave the factories on Newton intact."

"Or think they could defend themselves from God knows who, even if the Feds did," Mary elaborated for him.

"Exactly," Jack said. "It's like we're chess players planning the middle game but expecting a miracle to save us in the endgame.

Am I missing something here?"

"Only that life isn't chess," Mary said. "You can't see the whole board or all the pieces. You can't even be sure what the rules are or they won't change. "

"And that helps me how?" Jack asked. He made himself smile to take the edge off the question.

"Jack," Mary replied with mild exasperation. "It's clear you think the people running the Federation, the SDF really since that's the only Federal institution that really counts out here, are about to do something problematic."

Jack squirmed. He hadn't felt so uncomfortable since his Aunt Edna had caught him with his hand in the cookie jar when he was just eight. It was embarrassing being a grown man and feeling like this. "That's unfortunate, since I'm really not supposed to talk about it," he said, feeling somewhat exasperated himself.

Mary sighed. "It's a trick I've read about early space age officials using," she said. "They tell you something you might figure out for yourself, but in secrecy, which keeps you quiet. Pretty soon nobody is willing to discuss anything sensitive and then when bad things happen everyone is surprised because nobody who had any information would even discuss the possibility."

Jack frowned at her. He wasn't completely sure what she was saying, but he thought she was suggesting Dr. Smith had played him. "I don't think my sources were trying to do that," he replied.

"Maybe not. Perhaps not intentionally," Mary said. "Doesn't matter though. Discretion is important, but sometimes if the result is shutting down necessary conversations, it makes you complicit in preventing people from being able to deal with problems."

"I don't want to do that," Jack said.

"I know, Jack," Mary said. "If I didn't, we wouldn't be having this conversation."

"Good," Jack replied. "You were saying?"

"Pretty clear Federation is soon going to have the SDF do something game changing," Mary said. "That's been clear to anyone paying attention for a while. No need for shadowy in the know figures to pass on hush hush, burn before reading tips to figure that out."

Jack winced. He wasn't completely sure she was right about

that, but he did feel like a bit of a jackass. He was pretty sure Ted Smith hadn't meant to put him in this situation, but the Newtonians, even Ted who wasn't as bad as most of them, did tend to think they were smarter and better informed than everyone else. "And you think this means something I've missed? Jack asked.

Mary didn't answer right away. She took a sip of her tea and eyed him. "No you haven't missed it," she said, "but I don't think you're fully facing up to it either. They're going to try and change the rules. They're going to try and make it a fait accompli. Do it quick, surprise everyone, and have it done before anyone can work up any opposition to the new order."

And there it was. She was asking if he'd go along with that or fight it. An ugly decision, which was why he'd been trying not to think about it. Clear once he did though, even if it make him queasy. "I won't go along with that," Jack said. "I've sworn an oath to the Federation as it is. I'm not looking to cause problems and it wouldn't be good for business. That said no one is going to unilaterally force me or Ad Astra to break our promises to our customers."

"You're willing to rebel?" Mary asked, her tone altogether too calm.

"Ad Astra is an independent neutral business that's not going to take sides in any coup or rebellion," Jack said, biting out each word clearly.

"You think you can make that work?" Mary asked.

"I'm going to damn well try," Jack replied.

5: Mind Games

Jack was feeling grim.

Jack was supposed to be evaluating spreadsheets, or at least reading reports. If this was what success brought, maybe he should have remained a failure.

The Bird of Profit would be jumping for Alta Iberia within the hour. Jack wondered if a quick trip to bridge to be there for it would be amiss. A break might be good. On the other hand, he tried not to seem like he was peering over the shoulders of the people who worked for him.

He knew he had to trust them. He knew that was important that they knew he trusted them. Still, he was a hands on kind of man and not one who trust came easily to.

He was an honest one though. Proud of it, too. Didn't make him immediately popular with everyone, but there were people who appreciated someone who talked straight and could be trusted. He should build on that. Get trust, give trust, get more trust. Round and round.

And thinking of trust, Jack thought, while fiddling with the stylus he was supposed to be using to manipulate figures on his computer screen, he certainly trusted Mary Waldgreen.

He trusted her both to be honest in what she said, and to be well informed and intelligent in her thinking, as well as just plain perceptive. Her character was just as real as the input device in his hand and the seat upon which his poor sore butt was sitting.

Ha. Two action points emerged from that thought.

One, he had to take her belief that he and Ad Astra might have to take sides against the Federation seriously. That despite the fact that it was plain undesirable in of itself and ran against the loyalties he'd held his whole life. Also the idea was at best quixotic, more accurately it was borderline insane. The Federation controlled all of humanity's existing purpose-built military vessels.

Jack knew there had to be a few illegal ships belonging to trading clans, pirates, or Beyonders out on the fringes of human settled space. He also knew they had to be few in number. He figured they had to be much inferior in quality, too. People were spread thin on the Frontier. They were hand to mouth generalists not specialized in heavy industry.

That was completely ignoring that the vast majority of FTL transports and passenger ships were Federation licensed and controlled. The vast majority of humanity and its governing elites belonged to the Federation. The Federation's control might be light and only grudgingly acknowledged, but it was real for all of that.

Opposing the Federation was madness. Good reasons if they existed couldn't change that.

The second point was he needed to get off of his ass and move around some. That at least was something he could do.

The crew of *The Bird of Profit* were good people. So was their captain, Captain Joshua Greyfields, or Captain Joshua as Jack thought of him. He shouldn't worry about offending them. Friends would understand a natural desire to watch the ship's jump from the bridge.

He'd get a drink from the mess on the way up. Merchant ships were more relaxed about having food and drink on the bridge than the SDF. With that thought Jack put his stylus down, locked his computer, and heaved himself to his feet. It was a couple strides to his cabin door. He nodded to a crewman in the passageway as he exited. The crewman, an engineer, acknowledged his greeting in an absent minded way. He hurried by focused on a hand held tablet.

Amused, Jack watched the crewman bustle aft. To his chagrin, he couldn't remember his name. It was obvious that the crewman had recognized Jack but wasn't overly impressed by his high and mighty status. Making sure engineering's checklists were all ticked off before jump being much more important. Jack approved of the man's priorities. They cheered him up.

Maybe, just maybe, he took himself too seriously.

Didn't mean he didn't have an important job, but after all, no one could be responsible for all the rights and wrongs in the universe.

The good Lord knew he had enough immediate problems. Not the least of which was setting up an interstellar trading company and then running it. Worse running it from a different place from the one it'd started in.

Jack just missed walking into yet another crewman he recognized as a comms specialist on the way into the mess. "Sorry, Martha," he apologized. He lined up at the coffee machine behind a couple of other crew members. They were all busy getting ready for the coming watch change and jump. No one paid him much mind beyond nods of acknowledgment. He enjoyed it.

He contemplated their coming jump and planned route as he poured his coffee. The New Lustania to Alta Iberia to Nova Britannia to Jefferson back to Hanshan route was a side loop to the more trafficked New Lustania to Al-Alhadeen to Hanshan route. Each link in the chain being only a single jump made the route a short one. Most habitable worlds didn't happen to be so close together. Less fortunately the planets in question were similar both in their natural endowments and their development. They were all earth sized, half ocean and had a couple of large but not huge continents in their temperate latitudes. They'd all been terraformed from a base of very primitive native ecologies. They'd had oxygen atmospheres but no advanced large multi-cellular life forms.

As a result, the products they produced were all similar. It was doubtless a good thing that in the long term that they were self-sufficient in everything but very high end manufactures and novelties. Too bad it didn't make for profitable trading.

Ad Astra could expect to carry most of what trade there was, but that was limited and the profits from it thin. It was going to be necessary to nurture both markets and production on this route.

Local exports in particular. They could all be expected to import as many high-tech items from Newton as they could afford. The same was true of mid-tech items from Hanshan, and coffee and other exotic foodstuffs from Al-Alhadeen. He was going to have to help them find things to export. Fish, grain, hides, and beef just didn't make the cut as high value specialty items.

So that was an action point. He had to find new exports for each of the next few worlds.

Jack was feeling much cheerier as he stepped onto the bridge to find a watch changeover in progress. Made the place much more crowded than usual. Not the best timing on his part. Still, he'd identified a clear goal, and that was good. He claimed himself an observer's position to the aft of the captain's chair, hard against the back bulkhead where he could see the entire bridge.

Jack sat and watched the crew hand off their stations to those relieving them. They were relaxed but very professional about it. Not overly formal but thorough. They weren't making sloppy assumptions. This was a tight ship as well as a happy one.] warmed Jack's heart.

He hoped the new HQ he was going to be establishing at Jefferson, probably on Washington Station, would work out as well. He wondered if he ought to ask Captain Joshua to lend him some of the ship's personnel. Moe could use them to supplement the people he was bringing with him. They could help him get established, at least.

A couple of Miriam's girls from Al-Alhadeen might be appropriate too. Later on they'd be hiring locals, but at first Jack wanted people he'd already got a feel for. People he could be sure were loyal to Ad Astra.

So that was another action point. Excellent.

Politics. Not so excellent.

Not something he could delegate to any significant degree either.

In his initial swing along this route, he'd concentrated on generating general good will and on finding both cargoes and some investment. He hadn't had any strictly political goals. He didn't have a genuinely good grasp of local politics in any of the systems on the route. He was a bit better informed on Jefferson than Alta Iberia or Nova Britannia as a result of being attacked there by a competitor's criminal gang. Also because local anti-Federation elements had sought him out. In neither case had he initiated or even appreciated the interest shown.

Thinking about it now, that had been short sighted on his part. What had seemed like hassles at first were might have been opportunities he should have followed up on. One thing was for sure if Ad Astra's HQ was going to be in Jefferson system he needed to be on top of the local politics.

Yet another action point. He was building quite the To-Do list. It was good. Knowing what needed to be done was half the battle.

If there was a falling out with the Federation the Jeffersonians looked to be his most likely source of allies. The El Doradians held out promise too, tricky and violent lot though and literally on the fringes. Marxians and Heinleiners also weren't big supporters of the Federation. They were both too ruthless and devoted to their own self interest for that. That said, he couldn't expect to deal with them successfully from anything other than a position of power.

Hanshan and Al-Alhadeen were very different as cultures. They were identical twins in regards to their attitudes towards the Federation and the outside world in general. They both regretted not being able to wish the rest of existence away. They'd not lend anything more than lip service to either the Federation or groups opposing it. They were definitely in the "a pox on all your houses" category. They traded because it profited them more than it pained them.

He'd not get any help there, but neither would the Federation. If he played his cards right, their neutrality would benefit Ad Astra more than it would any faction in the SDF trying to bring the company to heel.

Beyond Hanshan there was El Dorado. A with the most earth-like non- planet Jack had ever seen. Occupied by the scariest and most contrary tribe of people he'd ever seen. Fortunately, they seemed eager to deal. Given their experience with wanna-be pirate king Foxall and being beyond the protection and effective control of the Federation both they seemed to instinctively understand how dangerous trying to stand alone was. Fierce and independent, but pragmatic too.

Jack couldn't help liking them. He knew they were tough and ruthlessly self-interested, but he also believed he could work with them. Have to be careful. Had to be sure he never appeared to be short changing them, but he did think could work with them.

He had hopes they might be a bridge to both the trading clans along the Frontier and the Beyonders on the other side of it. He didn't want the sector to cut its trading ties with the Federation's core, but he had to plan for the possibility. If nothing else some "exploratory" trips might provide an excuse to draw ships away from the main route back to the Core. It was a plausible excuse for keeping ships out of the New Lustania and Newton systems. He was going to have to do a bit of planning with the El Doradians to make that work.

Actually, it made a lot of sense. His original plan had been a backbone route from Newton to El Dorado through New Lustania, Al-Alhadeen, and Hanshan. From that backbone he'd planned two side loops. The first was to have been the Alta Iberia, Nova Britannia, and Jefferson one they were currently on. Marx and Heinlein would have been the other one.

He'd intended to set up a regular scheduled service despite long term demand not being high enough. Currently, Ad Astra was only profitable because of pent-up demand from the earlier disruption of trade. Both he and Moe had thought that the establishment of regular service would encourage the development of new export businesses that they'd been hoping would replace that demand once it tapered off.

Maybe it would have, maybe it wouldn't have. Fact was that plan wasn't looking viable anymore. Not in the face of the fact that ships visiting Newton were likely to be requisitioned and thereby taken out of service.

Logically, Newton and New Lustania were both going to have to be dropped from regular service. At least until ships going there were safe from seizure. So looked like a hub and spoke structure out of Jefferson was the way to go in order to serve their current customers. Also a good idea to push as many ships as possible out to El Dorado and beyond to trade on speculation.

It was a plan.

Jack watched the jump with new hope in his heart before returning to his office to pound out the details.

* * *

Cynthia strolled through Washington Station's high end shopping concourse with her eyes wide open.

She was here in Jefferson system to gather information. That and to smooth the way for Moe when he arrived to set up Ad Astra's HQ. She didn't have much time. The *Frontier Falcon* was only going to be in system for a few days.

Every day docked was extra cost. The freighter wouldn't spend any more time alongside than what it needed to load and unload. The crew would get a few hours off in shifts, to shop, drink and stretch their legs and that'd be it. Then they and Cynthia along with them would be El Dorado bound.

It shouldn't have been a problem.

A couple quick meetings with several CHSG correspondents to see if anything new had come up. A drink or a meal with a couple of personal contacts to get a better, more in depth feel for the state of the local political and economic climate. In between some quick calls to set up initial appointments for Moe and Jack when they arrived. Not critical work, but work that ought to help them hit the ground running.

Unfortunately, she'd already had some of those information gathering meetings and what she'd learned was disturbing.

People here were scared.

She wouldn't have been surprised to find them still a little jittery after the attacks on Washington Station, but this something else. They'd cleaned up the physical damage done with surprising quickness. To outward appearances, business had returned to normal.

It'd been months. The business people, shop keepers, and administrators of Washington Station and the rest of Jefferson system should all be calming down by now. They weren't.

Rumors and a series of individually small incidents had them all on edge. More to the point, they were specifically scared about being seen to do business with Ad Astra.

To Cynthia's immense frustration, it was proving almost impossible to nail down what or who had them scared.

One of her best contacts, a man she knew for a fact to be both brave and reliable, had told her what he could. "Cynthia, it seems silly when I put it into words, but we're all convinced there's some shadow organization still out there that doesn't like you folks," he'd said. "Doesn't like you and has the power to punish anyone that dares deal with you."

"It's not like you to be scared of shadows," she'd told him, hoping to prod him in his pride. "What have they done, really? Who are they?"

The man had scrunched up his face and shook his head. "Damned if I know who they are," he'd said. "Could be the same drain humpers what blew up half of Washington, but don't think so. It feels different. They're slyly slick, whoever they are. Nasty, cruel and they know just how to hurt people but they're sneaky about it."

He'd wanted to talk. A beer and a sympathetic ear was all that it had taken. An interjected "How so?" from Cynthia and he went on.

"Short anonymous notes left on devices or little pieces of paper where nobody should be able to reach," he'd said. "They just say watch your step and stay clear of troublemakers and foreigners because you and those you love can be hurt."

"That's not enough to scare a man like you," she'd replied.

He'd sighed. "It's easy enough to be brave in the moment when it's just you," he'd said. "Not so easy when it goes on and on and it's your friends and family they're threatening." He'd paused and looked at the knuckles of his hands.

"Go on," she'd said.

"Typical shit in a way," he'd said, rallying. "Dead kitten, blood splotches on the pillow, pictures of your kids they shouldn't have had the access to make. The whole horrid litany. You know it."

"Afraid so," she'd confirmed. Only one brush with a modern mafia and another more in depth experience with some terrorists on a struggling colony that'd been seeded with two incompatible ethnic groups, but it was more than enough experience for a lifetime.

"Not even any finger breaking or other quality one-on-one time," he'd said then. "But it's like they're everywhere all the time. Constantly watching, ready to act just as much as they need to." He'd looked up at her. "And Cynthia it has to be a 'them'. There's the feel of there being one evil master mind behind it, but no one person could be tracking so much and acting on it so promptly."

"You're sure?" she'd asked, knowing full well one could never be certain about something like this.

"Absolutely certain," he'd answered.

She must have looked startled. "I asked around," he'd said. "It was that that did for 'Poppy' my kid's cat. Not just me. Everyone I talked to. Watched closely. Disciplined promptly."

Somebody bumped into her. "Sorry, miss. You okay?" a harried looking man asked her. She was in a brightly lit shopping concourse, not the shadowy corner of a dockside dive.

"Fine, fine," she said. "Just day dreaming. My apologies. It's okay."

"Good then," the man said. He looked like a deliveryman of some sort. "You're sure?"

"Absolutely," she said.

"Great. Have a good day then," he said before turning and rushed off somewhere.

Cynthia stood there feeling stunned and somewhat worried. This wasn't like her at all. She was energetically action oriented, decisive and always alert to her surroundings. She didn't wander around in a day dream like many of her school friends and at least one of her sisters. Particularly when she was already making a point of trying to especially observant because she was looking for hints about a problem she knew existed. Could she be starting to get old already? Was she really that spooked by the situation? Could it be both those things?

Who knew? Wouldn't help to worry about it. Not right now. Limited time. Things to do. People to see.

She'd been trying to assess the mood of the station while walking to where she expected to meet her next contact. She'd also been hoping to pick up on subtle details that might give some clues about what was going on.

She looked around. Sadly, all she saw was a shopping concourse that looked much like a dozen others she'd seen on various stations and planets. It was a high end place, glittering with wealth and discretion. Took a certain level of population and wealth to support such a place, but given that she saw nothing unusual about it. There was no hint of the pervasive fear that her inquiries suggested lurked under the surface.

That was odd. Now that she thought about it both the criminal mafia and the terrorists had had a subtle effect on the whole tone of society. They'd created an atmosphere of subtle wariness and distrust. People were slightly distrusting of each other, especially strangers. They kept a certain distance. They kept their guard up. They gave the sense they knew the world wasn't entirely safe.

The people here on Washington Station and in Jefferson

system generally had just been subjected to attacks that had literally blasted their daily routines wide open. She had good evidence of a continuing program of intimidation. People here had good reason to feel unsafe. Good reason to be wary.

Yet standing here, she wasn't feeling it.

Mid-day on a work day, they were most absorbed in their own affairs. Not many of them were just idly chatting like the lady at the flower kiosk and a woman shopper. They also weren't acting wary. When they did acknowledge each other, they were bright and friendly in a passing way. They weren't sullen and wary in the way Cynthia had seen people living in constant if low grade fear become.

Cynthia stepped out of the middle of the pedestrian traffic and spun around slowly, looking. It was true people were relaxed. That guy there who'd just bought an ice cream was being careful not to make a mess, but he was happy. That lady with a toddler was a little exasperated with the little guy dragging his feet, but she didn't seem alert to the possibility of threats to him. The odd shop keeper or assistant loitering by the doors of their shops greeted passers by with little nods and small smiles and a few friendly words. There was no edge to their manners.

Maybe it took time for a place's mood to reflect new threats?

Maybe not, maybe whoever was behind the intimidation was just that targeted and subtle. Not a pleasant thought.

Well, didn't look like just standing here was going to resolve the question. She had a place to be. She was looking for a shop. A silverware shop from which Jack had bought a very interesting print. He'd reported a very interesting story about that shop's owner.

Cynthia had originally, with some regret, not planned to visit the place herself. Her plate was full enough.

Now, however, she was looking for answers and not finding them in the usual places.

Perhaps the owner of Revere's Silverware could help.

She moved on.

***

John Malcolm walked the halls of Washington Station's "Docklands" like he belonged there. Only made sense since he did in fact have a lot of legitimate business in this part of the station.

As well as a lot of not so legitimate business. Not technically illegal business because of laws passed in secret years before. Those laws authorized special Federation agents to ignore all other laws. They did so on their own sole discretion. They were only subject to review by their immediate superiors. Those agents and their superiors both worked in the utmost secrecy. No need to disturb the populace. The populace were, as they should be, content to believe the Federation to be distant, ineffectual, and rule bound.

The people were happy thinking that. The Federation's Special Operations Directorate was happy to let them think that.

John was one of the Directorate's special agents. He had kept close tabs on the population of Jefferson system for the Federation. He'd tracked their moods. He'd tracked their fads. He'd followed their merely criminal activities, and their subversive ones too.

After an initial period of familiarization, it'd been rather boring.

He'd often hoped for a little more action. He'd wondered more than once if any of his long detailed reports were being read. He didn't get much feed back. None, in fact. Could be they were filed and never read. He wondered if he had sacrificed his life for nothing.

Now he was quite busy indeed and missing those quieter days.

But at least he knew he hadn't been completely wasting his time. It was his earlier preparations carried out over years that were enabling the current Psych Ops. The operations SDFHQ had ordered him to carry out as a matter of the highest priority.

He'd worked his way into a position high up in in-system shipping. He'd made a point of being frequently seen throughout the Docklands running legitimate errands. Legitimate if sometimes rather trumped up. If he hadn't, he wouldn't now have the unquestioned access to the Docklands that he did.

That access was critical.

Being from Earth and well educated, John knew the history of the term "Docklands". It meant the part of a city next to the docks. Usually a dirty and unsafe part, but also usually a busy and essential part. Most cities were transport hubs. Even those who weren't were heavily dependent on shipping to provide their needs. Cities that weren't capitals also had to export the goods to pay for those needs.

John suspected most Jeffersonians didn't know the origin of the anachronistic "Docklands" label. That didn't change the fact that this part of Washington Station exactly filled the ancient function of a dockland. Its storage spaces, access ways, offices, and machinery provided an essential interface.

It was extremely handy that most of population couldn't be bothered to think about the "Docklands". It let John and his activities fly under the radar. It was even handier that other essential functions had been co-located in the Docklands. Essential, but gritty and boring, like distribution and environmental housekeeping.

The station's access corridors and the small automated carts that mostly used them were functionally invisible. People could see them, only they didn't bother to. They were everywhere but of no interest.

Someone with access could use them to go anywhere, to fetch and deliver almost anything. To do so almost entirely unnoticed and when noticed to go unremarked. It was a power that might seem unremarkable. In fact, it was pervasive and most flexible. It was one the Directorate taught its operatives to use well.

Just as they taught them to use control over a target's environment to influence them.

It again required direct access to the control center for household environments. Fortunately, at least for the Directorate and its agents, it was generally not difficult to achieve such access. It only took a little patience and planning.

Being from a planetary surface, Mother Earth's in fact, John wasn't unfamiliar with the ancient practice of householders fully controlling, and being fully responsible for, their immediate surroundings. In space, on ships and in stations, that wasn't normal. In fact, it wasn't even normal on most planets in large cities.

Modern people, of moderate means and below, outsourced the care of their air, lighting, and cleaning. Outsourced it to the engineering department or their landlords. They didn't think about where their water came from. They didn't care where it went. They thought about where their crap, garbage, and other waste products went even less. They didn't think about who kept their air and their living spaces clean. That was something most people quite willingly outsourced to the responsible authorities.

The responsible authorities who in turn handed the regular work off to machinery and not too well respected minions. Usually for efficiency's sake they centralized the necessary mechanisms. They also automated them as much as possible. As much as the laws against anything resembling artificial intelligence permitted. Truth be, they tended to skirt those laws as closely as they could.

Very convenient for John and those like him.

The uninformed might think environmental controls were either working or weren't.

The Directorate and those it trained knew better.

Human experimentation, of course, was banned. The Federation after all was a civilized society with a government that respected civilized norms.

There had been times in the troubled past, less civilized times, with less civilized, or less effective, governments during which such experimentation had occurred. When the Federation was being formed certain of her servants had thought it would be wrong to destroy the records of knowledge gained at such a cost in human misery. And so the Directorate was possessed of detailed and scientifically solid information of just how imperceptible changes to a person's environment could make them miserable.

Small changes in carbon dioxide levels, or in other contaminates, could make a person constantly and slightly sick. Slightly in the short term.

Lights flickering too fast to be consciously detectable could also induce headaches and a general feeling of malaise. Humidity and temperature levels that weren't quite optimal could have effects over time. Also, this was cumulative in a variety of ways Spec Op agents were well trained in.

In particular they knew sleep, after air and before water, was necessary to good human health. Good sleep was a vital human need. They had many tools for preventing good sleep.

And so John found himself practically trotting from the distribution center to the environmental housekeeping center. In the distribution center he'd arranged a special delivery to the child of a man who'd thought he'd got away with talking to Doctor Cynthia Dallemagne. The housekeeping center would help John make sure that message had the desired effect.

Talk about lack of sleep, John was finding himself too busy to get as much as he needed.

The laws against excessive automation weren't totally ineffective. Neither were the resources of the Special Operations Directorate infinite. He could have used the help of another fully trained and trustworthy agent, or two, but he didn't have it. He had employees drafted by various means into helping him. He had some paid or coerced agents. All of them knowing no more than they needed to. None of them fully trained up to Directorate standards. Meant he had to do all the special work himself.

In some sense, Psych Ops were a battle of attrition.

So here he was in front of the access hatch to Environmental Housekeeping Central. A quick look around and as expected nobody in sight. A pause to listen and just the hum of machinery and the barest whisper of moving air. No sounds of people.

He let himself in with the key he wasn't supposed to have.

Despite having no time to waste, he paused to take in the view. It was like being in a cathedral of small organ pipes. The ceiling was several people lengths above him. The huge space was consumed by long tall racks of piping with little panels of small valves roughly every square meter. If John had had any valid reason to access the station's documentation he could have found the exact number. In any event, every room, space, and office was mapped to one of those valve laden panels.

Environmental control was almost entirely hydraulic and electro-mechanical. There was no way to remotely hack these controls. Humanity had learned its lessons during the Times of Trouble that had culminated in the Federation's formation.

As an additional feature these controls were supposed to be immune to attack by Electromagnetic Pulses, EMP. At the time of their design that had been a worry. John thanked the heavens that it had turned out to be an unjustified one. Thanks to the Federation keeping the peace, no station had every been subjected to nuclear attack.

As usual, he paused to make sure no one else was there. There never was, but he was well trained.

Still, he couldn't help wondering if some of the panels had been touched since being installed generations ago. Supposedly the controls were adjusted every time a space changed use like a new family moving in or family members moving out. They were supposed to be at least checked.

John, however, had fiddled with a quite a few sets of valves. He'd never seen much in the way of signs they'd ever been touched. In fact, he'd learned to carry a small container of light penetrating oil and a wrench since the controls were frequently stuck.

Enough of that. With no one else here he was free to get the tall wheeled step ladder he needed from its storage place. Hard to do that unobtrusively. Pushing the ladder into place, John then climbed to the panel he wanted to adjust.

A slight change of timing with the quarter rotation of a set screw. A little narrowing of the dead space for a control setting. Presto the environmental controls for his target's sleeping quarters could be guaranteed to be ineffective. Ineffective but also constantly and disruptively going off and on. They hadn't been optimal before either, but people could get used to anything with time. Keeping them unhappy meant changing the nature of the discomfort at regular intervals.

John inspected his work and sighed to himself. It was nice to be able to use his decade plus old training finally, but he'd rather not have.

There was always a very slight but real chance of exposure involved in such work. Also Psych Ops might not mean gross physical damage to people but it was still nasty. Psychologically targets were almost certain never to be the same again. In the extreme it could even kill, albeit somewhat indirectly.

His orders, however, had been clear. He was to prevent Ad Astra from opening offices in Jefferson system if he could. If that was not possible he was to render them ineffectual.

Initially at least he'd been ordered to use only Psych Op methods. There'd been a strong hint that more direct physical methods should be employed if the less direct ones failed. If it was up to John that wasn't going to happen.

Only it seemed clear that his bosses back at SDFHQ had some sort of master plan. A master plan they were apparently willing to go to some extremes in implementing.

It was way above John's pay grade.

He'd be a good soldier.

He'd obey his orders.

* * *

Jack was all kinds of unhappy.

He had plenty of real reasons to be.

He'd arrived in the Jefferson system on board *The Bird of Profit* and docked at Washington Station, hoping he'd find Ad Astra Venture's new HQ up and running. Truthfully, he hadn't really expected that. Moe Libreman and his people hadn't been scheduled to arrive that long before Jack. They wouldn't have had that much time to get set up.

Nevertheless Cynthia should have got the ball rolling and both Moe and his people were very capable as well as hard working. And Moe knew how important this was. Jack had had his hopes.

He'd been very disappointed. Discouraged even. Cynthia had come and gone. She'd made some appointments and gathered some information. So far, so good until he'd read her report on what she'd found. Cynthia was a cool one. She didn't exaggerate, but she didn't pull her punches either. Her report had been a hard punch in the gut.

They were still facing major opposition in Jefferson. Its source was unknown, but Cynthia felt it was different from the earlier secret opposition they'd met there. Jack wasn't sure if that was good news or bad. Guess it was what it was. What was definitely bad was that the people they needed to deal with in order to set up here in Jefferson had been threatened. Certainly here on Washington Station, but Cynthia suspected system-wide. They'd been successfully intimidated into refusing to deal with Ad Astra.

Moe had not even been able to rent office space. In fact, he hadn't even been able to find personal living quarters for himself and the half dozen people he had with him. Currently they were living in the transient quarters for spacers and other people just passing through the system. The management had been hinting that their welcome wasn't indefinite.

Short of people actually being hurt, Jack couldn't imagine how the situation could be worse. Probably a lack of imagination on his part, but it was still very bad.

And so oddly enough, he'd found himself here. Here waiting quietly in the dark in a little girl's very girly and childish room with only ex-Sergeant Jackson for company. One of the very few locals willing to even talk to Jack had had his family threatened for that effrontery. Some creepy bastard had left him a note, in a supposedly private place, to the effect that the little girl who the room belonged to might be unhappy with her father's misbehavior. It had asked how the man hoped to explain that to his daughter.

The man in question loved his daughter. He also didn't like being threatened and wasn't convinced giving into the threats would make them go away. Not permanently. As he'd said to Jack "Give into bastards like this and they own you forever. You're never free from the fear of them. They like it that way."

Jack didn't ask what experience had led the man to that conclusion. He was just happy that the fellow had been willing to help him. Help him to the extent of letting two grown men, strangers, spend the night in his daughter's room waiting for the bastards in question to try and make good on their threat.

He'd been sitting here in a corner with Jackson in another corner, in the dark, not moving, waiting quietly for something to happen for a couple of hours now. It was amazingly hard, and he'd been feeling sillier and sillier as time passed. Only the twin facts that Jackson had thought this was a good idea and that they had no other leads kept him at it.

More minutes passed and then he heard a slight sound. He thought it might be the sliding door off of the kitchen to the service tunnels. Jack had made good use of such tunnels on Slovo Station in escaping the first of several attempts on his life.

Jack had grown up on a planetary surface and moreover in a rural area on a farm. Farmers did their own procurement and waste disposal using their own trucks to haul what couldn't be made or recycled on site back and forth from the local village.

It was different in the cities and on stations. People in those places had the front door to corridors for people. Waste and deliveries went through automated backdoors that folks seemed to have trained themselves to ignore. Ignore to the point the didn't seem to see them or ever think about them. It was just everyday magic they couldn't be bothered to notice. Much the same way they never thought about where their food, especially their meat, came from.

Jack wondered what automated delivery their host had forgotten to tell them about. He glanced at Jackson. He could tell the ex-sergeant was making an extra effort to be still and quiet. Made sense many delivery carts were designed to avoid rooms they detected people in. Like servants of old they were supposed to be unobtrusive. Jack followed suit; not moving and trying to breathe as slowly and quietly as possible.

A delivery cart trundled right into the girl's room. It was completely quiet and not much more than a moving lighter square area in the darkened room. It wasn't anything more than a platform on wheels. It had something on top. Jack couldn't quite make out the shape. Jackson was closer Jack wished he dared ask him what he saw.

Jack was blinded by Jackson suddenly turning his flashlight on. Instinctively he covered his eyes with the back of his hand. Blinking he lowered his hand to look at the delivery cart and its cargo. The cargo turned out to be a teddy bear exactly like one the girl already had. Except the new toy had been, what Jack could only call, desecrated.

The teddy had been ripped open from crotch to belly and up and blood splattered all over the wound. A note was pinned to it.

The delivery cart whirred and began to retreat.

Jackson cursed and kicked it over, violently flipping the thing over onto its back. Its wheels spun uselessly in the air.

Jack, wondering at the unusual loss of calm by the ex-marine, moved over to where the teddy bear and its attached note had rolled.

He read the note. "*It's just a teddy bear. This time,*" it read.

Jackson looked over Jack's shoulder and grimaced.

"What?" Jack asked.

Jackson looked away and sighed. "I should have known," he said. "I've seen this sort of thing before. This has SDF Special Operations Directorate Psych Ops written all over it."

"Okay," Jack said, "we knew there were elements in the SDF that didn't like us. Are there ways we can counter this?"

"Yeah," Jackson said. "This sort of thing requires direct access to housekeeping. We can block that."

"But?" Jack asked. He'd clearly heard some sort of "but" in Jackson's tone.

"But," Jackson answered, "means whole station is going to hear about what's happened. You can be sure that they're going to be hopping mad and looking to take it out on someone."

"Not us I hope," Jack said.

"No, but you ever see a civil war, Jack," Jackson replied. "They're not pretty."

"Jackson, we didn't start this fight," Jack said.

They hadn't but Jack damned well intended to end it.

6: Indigestion

Jack was tired. He'd even got over his anger some.

He had good reason to feel tired. He'd been up all night. First on the stakeout in that little girl's room. Afterwards in pounding out how to react to what they'd learned.

Jack would've liked to have slept on it. The girl's Dad had been angry though and eager to take immediate revenge. Jackson had deadpan recommended immediate action. Action before their hidden opponent discovered their cover had been blown and acted to disengage and save as much of their assets as possible.

And so they'd spent the last few early morning hours contacting a carefully selected sub-set of the local volunteer militia. Contacting them and then convincing them they needed to put guards both on the housekeeping spaces in the Docklands and on the docks themselves. They'd even eventually convinced the station authorities to put a temporary freeze on all traffic on and off of the station. Sometime during the next day, those authorities would be inspecting the housekeeping logs and spaces for unauthorized access and tampering.

Jackson had no doubt they'd find something, so neither did Jack.

That all done Jack would have liked to have had a drink with

Jackson and gone to bed.

Unfortunately Washington Station didn't have any twenty-four-hour drinking establishments, and Jack needed to think up some medium-term plans.

So here they were in a diner that offered all day breakfasts watching the station slowly start another day.

Jackson had ordered them both a big breakfast. He was methodically chowing down on his and not talking much. He understood Jack needed time to get his head on straight and to think.

Jack appreciated that.

The breakfast wasn't bad. Standard fare; artificial scrambled eggs, fried meat strips, and toasted bread with spread, it was slightly greasy but warm and filling. It was a breakfast that could have been found any morning, almost anywhere in human settled space. It was comfort food. It was helping Jack settle down and center himself.

Jack sipped his coffee. The coffee helped too.

He needed to think.

Best not to make any big irreversible decisions and immediately act on them. He trusted that with Jackson's help, they'd already done everything they had to do right away.

On the other hand, part of leadership was giving clear direction. At the very least, you had to give the impression you knew what you were doing. You always had to have some sort of plan.

Before going to bed Jack was going to have to leave Moe and Captain Joshua messages quickly updating them on what had happened.

When he got up, he was going to have to have some sort of plan on how they were going to proceed. Off cycle and sleep lagged from just waking up wouldn't be the best time to be formulating such a plan.

So he needed to sketch out something now. Now before he retired. He could change it later in the light of new information or simply because something came to him.

First things first, make sure they'd solved the problem of nobody wanting to deal with them. He'd have to have Moe try again after giving everyone time to get the news. That'd have to be part of his orders to him this morning. He'd sleep while Moe handled it. A quick reality check wouldn't hurt though.

"Jackson," he said. The ex-marine looked up. "You figure now that we've figured out how the bad guys been intimidating folks that'll put paid to it? Are we done?"

Jackson nodded. "Yes," he answered. "These sorts of operations are like magic tricks once the audience knows how they're done they lose their power."

"Great," Jack said. It was good he ought to feel better about it, really. "Do you think we'll catch who was behind it?"

"No," Jackson said, sighing. An unusually emotional display for him. "We'll get a part of their network. A bigger part, maybe most of it, if we do it right and are lucky, but we won't get it all, let alone who's behind it."

"Is that's what's bugging you?" Jack asked.

Somehow Jackson managed to put on a stonier than usual face. "No, no, it's not," he answered. "It's recognizing this must have done by part of the Federation. Never did this sort of dirty work myself, but I did lead a few escort teams to agents being dropped into hot spots. Hard not see what they were doing. Also, even SDF Spec Op agents get lonely and talk too much at times."

"Hard to believe that last," Jack said.

"They might be 'special' people," Jackson replied, "but they're still people, Jack."

"Not people you're too happy with right now?" Jack asked.

"No. It's not that," Jackson said. "No way this sort of thing is ever pretty or not morally debatable, but it's a fact that the Federation has been a force for peace and stability and it's a fact that it's been stretched too thin to use normal above board means to keep that peace."

"Okay," Jack said by way of urging Jackson to continue.

"Jack, we're both ex-SDF," Jackson said. "From what I've seen you're like me, you believed in the mission even when you didn't necessarily like the way it was tackled."

"That's right," Jack confirmed.

"Let's be clear here," Jackson went on. "Me and the boys, we were only sort of 'ex' at first, but we're all in with you now. You've proved yourself to us."

"Thanks," Jack answered. He was flattered. He was also a little dismayed that maybe his security's loyalty had been divided at one time. He wasn't good at handling emotion, but he knew enough to accept what Jackson was saying graciously.

"Just the same, it was Captain Taylor that assigned us here," Jackson said in a tone more contemplative than usual. A little like he hadn't really thought the matter through before. "None of us ever saw any real contradiction between helping you and serving the interests of the SDF and Federation. Figured we were all paid up members of the good guys whatever misunderstandings might occur."

Jack hesitated to ask, but it was necessary. "And now?" he said.

"And now I'm pretty damned sure there's a good portion of the SDF that never deserved the trust I had in them," Jackson said.

Jack said nothing as he watched Jackson struggle with feelings he'd never guessed at.

"Bitter truth is, Jack," Jackson said. "I don't think the SDF and the Federation were ever worth the loyalty I gave them. The loyalty I taught my men to have. Not anymore. It hurts. I built my whole life on that loyalty. It was my bedrock, and it's crumbled away."

"I'm sorry, Sam," Jack said, using Jackson's first name for the first time. Only reason he even knew it was because he'd read the man's file.

"Yeah, well," Jackson said, then paused. "Really, the only thing you need to know is however messy this gets you can trust me and the boys."

"Never thought otherwise," Jack said.

Jackson just nodded solemnly in reply.

"I'm not convinced we're facing down the whole Federation quite yet," Jack said. "This could just be a few bad apples or some sort of mistake. Going to still try and keep Ad Astra neutral."

"You're more trusting than I am," Jackson said.

"Don't worry, I'll keep my guard up," Jack said. "I know you'll help me with that."

Jackson nodded again. A sharp, definite gesture.

"Think we're done here in Jefferson," Jack said. "Unless Moe tells me otherwise, I'm going let him deal with setting up here. We have business elsewhere, out at El Dorado and on the way there. Folks there won't be lining up to take sides yet. We're going to have to work with that."

"Makes sense," Jackson agreed.

"So we stay on guard. Keep an eye out for skullduggery. We try to line up allies," Jack summarized. "We don't try to force them to take sides right away. We keep our options open. We try to at least look neutral."

"But we have to know who our friends will be when the crap starts to fly," Jackson finished the thought.

"Exactly," Jack said.

* * *

Dr. Ted Smith had thought his last family dinner tense enough.

The current meal, at which Admiral St. Armand was a guest, was proving much tenser. The Admiral was the commander of a Carrier Battle Group centered around the carrier *Saratoga*.

It'd been years since a carrier had been deployed outside Core space. Even then that had been a Task Force tailored to fight pirates. It'd been built around an escort carrier.

The *Saratoga* was a full sized battle carrier and had twice the major escort ships that the earlier Task Force had disposed of. Two cruisers and a half-dozen destroyers to be exact. Nothing like it had ever been deployed outside of Core space before, and certainly nothing like it had ever been seen in the Newton system.

The Admiral commanding the force was a man in considerable demand. All the more for the facts that the Battle Group wouldn't be lingering long in system and that news of the fighting on the Frontier was in high demand.

Ted's mother had been over the moon when she'd learned Ted's brother Mike had invited Admiral St. Armand to dinner and that he had accepted.

Ted had had to feign similar enthusiasm.

He supposed he ought to be happy the Admiral hadn't demanded to see him in person upon learning none of the FTL transports usually found in Newton happened to be present at this exact point in time. As the only officer and board member of Ad Astra Ventures in system and available to be asked about this strange coincidence, he'd expected to be called in and sharply questioned.

It hadn't happened.

Instead, he found himself sharing a meal with the man he'd expected to be interrogating him.

Somehow he wasn't convinced he was quite off the hook.

Admiral St. Armand had been the very picture of a gracious

guest. He was currently seated between Ted's mother and his brother Mike. They all seemed to be having a great time exchanging small witticisms, most of which Ted couldn't make out over the bickering of the children at the kid's table and everyone else's conversations.

The Admiral himself despite his good manners and apparent cheer wasn't a reassuring figure. He reminded Ted of an aristocratic bird of prey. Sharp featured, sharp eyed, alert with excellent posture and precise in his movements and speech both.

Ted didn't believe for a moment that he'd been overlooked by the Admiral. He wasn't sure what the Admiral's game was, but likely he was softening Ted up for a few innocuous sounding but potentially deadly questions.

He managed to choke most of his excellent roast beef and vegetables down before the expected questions came.

"So, Dr. Smith, can I call you 'Ted'?" the Admiral asked Ted across the length of much of the table. "I mean there are so many 'Dr. Smiths' here it's confusing." The Admiral smiled at Ted's mother to show he was joking. His mother giggled and smile back. Ted was mortified. He understood his mother was proud of her brood's accomplishments, and of her own for that matter, but the Admiral was playing her shamelessly. At least his brother Mike seemed a little more serious.

"Certainly, no problem Admiral, it is my name after all," Ted replied.

"Call me Henri then," the Admiral said.

"Very well, Henri."

"I wish we had longer to talk," the Admiral said, "I have many questions for you. Would you mind helping me with just a few maybe?"

Ted's mother beamed at him from the Admiral's side. She wanted him to perform for the Admiral and to make him happy. She had no idea what was going on. Mike on the other side of the Admiral likely did. Not that it was making him happy. Mike was probably the reason this conversation wasn't happening in a more formal setting.

"Of course," Ted replied. What else could he say? "Whatever you like. Do we share an interest in history?" Ted could play games too.

The Admiral smiled and his eyes twinkled sharply as he fixed

Ted with them. "Indeed we do," he said. "Although right now I'm more interested in making history than reading about it. Duty calls you understand. I'm curious how an academic, an historian, ended up on the board of the main local shipping company."

"It's a strange story," Ted answered trying to sound like it was one he was eager to tell and maybe embellish some.

"I'm sure it is," the Admiral said dryly.

"Well, a lot of our graduate students and post-docs are active in field research," Ted said. "Documenting history as it occurs rather than waiting for someone else to write it down as it were."

"I'm familiar with bureaucratic mission creep," the Admiral commented.

"We like to think we do good relevant work," Ted said, attempting to portray a man slightly miffed at being caught morally offside.

"I'm sure you do. You were saying?"

"Fieldwork," Ted replied. "It's rather messy and unpredictable." Mike snorted he'd often told Ted the social sciences were too messy, ill defined, and unpredictable to be real science.

The Admiral with a slight tilt of his head indicated he'd rather Mike not interrupt the conversation.

"As academics trying to do clean science that's a problem," Ted continued. "But sometimes it lets us be helpful to local authorities. We notice or stumble across things they've missed."

"Very interesting," the Admiral said. "I trust you always come down on the side of the law and not that of your informants when you learn of illegal activities."

Ted was careful to keep his face blank. Of course there was no way his people would rat out their informants as soon they suspected one of them might have infringed one of the many rules, regulations, and laws the Federation had promulgated during its long existence and never ever removed from the books. The Admiral knew that too. He was just letting Ted know it was something else that could be used against him. "Of course," he said. Honestly if technically, all his people knew better than to explicitly implicate their sources in their reports.

"That's good," the Admiral said with a thin, apparently genuine if predatory smile. "And just what did one of you stumble upon that led to you becoming involved in shipping?"

"My associates participate in studies throughout the sector," Ted replied. "Also some of them directly study the local interstellar trade patterns. So we're intimately familiar with local shipping interests and trade patterns and tend to notice changes."

"How convenient," the Admiral said. "I'm afraid though that my time here is limited. As pleasant as the company here is," he smiled at Ted's mother, "I'm going to have to leave soon. Could you give me the short version?"

Ted swallowed. He'd hoped to follow the usual bureaucratic dodge of burying the truth in a blizzard of words with multiple interpretations. "At the cost of simplification," he finally got out, "we noticed that one company had managed to procure a de facto monopoly of local shipping."

"A disturbing development," the Admiral noted.

"Indeed," Ted agreed. "What was worse was that our analysts couldn't see how that company could be making money operating the way they were. Our field workers also reported a whole series of rumors suggesting their business methods were less than honest." This was all now well known by the public, at least within the sector.

"I'm aware of the New Byzantine Trading story," the Admiral said. "It was a big enough scandal that even the public back on Earth heard about it."

"Dreadful business," Ted's Mother said.

"Yes it was," the Admiral agreed. "Not clear what its academic interest was, though."

"Monopoly and competition, especially in a heterogeneous regulatory environment," Ted replied, "have long been topics of scholarly interest. More so to economists traditionally, but my department has long felt that economists deprecate historical and social context to the detriment of complete understanding."

"Newton's historians seem to be a rather nosy group who like to ignore traditional boundaries," the Admiral commented.

"We follow those noses and the data where they take us," Ted retorted. "We don't let turf wars deter us from seeking the truth."

"Bravo," the Admiral said. "And how did the truth lead you to membership on the board of a shipping company?"

"Well, when I heard there'd been a break in at one of New Byzantine's local warehouses," Ted said. "And that contraband had been found I immediately recognized this was the clue as to what was going on that I'd been looking for."

"I see," the Admiral said.

"I was beside myself with delight when I heard they had a suspect or at least a witness in custody down at police HQ," Ted said. "We'd helped the police when they'd had trouble with off worlders before so I had some favors to call in. Rushed right down to interview their detainee."

"Captain Black," the Admiral supplied. "Formerly an NCO in the regular SDF. Now has a commission in the reserves as well as being the CEO of Ad Astra Ventures. An interesting career path and set of conjunctions, wouldn't you say Ted?"

"Indeed, Admiral," Ted agreed. "Not that I knew any of that at the time. Most of it was in the future, in fact. Actually I was rather disappointed as it seemed he really didn't know much of interest to me regarding the incident or New Byzantine Trading in general."

"But you managed to strike some sort of deal with him?" the Admiral asked.

"Yes, the Captain stood to benefit from my putting in a good word for him," Ted said, "and I had use for an informant in circles that weren't that welcoming to curious academics. Also I suspected that having come to New Byzantine's attention in conjunction with a PR disaster, they were likely to seek him out as a person of interest."

"So you stuck the Captain out as bait and waited to see wh came sniffing around," the Admiral said.

Ted looking past the Admiral saw a dawning awareness laced with surprise and anger appear on Mike's face. The Admiral, at the very least, had a strong suspicion of what Ted's job really was. Also of the sort of cold blooded calculations it required. His brother hadn't had a clue.

"Just how violent and criminal New Byzantine turned out to be was a shock," Ted replied. "I had one of my best people keeping an eye on him and when things went south, she immediately brought both the local police and the SDF into the picture."

"I have read Captain Taylor's reports," the Admiral replied.

"Then you know precisely how closely we co-operated with the SDF in defeating Foxall's plans to use New Byzantine Trading as a cover for establishing a personal pirate kingdom."

It was Ted's mother's turn to look shocked. In fact, a number of the remaining family members around the table were starting to tune into the conversation. Mike was looking both grim and attentive. The Admiral had thrown the cat amongst the pigeons. Ted didn't think for a second it was accidental.

"Pirate kingdom?" Ted's mother asked. "Surely you two are kidding an old woman?" She glanced rapidly back and forth between the Admiral's and Ted's faces. Ted could see Mike getting angrier, as if he thought Ted had deliberately played some sort of ugly trick on their mother.

"Not such an old woman, Laura Jean," the Admiral said to his mother in what Ted found an entirely too familiar, as well as oily slick, fashion. "One with an altogether too modest son. We decided to minimize just how dangerous the threat turned out to be so as to not frighten the public."

"So you're serious?" Ted's mother said, peering at the Admiral. She wasn't stupid. She was beginning to realize that perhaps the Admiral had been playing her.

"Extremely," the Admiral leaned back and sipped some wine, making sure he had everyone's attention. "Your son Ted as a result of his studies." He gave the word "studies" an edge. "And many of us in the SDF leadership, because it's our job, have been aware of some very serious threats to the Federation's peace and stability. In this sector and elsewhere."

"And nobody's told the public about it?" Ted's mother asked. Ted was finding Mike's reaction more interesting. He was beginning to look worried as well as angry. Mike was just starting to realize that his various transgressions, whatever they were, had not gone unnoticed. Unmentioned, perhaps, but not unnoticed.

"Nobody suppresses the news," the Admiral said, "but it wouldn't serve any useful purpose to help the general public connect the dots either. The Federation has people whose lives are dedicated to dealing with such issues."

"You're one of those people, Henri?" Ted's mother asked the Admiral. She was back to being rather adoring. To Ted's professional relief and his personal discomfort. He supposed even older women and mothers had a right to have feelings.

"I am not going to be modest," the Admiral replied. "And in fact it's no secret the whole expedition I'm leading is intended to cut off Beyonder assistance to dissident and criminal elements within the Federation."

He looked around to make sure everyone got the point. His gaze paused on Mike before stopping at Ted. "And so is Ted, as modest as he likes to be about it."

Damn, the Admiral had completely outed him to his family.

"I am the head of the '*Current* History Studies Group' after all," Ted said. "Personally I think it's useful to study older events at leisure and from a distance that allows some perspective, but the powers to be like to be kept up to date on what's happening right now. They also control my budget, so I do try to be accommodating."

The Admiral smiled. He'd made his point. Seemed like he was willing to allow Ted some shreds of plausible deniability. "A commendable attitude, Ted," he said. "As I said earlier, I wish I had the time during my current stay in Newton to take fuller advantage of it. Later on my return trip perhaps. Right now however my professional need to deal with my Battle Group's logistical support means I have need of you in your role as the chairman of Ad Astra's board."

"I'll help as best as I can," Ted said. He had little choice, after all.

"Captain Taylor wasn't as clear as he could of have been about exactly how Ad Astra came into being or why Newton was so deeply involved," the Admiral replied.

"As I think you realize, Captain Taylor and his marine detachment were absolutely critical in rooting out Foxall and his pirates," Ted said.

"Taylor showed a great deal of initiative," the Admiral said. His tone left the issue of whether he thought this was a good thing an open question.

"He had little choice," Ted said. He made no effort to hide his feelings of exasperation. The SDF had given Taylor an almost impossible task, and now they wanted to carp about how he'd achieved it. "Hunting down and destroying Foxall's pirates was hard enough. Cleaning up the mess that was left was harder. It was a minor miracle that we managed it. I'm proud of all of us that we did."

"But not so proud as to brag to your family about it?" the Admiral asked.

"As you pointed out, Henri," Ted said. "We couldn't tell people what we'd done without also telling them how close we'd come to catastrophe, and that didn't seem wise. Some people would have panicked. Even more would have started to doubt our current leadership. Social and governmental break down wouldn't have been good for anyone."

"On the behalf of the leadership of the SDF and the Federation generally," the Admiral said, "allow me to thank you for your efforts and your self restraint."

"Thank you, Admiral," Ted replied.

"We would, however, like a fuller understanding of just what the nature of your solution was," the Admiral said. "The better to understand how you can help us and the people of the Federation in the future."

"Certainly, Admiral," Ted replied. "I guess Captain Taylor was too busy with his normal duties in the sector to entirely keep himself up to date, let alone to report back to SDFHQ in the fullest manner."

"That does seem to have been the case," the Admiral agreed. He did so rather dryly. They both knew Taylor hadn't wanted his distant superiors jogging his elbow. Easier to seek forgiveness than permission.

"Well Foxall and his organization were our immediate problem, and it was close-run thing dealing with them," Ted said. "I can understand if Captain Taylor downplayed the risks he took. We were damned lucky they worked out, and that we got some help from unexpected quarters. If we hadn't been, you'd have been fighting pirates here in the middle worlds not Beyonders out past the Frontier."

"Perhaps," the Admiral said, "but you're speculating about complicated events that simply didn't happen. I have no idea myself how the politicians back on Earth would have reacted to such a scenario, and I daresay I have my ear more to the ground in that respect than most."

"Yes, I don't doubt it, Admiral," Ted agreed. "I'm afraid most of us in the middle worlds rather take Earth for granted and don't really understand complexity of the politics there."

"Also understandable, Ted," the Admiral said. "I wish we had more time to discuss it."

Ted took the hint to get to the point. Pausing to think, he glanced about and realized he had the rapt attention of not just his mother and Mike but all the other adults at the table. Well, at least he wasn't having to shout over other conversations. Scant consolation that was. "Well, whatever the reality of the situation was," he said, "all of us in know were in full out emergency mode scrambling to deal with the biggest and most immediate problems the best we could."

"Understood, you were too busy fighting alligators to have time to drain the swamp as we say back home," the Admiral said with an encouraging and kindly smile.

Ted knew better than to be deceived by that. He chose his next words carefully. "So leaving out how we got there, and to describe the key problem concisely," he said, "Foxall's organization had managed to subsume most of the shipping key to keeping trade going in Epsilon Sector. When we destroyed that organization we left the infrastructure necessary to the sector's continued prosperity in pieces."

"Understood, and exactly how did you go about picking up those pieces?" the Admiral asked.

"In a word, carefully, Admiral."

"Specific concrete details, Ted."

"It was a mess," Ted replied. "We were making decisions while only guessing at the actual facts we should have had. Most of the FTL freighters vital to Epsilon Sector's trade were caught up in New Byzantine's bankruptcy depending on exactly where they were when it hit. It looked like they'd all either end up getting bought by interests outside the sector or tied up alongside while their ownership was fought over in the courts."

"And meantime most local trade would be at a stand still. I see," said the Admiral. "Was this a purely hypothetical problem?"

"No," Ted said, "Most stationers and planet dwellers wouldn't have noticed, but with only a few small independents carrying FTL cargoes freight rates spiked through the roof. That was where and when shipping could be found at all."

The Admiral frowned. "My staff has been prioritizing our staging out to the Frontier and the planning of our operations once we're there," he said. "That said, I should have been better informed about this."

"Some of my analysts have been theorizing that our current social structure makes it impossible to actually handle all the information decision makers at the planetary level and above actually need," Ted said.

"Have they proposed any useful solutions to the problem?" the Admiral asked.

"I'm afraid not," Ted replied. "We're on our own there, Henri." He grimaced. "Situation was made worse by a lack of trustworthy crews, and an additional lack of real trust between those of us who'd come together to take Foxall down."

"Go on."

"So Captain Taylor, our Dr. Dallemagne and Captain Black had taken the lead in dealing with Foxall so they were at least conditionally trusted by most of the actors in the sector."

"Captain Taylor's discretion most certainly did not extend to starting and running a commercial shipping company," the Admiral said.

"No, but his blessing by agreeing to be on the board was necessary to setting up one everyone would trust," Ted replied. "Also it offset the fact Dr. Dallemagne, myself, and Mr. Libreman were all involved. That might have suggested Newton was using the crisis to dominate the sector's shipping."

"And the three of you had to be involved why?" the Admiral asked.

"Because even with getting some crews to work on speculation, and with contributions by local planetary governments, we still needed a lot of money to buy New Byzantine's ships at auction, to pay crews for many of them, and to buy cargoes to put on them," Ted said. "We got that money from bankers here on Newton and they wanted local people they felt they could trust."

"You made deals with Marx and Heinlein to say nothing of some rather shifty operators out of El Dorado," the Admiral said.

"We made whatever deals we could," Ted said. "Did I mention we were scrambling in the absence of any good information?"

"It seems to have worked out," the Admiral said.

"It's all still an under capitalized and fragile house of cards," Ted said. He fought down the urge to sigh and stepped out of character. Looking around at his family and some of their close friends with as serious as a countenance he could manage, he spoke, "And that is something that must not leave this room. Our sector's business climate is fragile and a loss of confidence could collapse the sector's economy. None of you can spread any rumors."

"Allow me to second Ted's point," the Admiral said, looking around coldly. "Rumors detrimental to the security of the Federation will be looked into by both the SDF, and by the Federation's Bureau of Investigations. Those found to have been spreading them will be prosecuted. I trust I've made my point."

A few of the family got over their shock to murmur agreement. Ted's mother and his brother Mike just looked grim. From the hard looks they were giving him he knew they'd have questions for him later. He also knew they'd not be happy when he refused to answer them. "Thank you, Admiral," he said. On this he and the Admiral could agree.

"You're welcome, Ted," the Admiral said. "I do understan how your lack of formal authority might pose security problems for you. So how is it that none of Ad Astra's freighters happened to be in Newton when we could have most used their services?"

"I'm not entirely sure myself, Admiral," Ted replied. He attempted to sound as rueful as possible. "Part of it is that Ad Astra is still not running on a settled schedule based on a sustainable business plan yet. In an ideal universe we'd have steady predictable customers and we'd be running a regular predictable service along established routes."

"I'm not a businessman myself," the Admiral said, "but that does seem to make sense. It's the way most larger companies seem to work elsewhere."

"Indeed," Ted agreed. "And it's certainly what we're aiming at. Unfortunately most of our current business still seems to be handling the backlog that developed during New Byzantine's ascendancy and got worse when they went out of business. Not helped by the fact our captains and factors seem to be operating mostly in their own immediate self interest."

"Even the ones where you own the ships and are paying the crews?" the Admiral asked.

"Even those," Ted affirmed. It did seem a fact that he and the board were more in the business of giving hints and suggestions, and hoping things worked out, than in one where everything was tightly controlled. Moe had complained more than once about that. "Unfortunately it turns out that it's just not possible to micromanage an organization over interstellar distances."

The Admiral peered at Ted with narrowed eyes. He didn't look pleased by this assertion. He paused, seemingly to think.

"Hmmm, in fact, the SDF doesn't try to do that either," he said. "We keep our fleets tightly concentrated even within systems. I don't know how actively businesses with interstellar reach are managed. I'll accept that assertion at face value - for the time being."

"Thank you, sir," Ted said. Ted was beginning to feel very definitely intimidated. "I should emphasize that most of the captains and spacers we hired were former independents. Most of the spacers for hire available in the sector used to work for New Byzantine. We weren't sure we could trust them. Given the violence and dislike between those men and the rest of the spacing community it was hard to hire even the ones we thought we could trust. Too much bad blood. We mostly hired former captains and officers from independent ships, gave them larger commands and let them find their own crews from among their friends and family."

"So you have no real control over the ships you've paid for and nominally own at all?" the Admiral asked. "Do your financiers know this?"

"They're aware that Ad Astra is a loosely structured organization," Ted answered. How aware was not something that had to be looked at too closely. "They also understand, as we do, that the company works as a commercial venture as long as everyone's business interests coincide. In fact one of the problems we have is that although our officers and crew receive sufficient salaries and benefits to live comfortably, they're mainly motivated by the prospect of large profits by trading on their own accounts."

"So they go where the money is not necessarily where you tell them to?" the Admiral asked.

"It's a feature not a bug as long as we're all agreed our primary goal is making money, Admiral."

"And none of them thought trading with Newton was a good way to make money?"

"Well they did last year and earlier this year," Ted said. It was fortunate indeed that the economics justified what had happened. "After we got started up most of our ships were other places, mostly places with an agricultural surplus. Some with a surplus of low and middle tech manufactures. Newton is too dry and underpopulated to have much agriculture or low tech industry. We sell high-tech items."

"Okay."

"What it means is they all loaded up meat, grain, luxury food stuffs, coffee, teas, toys, cars, pots, and pans, whatever they thought would sell here," Ted said, "and all rushed here to sell it at elevated prices."

"So why didn't I find the system full of those freighters when I arrived?" the Admiral asked.

"Two reasons, sir," Ted replied. He could hear the Admiral was getting impatient. "One you're really not going to like."

"Imagine my surprise," the Admiral replied. "Good news first and make it quick."

"You were too late, Admiral. They got here, dumped their cargoes mostly at a good price thankfully, loaded up with our high-tech goods, and left as quick as they could, trying to get back to the further worlds while prices were still good there. We did try to provide a little co-ordination, but frankly most of those people know their business as least as well as we do."

"Again I'll accept that for the time being. Your bad news?"

"Your security wasn't good, Admiral. Surface and station dwellers didn't hear of your expedition, but rumors were rife in the shipping and spacer communities. Nobody leaked any explicit plans that I know of, but the change in SDF deployment patterns provoked widespread comment. Also, your advance purchasing agents for supplies were very clumsy."

"I'll take those observations under advisement," the Admiral replied. "Unfortunately my staff is already overworked and I can't afford a major housecleaning right now. So you knew we were coming."

"No, sir, I didn't," Ted replied. "But everybody guessed something was going to happen, and the entire spacer community is gun shy after the New Byzantine mess. I don't know how many captains decided to be somewhere else out of an abundance of caution, but I guess it was at least a few of them."

"I see," the Admiral said grimly. "You understand it's going to be a matter of some interest in the post mortem the SDF does on this campaign as to why you and the other board members and officers of Ad Astra failed to hold ships in system despite suspecting they would be needed by us."

"If all goes well, Admiral. I hope they'll be understanding of the imperfections of your plan. If not, I imagine there'll be a lot of blame to go around. I assure you that I and the other officers of Ad Astra did our best to be good Federation citizens."

"Well, water under the bridge," the Admiral said. "Unlikely you or your cohorts did anything outright illegal. If you're helpful to us in the future, we may even let bygones be bygones."

"I'll continue to do my best."

"Yes," the Admiral said. "I'm sure you will. To make it a little easier for you, I'm going to ask my logistics officers to set up a depot here on Newton. We'll stock consumables and parts in it on speculation. If all goes well we may not need the supplies. In any event I'm going to work up paper work requisitioning any Ad Astra freighter that arrives in system. You will make sure that that happens."

"Yes, sir."

"And you will make sure those ships are loaded in a timely fashion and sent forward to my Battle Group."

"Yes, sir."

"And, perhaps, if all goes well there'll no need for the Federation to stand up a commission to study whether there's an issue with the sector's shipping being dominated by hostile interests. Understood?"

"Clearly, Admiral."

* * *

Cynthia sipped her coffee. It was very good. Not good enough to dispel her throughly rotten mood. She was tired of the bullshit involved in being a spy. In particular if she never saw the Al-Alhadeen system again it'd be too soon.

At least here in the offices of Hussain Avarim she didn't have to wear the heavy dark tent that passed for female outerwear in this benighted system. She'd been trained to be open minded and accept that different societies had different mores. She wasn't supposed to think her own culture was automatically superior in all ways. She was supposed to realize that if a particular cultural practice made no sense to her that the fault was likely her own. In such a case she was supposed to gather more information and open her mind to more possibilities.

Maybe she'd spent too long in the field and forgotten her training because whatever God or gods existed in heaven the more she saw of Al-Alhadeen the more she thought it was a medieval throw back of a rat infested and benighted hellhole. Just her personal impression.

"Something wrong with the coffee?" Mr. Avarim asked her.

"No, no, the coffee is superb," Cynthia answered. She fled a twinge of guilt. Hussain Avarim had been nothing but gracious and helpful. "This is a difficult system for a woman to work in."

"Yes, you're supposed to be Captain Black's eyes and advance agent here."

"Which is difficult when almost no one will talk to me and almost everywhere I go I have to have both male and female chaperones."

"Have Omar and Tasha failed to be entirely helpful?"

"They've done everything that could reasonably be expected and more. The situation is simply very awkward."

Hussain Avarim pursed his lips and sighed. "I'm afraid I understand all too well. Our culture's attitude towards women is unusual, perhaps unique, in the modern Federation. I do believe even back on Earth they practice a very dilute version of our religion."

"Some of Al-Alhadeen's products like this coffee are absolutely outstanding," Cynthia said. "And the system is a key link on the Marx, Heinlein, and Hanshan loop, as well as an important staging point to the Frontier and El Dorado in particular."

"And if it wasn't the rest of you in the Federation would boycott us completely," Mr. Avarim said. "I do understand."

Cynthia nodded and took a breath. She felt bad. Mr. Avarim himself was a reasonable man. He hadn't created the situation and was working hard to change it. "Practically speaking," sh said, "I'm supposed to be Ad Astra's eyes and I'm all but blind in this system."

Mr. Avarim frowned and nodded. "You have me," he said.

"Yes, and you've been very helpful."

"And you'd prefer to use your own eyes and have independent sources of information," Mr. Avarim said. "Again I do understand. I think you might find a close questioning of both Miriam and her girls and Captain Greyfield rewarding."

"You do?"

"I do. As you know separating noise from signal can be very difficult in our business."

"But?"

"For one the good Captain has loaded far more in the way of

luxuries like our fine coffee than has been his wont on previous trips."

Cynthia took a moment to digest that. "He's selling product on," she said.

"That does seem likely," Mr. Avarim agreed.

"Ultimately the only possible end customers are the Beyonders."

"A logical conclusion."

"Maybe not the exact same Beyonders the Federation is now at war with, but illegal at best."

"At best," Mr. Avarim agreed. "I must confess that myself and my colleagues here in Al-Alhadeen have not been overly curious about the final destination of the products we sell."

Cynthia snorted. "No, I imagine not."

"Those New Byzantine dogs upset many cozy arrangements of long standing."

"It might have been nice to have known about some of those arrangements earlier," Cynthia said. "Particularly the ones involving our own captains for which Ad Astra might be blamed by the Feds."

"Please forgive me," Mr. Avarim said, "but our original arrangements with Dr. Smith were largely mercenary ones of convenience. It has been a pleasure getting to know you and Captain Black, but you've also been working quite closely with the SDF in the form of Captain Taylor."

Cynthia allowed herself a sigh. She did in fact trust Mr. Avarim as much as she trusted anyone. "It was necessary and Taylor at least is both reasonable and dedicated to the greater good."

"Not something, unfortunately, that can be said of the Federation and the SDF in general."

"No their internal politics are obscure, volatile, and uncertain. You can make deals with particular individuals but it's never clear if they're going to be able to keep them even if they want to."

"Captain Taylor is getting promoted and sent back to the Core I hear."

"That's what he's told Ad Astra's board," Cynthia confirmed. "We thought our main problem was going to be dealing with whoever replaced him."

"You're letting them place who ever they want on the board?"

"We don't have any formal arrangement," Cynthia said, "but it might be hard to ignore any suggestion that came from the SDF."

"In these unsettled times it might be best to be in no hurry to fill Taylor's seat."

"That makes sense. You've heard the news about the fighting on the Frontier and an SDF fleet arriving at Newton?"

"A few reports lacking detail. Surprising, if they're confirmed. The SDF had greater forces on the Frontier than previously believed, they managed to surprise the Beyonders and seize major settlements if the rumors are true."

"I trust the reports I have from Newton," Cynthia said. "They say the SDF has deployed a full strength Carrier Battle Group. Only makes sense that they're on the way to support the operations on the Frontier."

"Agreed," Mr. Avarim said, "many of the fellows I suspect may have been trading with them have been going around with long faces."

"We didn't see this coming," Cynthia said. "Nobody I know of did."

"Do you see yourselves making a change in plans?"

Cynthia noticed he'd not precisely specified who he was talking about. Was it the CHSG, Newton, Ad Astra, or her and Jack? It wasn't clear, and she wasn't going to clarify for him. "No," she replied, "we're in a difficult place. We can't afford to offend the Federation, but we can't afford to meet all the demands they're likely to make of us either. In particular we need all the friends and business associates we currently have and don't plan to alienate any of them."

"And your plans to achieve this balancing act are what?"

"Our plan has been to keep our heads down and wait for the Feds to go back to the Core worlds and resume ignoring us."

"It has been said hope is not a strategy. Or a plan I would think."

"There might be some faction in the SDF that thinks they can impose tighter control outside the Core worlds but history is against them," Cynthia said.

"Many causes have thought God or History favored them, but neither seem to, in fact, play favorites."

"It's a shitstorm," Cynthia retorted, "but all I can do is help Jack dodge between the raindrops of crap."

"So it'll be up to Captain Black?" Mr. Avarim asked.

"Yes, I'll give the best advice I can and I'll try to work up some contingency plans, but we're going to all have to act decisively and together when the time comes," Cynthia said. "Means we need one decision maker and one everyone will follow. That means Jack."

"That makes sense."

"You'll keep us informed and help when needed?"

"I will," Mr. Avarim affirmed.

* * *

Jack had thought the last few years had inured him to odd surprises.

Seemed not.

The last of the increasingly worrisome notes Cynthia had left behind for him had directed him to his current meeting. Like all of her notes it had been oblique and cryptic. *"Potential business contact with exciting, must check out, opportunity to expand trade. Meet in Hanshan at Mining Depot 0413. Main dock 2453-07-14:0730Z."*

Mining Depot 0413 was small, well out of the main deeper part of the Hanshan system's gravity well, and had definitely seen better days. He'd found a trading clan vessel waiting for him there.

Extremely odd on two counts.

For one, it was most unusual to find a trading clan ship so far into the Federation. The Core worlds and the middle worlds had a fairly substantial and regular demand for shipping. The shipping firms that served them provided a regular, dependable service and usually managed to make a profit at it. That was not the market the trading clans served.

The trading clans traded irregularly as they saw opportunities. They sent out expeditions on speculation to smaller, further out, largely self-sufficient settlements with little to no regular contact with the wider universe. They operated close to, and many believed beyond the Frontier. They did not usually travel to well established middle world systems like Hanshan.

Especially not like Hanshan.

The trading clans valued their independence. They didn't like close scrutiny by government bureaucrats. Not the Federation's bureaucrats, and not the bureaucrats routinely found on well populated planets. So they avoided them. And as long as they did so, the Federation by and large was willing to benignly neglect them. They did after all provide services that would have otherwise involved much more expensive and unrewarding effort on the Federation's part.

So Jack was already curious when he arrived at the main hatch to the *Chang's Pride*.

He was greeted there by a single man, lean in a dark ship suit and middle aged in an indeterminate way.

"Lionel Chang, my friends call me 'Leo'," the man said extending his hand.

"Call me Jack, Leo. So what's this all about?"

"It'll be easier to show you than to explain it," Leo said. "Then we can discuss it. Follow me." With that he turned and disappeared into the ship.

Jack followed.

Jack had seen a lot of ships in his day. He found you could tell a lot from seemingly inconsequential details.

The *Chang's Pride* was clean, tidy and well maintained. This was not a ship with a sloppy crew or down on its luck. Although Jack wondered where the crew was. It wasn't like Mining Depot 0413 had a lot of amusements or a big shopping district. Moreover, it was apparent the ship's crew area was bigger than was usual for the freighters Jack was familiar with.

"Big crew area," Jack commented.

"Clans are family businesses and we spend more time than most on our ships," Leo replied glancing back at Jack. "For many of us they're our true homes."

"New too," Jack said. Which was even more unusual. The clans were not the first in line for new Federation FTL drives, so their ships tended to be old if well kept.

"Yes, and there's a story there, but it can wait until later," Leo answered, not bothering to look back at Jack this time.

"Okay," Jack said. If the man didn't want to talk, there wasn't much to be done about it. Also, he realized they were heading aft to the engineering spaces, and he didn't mind being left free to look around. Engineering tended to be one of the most sensitive areas on a ship, almost as much as the bridge. Guests weren't invited to either casually.

To his even greater amazement, Leo led Jack to the ship's jump drive compartment. An inspection hatch in the huge containment vessel for the drive had already been removed.

Leo turned to Jack and gestured at the open inspection hatch. "You're familiar with the labeling of drive information plates?" he asked.

Jack hadn't been in engineering, he'd started as a fire control man and retired as a senior combat tech. Engineering techs didn't get sent on boarding parties, however, so Jack like most non-engineering techs had been throughly instructed on how to determine the origin and nature of a ship's drives.

"Yes, I know the format it's not complicated," Jack replied. "Standard boilerplate words 'Solarian Federation AD'. An 'L' or 'N' for Luna or Newton, six digit serial number with leading zeros and a quality rating A to F. Never saw anything more than a B, mostly Cs."

"Well, take a look you'll find this interesting," Leo said. He pulled a small flashlight out of a pocket and handed it to Jack.

Jack wasn't sure how interesting dry technical information could be though he'd certainly memorize the serial number to check up once he got back to his own ship.

He stuck his head into the inspection hatch and looked around at the exposed Anderson coils. Anderson coils were the magic sauce in FTL engines. Nobody Jack had ever met had any idea how they were made or they how worked. They weren't that much to look at though. They didn't look that much different from the coils in a big electric motor or generator.

These coils were a slightly different shade of copper red from those Jack had seen before. They were also shinier. They seemed pretty new, maybe a couple of years old. That was a surprise. Even if the *Chang's Pride* was herself relatively new Jack would have expected the coils to be recycled from an older ship.

He then looked at the information plague. Might as well get a serial number. Also be interesting if this drive was from Newton or Luna.

What he saw shocked him. It took him a minute or two to absorb it. Leo chuckled behind him.

Instead of the usual words "Solarian Federation AD" he instead read "NJS AD FC Series C:". This inspection plate was asserting that these coils had been manufactured outside the Federation. The "NJS" had to stand for "New Jerusalem Society" the largest of the Beyonder groups the SDF was currently engaged with. "AD" no doubt stood for "Anderson Drive" just as it did on a Federation coil. "FC" he could only guess at, but "Federation Compatible" seemed a reasonable one. Suggested they had were also manufacturing drives not compatible with standard Federation equipment. "Series C", well that could be disinformation, but taken at face value that suggested two other series, "A" and "B:.

Jack could not for the life of him imagine why someone would place disinformation on a plate that already read like something out of bad speculative fiction. Finally, there was a five digit serial number "00059". Guess six or seven digits would have been even more surprising.

Jack carefully retrieved his head and shoulders from the inspection hatch and thumped his ass down on the deck.

"That was interesting," he said. "This isn't some sort of joke, is it?"

"No joke," Leo said. "Go ahead, take a few minutes to think it over."

"I'll do that," Jack replied. If this information was accurate, and it was an odd and extremely elaborate ruse if it wasn't, the Beyonders had managed to break the Federation's monopoly on FTL drives. What's more they appeared to have done so some years ago, and to have produced a large number of drives of a variety of types. The lack of a quality indicator was also interesting. Perhaps they just didn't bother determining drive quality, but Jack had a feeling that perhaps they'd mastered the art of producing ones with consistent quality.

If so not only were the Beyonders producing acceptable FTL drives they were producing ones better than the Federation's and in similar numbers.

Jack felt giddy. He felt another odd emotion. He thought maybe it was hope. It hurt. It was like the feeling coming back to limb after you'd been sitting on it and it had gone numb. If there were sources for FTL drives other than ones the Federation controlled his strategic problem of needing a Federation that didn't need him or his people had been solved. Solved at least in theory.

Jack wondered if maybe this was the motivation for the unprecedented attack across the Frontier.

"Let's assume this means what it appears to," Jack said. "Can they still make these things or have the Feds shut them down?"

"Good question," Leo said. "Don't know. News is sparse and unreliable. Think they hide their facilities somewhere far back, but don't know where. Don't know if the Feds have found them. Don't even know if the Feds know about them."

"Damn, what a mess," Jack said. Suddenly he had a splitting headache. It was all just too much to absorb at once.

"Amen, brother."

7: News

Jack was back on *The Bird of Profit*.
Still overwhelmed by the news Lionel Chang had brought him, he couldn't sleep.
It'd been less than a couple of hours, in truth. Most of that had been questioning Chang about his drives, and about how the war with the Beyonders was going. It'd hadn't provided much more in the way of solid information.
Chang didn't seem to be holding anything back. In fact, it was clear that Chang and his trading clan had gone out of their way to bring Jack into the picture. It was now obvious the *Chang's Pride* had been stripped of most of its normal crew and sent into Hanshan for the sole purpose of letting Jack know beyond a doubt that the Federation FTL monopoly no longer existed. The *Chang's Pride* had cast off and boosted for jump as soon as Jack had left her.
No, the problem was Chang simply hadn't known how the war was going. From what he did know, it seemed clear that it wasn't going according to either side's plan. The NJS, the Beyonders, had been secretly building their strength for years. The clans could tell that but didn't have a lot of detail. The Federation appeared to have obtained complete surprise with their attack. They'd taken

most of the Beyonder's major systems.

Only the SDF was now like the infamous dog that had succeeded in catching the car. If the Beyonder's had only had what the SDF had expected the campaign would have already ended in success for them. Unfortunately for them, it looked like they'd bitten off more than they could chew.

Chang and the clans didn't know how many fall-back positions the Beyonders had, and they didn't know how long the SDF could sustain its offensive. They only knew both sides had taken heavy losses and were now improvising.

Most of all Chang didn't know where the Beyonder FTL production was located and didn't know if the SDF had overrun it or not. He suspected not because that would have likely led to a blizzard of rumors, some of which would have leaked through to their informants. There hadn't been any such rumors yet. It wasn't even clear the SDF yet realized that the Beyonders had their own FTL. If their leadership knew, they weren't telling the rank and file about it.

It was a mess, pure and simple, and there was no way to tell who'd come out on top.

Best guess was that it was a severely negative sum game and lose-lose for both sides.

Most likely the Feds would reduce the Beyonders to a few hard scrabble refugees. Most likely they'd be badly hurt in the process. So badly hurt that they had to abandon both the Frontier and most of the Middle Worlds. The tax payers back on Earth already thought the Federation and SDF were an expensive welfare project for bureaucrats both civilian and military.

With regards to that altogether too likely outcome, the news Chang had brought had been intensely good. With the Federation the only source of FTL drives that outcome would have meant a new dark ages for all of humanity outside of the Core. Many populations in small settlements and stations weren't completely self-sufficient. Cut-off they would have faced slow but certain extinction. A mood of horror and despair that Jack hadn't even realized had been weighing him down had been lifted.

He felt buoyant. Down right light headed as it happened, which was odd given all the problems he now faced.

Before his prospects and those of all the people depending upon him had been limited and grim. There hadn't been much he could do besides to avoid as much collateral damage as possible from the Federation as it thrashed about in its death throes. He'd tried to hold out hope he'd survive and somehow manage to pick up and put together the pieces after the drama had played itself out. He'd mainly hoped the situation wasn't as bad as it seemed.

Now it turned out that in fact it wasn't.

Even if the SDF had taken out the Beyonder's ability to make FTL drives, it'd been proven that capacity was one that could be independently developed. There were likely people out there who could jump start the process.

Humanity in the Middle Worlds and beyond wasn't doomed to isolation in the dark. It was no small thing.

It also opened up all sorts of options and choices, which Jack had no idea how to deal with.

Might be a good thing, but it wasn't an easy thing.

One option had been closed, though. That was the one of remaining neutral. It was pretty clear now that Jack and Ad Astra were going to have to weigh in against the Federation.

Too bad they had no military power at all to put on the scales.

Too bad that abandoning Ad Astra's neutrality would likely mean Jack's assassination.

Bonaparte, whoever he was and whoever he worked for, had made that clear.

* * *

Samuel Jackson, now a genuinely ex-sergeant in the Federation marines, was a tough man and one used to exercising initiative in dangerous and uncertain situations. Charlie Foxtrot, Ka-Ka hitting the fan, run for cover sorts of situations.

He didn't scare easy, and he didn't freeze under pressure. He was copacetic under any and every circumstance.

His bosses knew it too. That was why they habitually delegated almost impossible tasks to him while providing a minimum of resources and warning.

Jackson treasured that reputation. It was useful.

As nice as pride was, you couldn't eat it. Being left free to use one's own methods to get things done, and having men willing to do whatever you asked them to, that was useful.

On the other hand, sometimes the responsibility was downright terrifying.

This was one of those times.

His latest, and he suspected, one way or the other, his last, boss had handed him a doozy of a job.

Jack Black hadn't told Jackson why they'd docked at an obscure mining station in the outer parts of the Hanshan system before moving in system. Neither had Black told Jackson everything he'd learned there. What he had told Jackson coming back from meeting whoever there, looking shell shocked and pensive, was, to quote; "Not going to be able to stay out of the fight, Jackson."

He'd then gone on to give Jackson a blank check to up both Jack's personal security and the defense of the ship itself. He'd gone further than that. He'd told Jackson, "I'm afraid we may have to take the offensive and find people and deal with them violently."

Jackson looked around Port Tianjian Station's main market deck, trying to get his bearings. He'd been so sunk in his thoughts as to lose track of where he was. He'd arrived in the area early because it was vital not to miss his appointment here. Still, it was never good to lose situational awareness.

A large display high up on a bulkhead gave the time. Showtime.

He made his way to an obscure door with a garish but strangely modest sign above it advertising the Stardust Lounge. It was a place that didn't even try to hide how seedy it was.

Moving inside, and stopping just to one side of the entrance to let his eyes adjust to the gloom, Jackson found the interior met the promise of the place's outside.

Heavy, metal, and faux leather, bolted down furniture crowded the place. Patrons did not. The carpet was thick and smelled of old booze. An old man in an old suit quietly molested a piano in one corner.

Jackson didn't have exalted standards, but he wouldn't have normally frequented a place like this. Then again, it wasn't really a place of entertainment, it was a meeting place for a certain sort of business person.

Jackson made his way to a booth a few tables away from the piano and its player. He found the particular businessman he was looking for there. He sat himself down.

The businessman in question was old, thin, worn and gray. He wore a suit that was just like him. He looked up from the beat up old tablet he'd been fiddling with, his face was strangely demonic in the light the tablet gave off. "I have arranged the deliveries you asked for," he said. "It wasn't easy on such short notice."

"And doubtless there'll be a commensurate surcharge," Jackson said.

"There will be," the gray little man said. "You should be glad it won't be more and that I was able to fill your order at all."

"I should?"

"You most certainly should," the gray man said. Rather more forcefully than Jackson would have expected. "If certain associates of mine hadn't made it clear that taking care of your principal was of the highest importance to them, I would not have been able to do so."

Jackson paused. This man wasn't supposed to know he was working for Jack or Ad Astra. They were swimming in murky waters here. "Mind elaborating?" he asked.

"Free of charge even," the gray man said. "Turns out you're a valued customer of ours. We have great hopes for repeat business should all our plans succeed." He made a facial expression that was probably a humorless smile.

"Great."

"Indeed," the gray man said, his smile somehow turning less fake. "Everyone in the sector with any responsibility and a clue is scrambling to arm."

"And?"

"And as a result prices are up and orders are backlogged."

"Interviews?"

"A few but given current circumstances contractors, especially ones meeting your criteria, are difficult to find."

"More expensive too, I imagine."

"I believe so," the gray man said, "but you realize we're only middlemen bringing you together in these cases." He paused. "We can arrange for both regular troops and special operators at reasonable prices, but I suspect you wouldn't be comfortable with all their associations."

"You mean they'd be loyal to Hanshan or the Tian Zhong Guo not us," Jackson said.

"It might be a distinction without meaning," the gray man replied, "most of the responsible authorities here have come to appreciate that Captain Black is a responsible person and a force for stability in the sector. We wish him nothing but continued good health and success in his ongoing endeavors."

"You do?" Jackson asked. This was news. In their previous experience with the people running Hanshan, they'd been cagey and very transactional. This new willingness to be pals was disconcerting.

"We have the greatest confidence in Captain Black," the gray man said. "The Federation's current efforts have greatly clarified our thinking as well as that of many others."

Jackson thought it far more likely that what he meant was that they were desperate and scared. Looked like they were shocked by the Federation's sudden willingness to act, and the strength of the Beyonder resistance. Looked like faced with a genuine crisis that the fractious local interests in the sector realized they had to get their act together. He didn't say that.

He didn't say much really except to hand payment information over to the gray man.

As he left Jackson wondered how he'd explain what he'd learned to Jack.

He was more used to action than talking about his gut feelings.

* * *

John Malcolm was bone tired.

Still, he needed to focus, and to look alert, as his men finished up searching their assigned sector of Washington Station's Docklands.

In addition to his two day jobs John was a lieutenant in the volunteer Jefferson System Space Guard. Specifically, in Washington Station's militia battalion. A battalion that didn't consist of much more than two under strength and under armed companies. One of which was John's mainly by the virtue of his being a graduate of the Academy.

Normally the position provided some useful contacts and only required attending a meeting for a few hours each month. Right now it was more like a second full-time job.

A second full-time job that with extreme irony consisted of searching for and rooting out the spy network John was running here in Jefferson system on behalf of the SDFHQ's Special Directorate.

He had little choice but to perform the task to the best of his ability. The entire system was beside itself with rage at the newest evidence of outside interference in its business. Demonstrating anything but the fullest and most effective devotion to his task would have risked casting suspicion on himself. People usually overlooked his having been educated out system, but they would remember quick enough given cause.

He looked up from the station blueprint he'd been reading to see one of his sergeants approaching. Bill Fillon by name, they'd shared the occasional beer after a meeting. Bill snapped off a salute that John returned. Just like they were in a real military.

"We're done, John, er, Lieutenant, ah, sir," Bill said.

"That's fine, Sergeant," John replied. He did so in a mild but professional tone. He carefully hid both the amusement and irritation he felt. "Muster and dismiss the men. Time to go home."

"Be good to get some sleep, won't it," Bill replied. Then he remembered John's day job. The one everyone knew about. "Oh, sorry, been busy hasn't it?"

"It has," John said. "But better to have too much business than too little."

"But you're not going to be getting much sleep."

"No, I'm not."

"Well, sir," Bill said, "I guess I'd better be going and not take up more of your time."

"Thanks, Bill."

John watched Bill leave the compartment they'd commandeered as his "Command Post" before sitting back down and sighing.

He wouldn't have minded some sleep, but the whole system was booming. Ad Astra had set up their HQ in Jefferson. As a result they'd been visited by more traders in the last few weeks than they'd seen in the entire previous year. All of them bringing cargoes to sell and looking for product to buy. Offering good prices, too. On top of that, they had supplies they needed for themselves.

The system's economy was being stretched to the limit to fill the new demand. The in-system shipping company John was Operations Manager for was busier than ever.

John was almost glad they'd shut down his local network, and he was of necessity remaining inactive for the time being. He barely had time for two jobs, let alone a third.

Almost, but not quite.

It'd been quite the personal setback.

Wasn't helped by the fact that from what he heard, the SDF campaign against the Beyonders wasn't going well.

He hadn't heard much back from SDFHQ, but he suspected they were having to come up with an entirely new set of plans, probably based on out-of-date information. It was a long ways back to Earth.

He hoped they'd have the good sense to sit back and let the dust settle.

He didn't expect it. He expected that for the sake of their careers they'd double down.

He expected when they did, he'd have a starring role in their new plans. After all, Jefferson was now key to the sector's logistics. The actors based here were the most likely candidates to lead a rebellion against the Federation.

He might not like it, but what he did here, or didn't, would matter.

Not that it was worth agonizing over it like this.

When he got his orders he would, like usual, follow them.

* * *

Jack and Jackson were sitting alone at a table in the *Bird of Profit*'s mess post the breakfast rush. There were a few remnants of their own breakfasts in front of them, and they were both on their second cups of coffee. They were attending to business.

The day had started with the ship's emergence into El Dorado. It was now on the long run into the planet Caelum. They had a longer than normal stop over planned in El Dorado, but they had a lot to do too.

Jackson had more tools and more people, but they all needed some trying out. Training facilities on freighters, big as they were, were limited. Of course, the training had to be geared to the objectives Jackson was given. Giving him those objectives was Jack's job.

"Going to need a twenty-four seven security detachment to protect our HQ in Jefferson," Jackson was saying.

"We can't recruit one locally?" Jack asked.

"Best not to. Not all of them," Jackson replied. "People have a hard time being tough with long time neighbors, let alone friends and family. Also, we know for a fact that multiple factions hostile to us have been operating underground in Jefferson."

Jack took a sip of coffee and thought that over. Jackson was just stating facts. It was what it was. "You don't think we can trust people we recruit in Jefferson?" he asked, seeking confirmation.

"Most of them, ones we screen carefully," Jackson said, "will likely be both loyal and well disciplined."

"That's good, isn't it?" Jack was feeling a bit puzzled.

"Yes, it is because we are going to have to recruit locally there," Jackson said. "We just don't have the bodies we'll need otherwise. Running operations everyday all around the clock means having to have three to four times the people you need for a nine-to-five operation. At a minimum. You need at least three shifts, people for the weekends and other vacations, and then because you have so many other people you need people to act as support staff."

"Damn," Jack responded. "Being ex-Navy I should know this. You're right. We're going to need some sort of command structure, aren't we?"

"Yes, figure that's something we can use training on Caelum for," Jackson said. "We pick out some prospects for command after seeing how they perform. Maybe some people will be better in support roles. Others we can just seed in among the local Jeffersonian recruits. We should try to recruit as many El Doradians as we can."

"Okay, run with that," Jack said. "It all sounds good." He couldn't help thinking at this point that Jackson might be another ex-NCO in the SDF who was capable of being more than just a trusted minion. Have to give that some thought.

"So is that all?" Jackson asked.

"I believe it is," Jack said. "I don't want to jinx us, but I think as busy as we're going to be that this stop over in El Dorado should be a break from people trying to kill us."

"Kill you mostly, Jack," Jackson said.

"And willing to go through you and your men to do it," Jack said.

"True."

"Anyhow the El Doradians are all in with us. They aren't inclined to being sneaky about it when they turn murderous either. Everybody else is pretty far away," Jack said. "No, I think we've got a little calm before storm here. We should make the best of it."

"Sounds good," Jackson replied as he stood up, picking up his plate and utensils as he did so. He wasn't a man who liked to leave messes.

 Jack followed suit. "Right, give me a plan in writing before we dock," he said as they walked to the scullery. "Just to make it official."

8: The Shadows Gather

It was mid-morning in New Cambridge, Newton's capital city and main spaceport, too early for Ted to be in a tavern.

Didn't help he hadn't had much sleep the night before. The tavern was one of those places that only closed for a few hours very early in the morning to wash out the stale beer and sweep out the drunks. Then they'd open again to serve breakfast.

This particular place was on the boundary between the university district and an industrial park. Wasn't far from the spaceport either. It catered to students in the evenings, workers in the mornings and after work, and drunks all day long.

It was one such drunk that had requested Ted's presence.

A request Ted was in no position to refuse. Not given that the drunk in question was the ranking SDF officer on Newton.

It didn't take him long to locate the man. He was sitting by himself, with nobody nearby, in a corner in the rear of the tavern. Seemed like the other patrons were giving him a wide berth.

Sitting down across from Lieutenant Commander William Chidley Ted could see, or rather smell, why. The man was rank. Apparently the tavern's cleaning staff had missed at least one drunk this morning.

Chidley didn't look good either. There weren't many homeless in New Cambridge. They were rapidly put back on their feet or if they couldn't fend for themselves institutionalized. He had seen some elsewhere and all of them had looked better than the Lieutenant Commander. His eye sockets were a squinting mass of dark reddish wrinkles through which peered two bloodshot orbs more red than white. The man was the very epitome of a drunk down on his luck.

He was also the man that held Ted's and likely Newton's fate in his hands.

"Good morning, Ted." Chidley seemed to be making an effort to sound cheerful. He contorted his face into a wide grin. Apparently the effort hurt as he then winced. "Arragh."

"Are you sure, Lieutenant Commander?" Ted asked. "What is this about?"

"Call me Bill, Ted. Not in uniform, and this isn't official. Highly unofficial really." Bill sprawled back against the bench he was seated on, took a deep breath, and belched. "Sorry."

"That's okay, Bill." Whatever Ted thought of him he had to humor William Chidley. "Bill" was not only in command of the SDF logistics unit based on Newton, mostly in New Cambridge's warehouse district, he was also the senior SDF officer in-system, and Ted's personal minder. Admiral St. Armand had made it clear Ted was to jump when Bill said to or else.

"What's this about you ask?" Bill stared at the ceiling for a while then heaved himself up to look at Ted. "Well, Ted, I got some information about our forces near the Frontier late yesterday. I've been sitting here trying to figure out how to explain what it means all of yesterday evening, all of last night, and most of the morning. I drank myself blind, passed out, woke up, and now I'm mostly sober with the worst headache you can imagine. Still don't know how to explain."

"Not good news?"

Bill laughed, then winced again at the movement. "No, not good news. I do believe we can expect the SDF units remaining out on the Frontier to be making a rapid strategic redeployment in our direction back towards the Core."

"I can see how that might be hard news to digest," Ted said. He tried to sound sympathetic. He was genuinely worried for Newton. He had no idea how the SDF would react to defeat. To his knowledge, it wasn't something they had any experience of. If they were fleeing the Frontier and didn't intend to stop before or at Newton would they be willing to abandon the valuable production facilities and supplies here intact? Or did military logic dictate a scorched earth policy?

"No kidding." Bill peered blearily at Ted. "Yeah, it ain't good news for Newton. And it's really not good news for you, Ted. But it's not you or Newton I'm most worried about it's me."

"You?"

"Yes, me." Bill spread his hands wide in a mock gesture of beatification, before clasping them over his heart. He smiled sweetly at Ted. "Me," he said. "Believe me or not, I used to be an idealistic young man willing to sacrifice all for the greater good."

"I'll take your word for it."

"Thank you, so much. As you can imagine there's been a lot of water under the bridge since." Bill leaned forward. "Neither here nor there, but I've got my reasons for drinking. You might feel hard done by, Ted, but I'm first in line to get diddled here."

"I've got to live here on Newton. You can go home to the Solar System, probably even keep your career in the SDF."

"Wrong on all counts. Wish I had the time to enlighten you. Not why I asked to talk to you. We have other business."

Bill leaned back. Ted was happy to be a bit further from his stench. He knew he had to tread carefully, but he was tired and fed up. The Lieutenant Commander had something to say, but he seemed to be having trouble saying it. Ted was in no mood to humor him. "So get to your point," Ted said.

Bill sitting up straight clasped his hand together on the table between them and looked Ted right in the eye. Ted was shocked to realize how lucid the man's bloodshot eyes were. As tired and worn as the face in front of him was, it reflected an intense intelligence. The drunk clown was in part at least a mask for the real man. Ted remembered the report he'd read on Chidley before meeting the man in person, the report had suggested someone highly intelligent and not just in a narrow way. Bill had real problems, but Ted realized he'd been sucked in by an act. At least in part.

"Okay," Bill said, "first thing you've got to realize is I'm intended to be the main scapegoat for this horrific fiasco."

"So?"

"So, I want to defect," Bill replied. "With conditions." By his tone he could have been reading a grocery list.

"Defect?" Ted needed time to process this. "To who? Conditions? What conditions? And what do you have to offer that let's you set conditions, pray tell?"

"To you and your buddies, Ted," Bill answered with a smirk. It was the sort of smile an assassin would give his victim before twisting a knife in their kidneys. "I'm not an intelligence wanker myself, but I know one when I see one."

"Then you should know intelligence wankers don't run things. They report to those that do."

"Normally maybe. Not normal times though, is it, Ted? Oh, I know you'd just like to hide like a spider in a dark corner of some library pulling on the strands of your web. Only occasionally though, mostly just observing with your oversupply of eyes. But neither one of us is going to get what we want, my dear Doctor Smith."

"A dramatic image that means what?"

"It means that when the dust settles you're going to be one of the poor bastards that has to put the pieces back together. Here in Newton for sure, given your friends I'm guessing in the entire sector."

"I'm flattered you think so," Ted said. "Assuming I'm in any position to do anything for you, what do you want? Why would I give it to you?"

"What I want is a safe home here on Newton and a job working for your brother, or at least the University. As a physicist. On FTL."

"With all due respect, Bill, an undergraduate degree, and a little masters work doesn't qualify you for a top job as a working physicist, not here on Newton."

"Glad to see you at least did your homework." Bill didn't seem in the least disturbed by Ted's opinion of his qualifications. "Imagine you also noticed I graduated the top of my class."

"You were recommended highly for the command track," Ted said. "It was suggested that this might have reflected your family connections. Your family has a long tradition of serving in the SDF and as senior Federation bureaucrats. You have a lot of relatives well placed to give each other a hand up."

Bill assumed a new expression. Sad and regretful, maybe? "It didn't. We do and we were. Your data is a little stale." He smiled wanly. "I applied to take the engineering track. It didn't make my family or the staff at the Academy happy. Also, it might have been that my attitude towards authority was less than reverent. I was a smart ass to be honest. I didn't care. I liked understanding how things worked, helping them to keep working, and improving on them. Eventually I hoped to transfer to FTL research and production and to improve it."

Ted sighed. For the first time he felt a twinge of sympathy for the man in front of him. Maybe he hadn't always been the cynical drunk he was now. Still. "I'm sorry for your dashed hopes, Bill, but we both know the SDF doesn't send its best and brightest into the Logistics branch."

"It's a dumping ground true." Bill paused and then snorted.

"What?"

"Ironically, and I know you're not going to believe this, I was tracked into logistics for being too smart."

"Really."

"Really. Not just that. Hard to be sure what was most important, but it didn't help that one of my uncles published a book."

"A book?"

"Yeah, a tell all novel. A true to life novel mostly with just a few names changed and maybe some characters conflated. It was a great book. It sold like gang busters."

"Good for your uncle."

"Not really. Uncle Thomas was more clever than smart. Wasn't good for the rest of us in the family either. His tale of embedded corruption, and worse comically bad incompetence and stupidity in the highest levels of the SDF and Federation bureaucracy was extremely popular. It even prompted some congressional investigations."

"So you think the corrupt bureaucracy wrecked your career because of a piece of fiction an uncle wrote?" Ted tried to keep the skepticism out of his voice. He didn't want to underestimate Bill again, but he did seem a little off the mental tracks.

Bill fiddled with a half full glass of beer that'd been sitting in front of him. The beer was completely flat. If Ted had to guess he'd think Bill had stopped drinking it hours ago. Stopped cold. What kind of man got throughly drunk and then quit in the middle of a glass? "I do," Bill finally said.

"I'm not a fan of everything about the SDF or the Federation bureaucracy in general," Ted said, "but forgive me if I'm a little skeptical."

Bill smiled wanly at Ted. "You're forgiven. I didn't see it, and my uncle underestimated it along with most of my, as you said, well-connected family. If we didn't see it why would I expect you to?"

"Very kind of you."

"No it's not. We tend to see what we want to. I'm sure in your line of business you understand that." Bill looked at his glass and chuckled. "Funny thing is is the novel was too accurate. Didn't just step on some important toes, but it described a situation too bad to be believable. Truth really is stranger than fiction. They waited until the publicity blew over, then all the careers in my family stalled. Not just mine."

"Tragic, but how is that relevant here and now?"

"Put in a good word for me with your brother and I can prove myself," Bill replied.

"Relations between my brother and I are somewhat strained right now," Ted said. "I can do that, but it will cost me."

"A down payment, Ted," Bill said. "I applied to the FTL production facility on Luna before my career went west. Gathered all the information I could about the place. Some of it through informal channels, you might say."

"And?"

"And it's huge. There's a whole city there full of workers and their families that are never allowed to leave. I'm not sure how much money the Federation pours into the place, the accounting was too tangled, but it's hundreds of billions at a minimum. And you know the biggest fact about the place?"

"No, what?" Ted figured it couldn't hurt to let the man tell his story if Ted could manage to learn something about the ultra top secret production facility.

"It produces almost nothing," Bill said grinning at Ted. "It produces less almost every year and the quality is constantly if slowly falling too. I didn't believe it at first. Went to a great deal of trouble to get the best figures I could. Many thousands of people, whole secret cities, a huge budget, and the place puts out less than a half-dozen new ship sized and quality FTL drives a year. Barely enough to replace those lost in accidents."

"That is very difficult to believe." Ted wondered why Bill was wasting his time with stories like this.

"It's something you can check for yourself once you know what to look for," Bill replied. "Just keep an open mind about it. What you have to understand is that it's not an industrial facility anymore run by businessmen, or engineers, or even scientists, it's a pork barrel project run by corrupt politically well-connected incompetents. Has been for sometime."

"I will do my due diligence," Ted said. He would despite being very busy already. "If true, I imagine this is important."

"Damned right, it's important. Know you haven't had time to think it through, but what it means is that your brother runs humanity's only viable FTL production facility. The Core fleet, SDF, and civilian transports both, has been a fixed size for years. Only the middle world and Frontier fleets have been expanding and Newton has been filling all that demand. You can check that."

Ted blinked. If he could pry accurate information out of Mike, it was true because how many new transports were built was basically public information. The numbers were low, shipyards few in number, and every new transport had to be registered. He'd never been tasked with collecting the information. Keeping track of events in the sector kept him busy enough. Still shouldn't be too hard. "I can. It'll take time. Okay, I'll look into it."

"You do that," Bill said. "And while you're at it consider the fact that maybe one reason we're talking is because I don't want some over eager, clueless SDF ship's captain to destroy humanity's only source of new FTL drives because he's not as well informed as we are."

"You're a regular altruist."

"I am," Bill replied. "And if this wasn't so serious it'd be amusing, you don't believe that. In any case your brother needs to disperse his supplies, machinery, and people to safe sites. I'll cover for it. You can do it openly and my bosses won't hear a thing about it. In return I want you to promise to treat my people right, give them asylum too, not prosecute them for just following orders."

It was beginning to dawn on Ted that Bill was serious. Maybe a little off his rocker and overreacting, but serious, and proposing some useful solutions to their joint problems. "I can't make any guarantees," he said, "but I can talk to some influential people and I think I can persuade them to be reasonable."

"Good." Bill looked at Ted expectantly.

Ted realized Bill was waiting for Ted to connect the dots. "Two points, I guess," Ted said. "One, you think the SDF might strike targets on Newton, is that right? Two, you don't think you'r going to be able to evacuate your people."

"Very good," Bill said. Ted didn't appreciate being condescended to by a smelly drunk, but his feelings weren't that important. "Those two points are not unconnected. Play ball with me and I'll do my best to ensure that the SDF units transiting Newton do so directly without having to approach the planet. I'll need all the help the local authorities can provide to locate supply dumps in space on the direct transit route through the system."

"Okay that's asking a lot, but I think I can convince my superiors it's a good idea," Ted said. "But it'll only take one rogue or detached ship to devastate Newton, won't it?"

"True," Bill agreed. "Like you said no guarantees, but the fewer ships that approach the planet and the less time they linger, the better. You should certainly step up your evacuations. You're not guessing about the threat anymore, and you don't have to hide your preparations any longer. Don't hurt yourself thanking me."

Ted sighed. "I guess I have to admit that what you're doing might end up saving countless lives."

"Good of you, but I'm pretty sure I can count them and that it runs somewhere from hundreds of thousands to millions of people," Bill said.

"Perhaps I'd be more impressed if you weren't using them as leverage to better yourself."

"Perhaps gratitude alone, even when it's forthcoming, doesn't buy food or pay the rent," Bill said. "In addition to all the advice, very good advice, and warning I've already given you, I can actively attempt to forestall efforts to dismantle or destroy your FTL facilities. I can tell my superiors that I've successfully seized control of them, that I can destroy them if it looks like I'll lose that control, and that my people are safe here. It'll help if Newton's authorities go along with the charade."

"So there'll no need for an orbital strike."

"Right. Also though random ship's captains won't be aware of it, both Admiral St. Armand, the expeditionary force leader and Admiral Arain in command of the standing forces in the sector are doubtless aware that Newton's production is not replaceable. They'll also be aware that without it they'll not be able to replace the ship losses they've taken."

"So an unholy mess, but there's light at the end of the tunnel."

"That's right. At least if you play ball with me," Bill said.

"Okay, I'll do my best," Ted said standing up. "If what you've told me checks out and I can persuade my superiors we have a deal." He held out his hand. "Shake on it?"

"Deal." Bill said, shaking Ted's hand.

* * *

Live blaster bolts sizzled by just tens of centimeters overhead. Cynthia pressed herself into the mud. A miss of a few centimeters was as good as a miss by a kilometer in a fire fight.

If she stood up and was killed it'd only be a training accident. She'd be just as dead. She felt she had good reason to be feeling a little uneasy. And for getting as intimate with the surface of the planet of Caelum, El Dorado system, as she could.

Turning her head, she saw one of her new recruits was feeling more than just uneasy. The poor woman was scared just short of witless. White as a ghost with big eyes.

"It's normal to be scared," Cynthia said. She thought she sound impressively calm. "You get more used to it. That's why we're doing this."

The woman, Kathy Collins, Cynthia remembered, nodded. "Yes, ma'am."

It was true the couple weeks of training they were giving their new recruits would make a real difference if it came to an actual fight. Cynthia regretted how likely that was. She'd rather be drinking wine in a resort than being shot at in a muddy field. Still, she had a job to do.

"Heads down, butts down, leopard crawl ten meters forward!" she yelled. She crawled forward in the slippery mud, using only her elbows and knees. Kathy next to her did the same. Good.

* * *

The *Bird of Profit* was in orbit around Caelum. Not docked. Jack could have ordered her left docked to the small station serving the planet, but it would have been rude and inconsiderate. Jack didn't figure he wanted to try the patience of El Dorado's people if he didn't have to.

And El Dorado wasn't set up in the usual manner of Federation mid-world colonies. Most of those had one at least semi-inhabitable planet with one major city on it and a large trade hub of a station orbiting above that city.

Some systems might have a large settlement out in their asteroid belt. If that belt was large or mineral rich. Or if the locals had a particular dislike of outsiders. If they wanted trade, but not to have foreigners too close. Al-Alhadeen came to mind as an example.

Generally, the local culture in a colony system was some exaggerated re-creation of one from Earth, the original settlers having emigrated for the very purpose of establishing a pure expression of their desired society. Mother Earth herself had become too crowded to allow that. No large group could go its own way. On Earth you had to compromise with other, different, people living on the planet.

But culture aside, Federation colonies tended to be built on the same general material template. One of the main things that endeared both El Dorado and Newton to Jack was that they both departed from that template.

Newton's belt was minimal and mineral poor. The planet itself had had a very earth like atmosphere, the local life had been somewhat more evolved than usual, but was very dry. Any earth-sized planet was going to have local areas where agriculture was possible, but Newton's weren't extensive. Neither was the planet mineral rich. Newton was never going to have a large population or much heavy industry. What it did have was the University and some high-tech industry. It had the flavor of a planet sized college town.

El Dorado was unique in a completely different way. It could have been settled in the Federation standard manner. It hadn't been.

Three major characteristics had distinguished it from the beginning.

First and most of all, it was a long ways out from Earth and the Core worlds, hundreds of light years in fact. The vast majority of Federation systems had been settled directly from Earth. Moreover, they'd been settled quickly, more or less all at once, if a period of a decade or two can be called all at once. They'd been settled by culturally and ethnically homogeneous people. The

Federation hadn't wanted to replicate Earth's divisions. Not El Dorado, it'd been settled by a second wave of settlers from other colonies, usually extended spacer families. Traders, miners, and ships crews with families gathered catch as catch can from all over. Misfits but self-dependent ones willing to trade comfort and security for the freedom to live their lives as they wanted. People who prized elbow room. El Dorado had a culture all of its own that hadn't originated on Earth.

Second, El Dorado's colonization had been spread out, sparse and sporadic. It had a large rich asteroid belt but no nearby markets for the minerals or manufactures that belt could provide. If there was such a thing as a subsistence level space age economy than that was what El Dorado's belt had. More than that was the fact, apparently unknown to the wider Federation, that the system's inhabitable planet, Caelum, was earth like to the point of requiring little or no terraforming. Jack could only imagine it hadn't been reached by the initial colonization surveys.

What it meant was that unlike with most colonization efforts, the planet's settlers hadn't initially needed to be concentrated in a few of the most habitable areas of their new planet.

Although it might have made sense on most planets to have waited a generation or two before starting their colonization. It turned out that most prospective colonists weren't willing to wait that long. The Federation for its part had been happy to get most of them off Earth and out of the Core worlds. So most worlds started off with a tiny, densely populated concentrated set of settlements.

Not Caelum, most of Caelum's surface was inhabitable right from the beginning and each rather small set of new settlers chose somewhere new.

Caelum's settlement wasn't just thin. It wasn't even continuous. It was one of widely spaced penny packets of people. People pre-disposed to preferring breathing space over luxury. There was no world dominating large city. There weren't even very many large towns.

Thirdly, El Dorado's development had been capital poor. There'd been no large Federation sponsored colonization project. One supported by the deep pockets of Earth's financial system. No, the people that settled El Dorado hadn't been poor, but they hadn't been wealthy on the level of governments, or mega-corps, or, especially, mega-banks. Oddly enough, large capital projects, which most major infrastructure investments are, require large amounts of capital. There'd been none of that in El Dorado's history.

El Dorado's development had taken place in small, very incremental steps. Infrastructure was only built as needed. And then only if it could be afforded.

And so Jack found himself onboard his ship, *The Bird of Profit,* in orbit not docked. The huge extensive docks of a major purpose-built trading station not being available in El Dorado. For historical reasons.

The complex interconnectedness of such things had never ceased to fascinate Jack. The chance to encounter them was one of his main pleasures in life and why he enjoyed interstellar travel so much. It had also built an understanding he hoped to put to good use in his new job as head of Ad Astra. If he could ever pull free from putting out bush fires and if he somehow managed to survive the current crisis.

But now right he was waiting in orbit around Caelum. Waiting and playing bait.

Jack had thought El Dorado was safe from the madness consuming the rest of the sector. He'd hoped for a few weeks of rest and training in preparation for the long trip back to Jefferson.

Turned out he'd thought wrong.

Scant hours before they'd detected jump emergences from an unusual direction. At least unusual in Jack's experience. He wasn't sure exactly how much the El Doradians had failed to share with him regards their trading patterns. He'd come to the realization that it was a habit with them not to share more information than necessary. They were very friendly people and not at all trusting ones. Not of outsiders and non-family.

The emergences had been those of three SDF long range FTL capable fighter craft. Apparently fleeing a military debacle out in Beyonder territory. As small as they were, and as tired as their pilots had to be, in the absence of any opposition those fighters could completely dominate the system. *The Bird of Profit* certainly couldn't either evade them or fight them. She was a sitting duck.

Jack had been awake when the emergences had been detected.

The watch officer had immediately pinged him and it'd taken him mere minutes to reach the bridge. It'd taken only a few more minutes to assess the situation and realize just how FUBARed it was.

The broadcast from the SDF craft that closely followed that realization only confirmed it.

"El Dorado system, this is Lieutenant Landes of the SDF. This system is now under martial law and lockdown. All ships in dock or orbit will remain so. No ships in transit will alter their courses for any purpose other than safety. Caelum station will prepare to receive our ships and to refuel and resupply them. Acknowledge your compliance or suffer the consequences. Landes out."

Jack imagined Landes must have spent hours honing that speech while in jump. It was just barely possible to build jump capable fighter craft. That didn't make them comfortable. Landes and her little group must be desperate. Didn't make them less dangerous.

Jack had checked with the station and his people on the planet's surface before replying to Landes.

"SDF fighters, Lieutenant Landes commanding, this is Captain Jack Black aboard *The Bird of Profit* in Caelum orbit, we will comply as necessary. Be aware you may not be the senior SDF officer in-system. Suggest we confer in person."

The Lieutenant hadn't mentioned his delay in replying, but it was clear it didn't make her happier. Despite the hours they had available, she'd not attempted a long discussion over open comms. "Black, Landes acknowledging," she'd replied. "Altering course to rendezvous *The Bird of Profit,* Landes out."

That had been hours ago and now Landes was about to attempt a docking with *The Bird of Profit* that neither it nor her fighter had ever been designed for. Her two wingmen were keeping watch, but it was still a sign of considerable trust. Or desperation. Or both.

In any event, if nothing went wrong Jack would soon be talking to the woman in person.

Landes turned out to not only be female, but even tired, disheveled and under considerable emotional stress, a very attractive one. A cloud of frizzy strawberry blond hair billowed out when she pulled her flight helmet off. Jack was impressed. She'd just pulled off a difficult maneuver after days in her cockpit.

He was also quite aware that being physically attractive was no advantage to an active SDF officer. Not the female ones, anyway. Being tall and blond seemed correlated to perceived "command presence" for male officers.

Jack stuck his hand out to shake. "Jack Black," he said. She took it tentatively, like it might bite, then leaned in and shook it firmly. "Anna Landes. You wanted to talk?"

"Yes. I believe I'm technically your superior here in-system, but I'm afraid there may be complications. Would you like a shower and a meal before we get down to business?"

Landes stared at Jack for a second before replying. She really was tired. "Something stinks here, Black, and it's not just me," she said. "What I'd like is an explanation of what's going on."

Jack had learned to smile when delivering bad news. Or even just saying things that weren't what people wanted to hear. A simple trick he now employed. "It's complicated, but the first thing you need to know is that you have to act like the professional I know you are," he said. "Can you do that?"

Landes twitched. Yes, she'd got the message despite the pleasant manner in which it'd been delivered. "Yes, sir," she replied. She straightened up without quite coming to attention.

"Good," Jack said. "Treating me with respect since I'm at least your peer and more likely, given my designated responsibility and seniority, your superior here, is a necessary start. I have to emphasize that this is particularly true because the situation here is political, uncertain and highly delicate. You mustn't undermine me. Understood?"

"Yes, sir," Landes answered. She looked more tired than angry now.

The benefits of training and discipline. How Jack had missed them. Besides Jackson and his people it seemed everyone he dealt with now had to be soft soaped, cajoled, flattered and reasoned with. Even when everyone knew ahead of time what the final deal was going to be they still wanted the respect of going through the motions. He did miss the real military at times. "Your people in the other fighters, can they wait another hour or two or do they need immediate rest and replenishment?"

Landes went flat-faced. "They've plenty of air and water. They got to sleep on the jump here. They're good for days."

Jack was careful not to sigh, instead he smiled wider. Nobody was genuinely good for days in a fighter, though professionals were trained to function despite it. It would have made what was coming much simpler if she'd ordered her men to stand down and come in for some R & R. "Great," he said, "that means it won't hurt for you to wash up and change. We can then discuss this over a meal rather than standing around in my docking bay. Follow me."

Landes looked like she wanted to complain, but like being clean and a real meal sounded good too. "Yes, sir," she said catching up with Jack and his security detail. Oh, to be young again. Somehow Jack suspected that Anna Landes if she played poker didn't win much.

At least she'd learned to shower and dress quick when needed. It was less than a quarter hour before they were sitting down to a hearty meal in the ship's main mess. Jack had actually been hoping to buy a bit more time.

Landes inhaled half a heaping plate of starch, meat, sauce, and veg before realizing time was passing. The low mass, nutrient rich rations issued fighter pilots for extended operations were deliberately not very filling.

She suddenly looked up at Jack. Jack had been picking away at his food much more slowly, more to keep her company than because of any real hunger on his own part. "Thank you for the food, sir," she said. "I'm sorry to be so paranoid, but the last few months they've been crazy. I volunteered to be transferred to this sector because I was bored and I didn't think my career was going anywhere fast." She paused and stared at her food.

"Somebody made promises?" Jack half asked, half volunteered.

"Nothing explicit or in writing." Landes spoke between bites. She was eating more deliberately now. "Excuse me, sir, but you're old for a lieutenant."

"I'm a lieutenant commander, but a reservist mustang on a technical track, also a mid-worlder," Jack said. He didn't mention that he also didn't have a command, let alone one with three fighter craft. Jackson and his men didn't count anymore. He also didn't feel she needed to know that although he had credentials he could show her, he didn't know himself what SDFHQ would say if she could somehow check with them. Fortunately, Earth and SDFHQ were months of travel away.

She nodded. Despite all the caveats he'd apparently made her day. Her relief was palpable. Her face brighter. Jack imagined she now thought all her problems were his instead. "Well different sector, Beta, sir, but I'm a mid-worlder myself," she said. "Lieutenant Commander isn't bad for one of us." She hesitated. "No offense from the ranks too, sir. That's rare. Lot's of ex-NCOs acting as lieutenants in technical slots, but don't often see one much beyond that." She frowned. "You've heard of Lieutenant Commander Torson?"

"Who hasn't?" Jack asked.

"I wish I hadn't, sir," Landes said bitterly.

Jack raised an eyebrow.

"They say he's brilliant and a dedicated officer, one of the few to have seen actual battle," she said. "He taught at the Academy too."

"But?"

"Well, Admiral Arain started this fight, and Admiral St. Armand and his Battle Group took it over, but rumor has it Torson planned it."

"I take it the fighting didn't go well."

"No sir, it did not," Anna Landes said with considerable heat her food temporarily forgotten.

"We've only heard bits and pieces here. Some of them hard to believe."

"It's a long and confusing story," Landes slowly chewed a bit of meat. She looked haunted. "I've been trying to deal with it day by day. Trying not to think too hard about what's above my pay grade."

"Understandable."

"I missed a lot of it," she said. "Drifting in an induced coma in my knocked out fighter for over a month during the worst of the campaign."

"That's horrible. Surprising too. I'd have thought one side or the other would have rescued you before that."

"We lost that battle and I refused to surrender to the Beyonders. They finished my fighter off from a distance and left me. Don't know if it was an accident, or mercy, or what."

Jack figured Landes was very lucky to be here and knew it too. He wondered if she'd have the nerve to be so hard nosed in the future. No wonder she looked worn.

"Not many of the pilots that I started the campaign with are still alive," she said. "It was a death march and Torson is the one who planned it. Apparently on the basis of inaccurate intelligence and expecting surprise we didn't get. We had traitors in our midst. They gave the enemy our plans and many of us died because of it. I might be bitter and paranoid, sir, but I've got my reasons."

"I understand," Jack said. "How is it you came to be here?"

"Beyonder's retreated deep into uncharted space." Landes paused to eat a bit more of her meal. She chewed pensively before continuing. "Admiral St. Armand's Battle Group followed and walked into an ambush." She looked at Jack to see if he had questions.

"I've a friend who's an historian who'll want all the details," Jack said. "Is that okay?"

"Might help to talk about it, sir," Landes said. "Not sure of them all you understand, but I can give a grunt's eye view. Pass on the rumors I heard."

"Thanks," Jack said. "Right now best give the short version."

"Yes, sir. So St. Armand and the ships he had left fled. The Beyonder's harassed them all the way back. We managed to keep the carrier, the *Saratoga*, spaceworthy but not fully operational. FTL fighters like mine and patrol craft had to screen it the best we could. It cost us. They gave me some raw pilots and orders to form the rearguard in one of those systems. Managed to draw the Beyonders off and the *Saratoga* and the remaining destroyers made it back through the main jump point on the route to Earth through Newton, but we were cut off."

"So you left the system moving laterally?"

"Yes, sir. Long trip and we weren't sure what we'd find here. We hadn't planned to come this way."

"So I'm guessing you and your men are shorter on supplies and more tired than you let on earlier."

"That's true, sir." Landes put her utensils down neatly on her now empty plate.

"My guards here have SDF marine training in EVA," Jack said.

"Not in uniform, sir."

"Technically we're acting on our own as civilians here. In fact they're trained marines who can retrieve your men and stand down your fighters without them having to take the risks you did."

Landes looked around at Jack and his omnipresent guard detail. She was visibly processing what he'd told her. "Still out on a limb here aren't we?"

"Universe isn't picking on you in particular, Lieutenant," Jack replied, "seems like the whole human race is out on a limb right now. That said best thing for you and your men is to trust me. I'll get you fixed up, keep you safe, and eventually when the dust settles I'll make sure you get home where ever that is."

Landes looked at Jack bleakly then sighed. "Very well, Lieutenant Commander, I'll tell my boys to stand down. Comms?"

"Follow me." Jack stood up and led her to the bridge as briskly as he could without sacrificing dignity. The sooner this situation was defused the better.

Landes didn't waste time on the bridge. She gave the communication officer a frequency and spoke as soon as it was set. "Ross, Gerry, let's not repeat the Alamo today." Apparently that was an ad hoc pass phrase of some sort. "Stand down. They've got trained marines who'll come out and fetch you. Food's good. Plenty of hot water. Haven't had time to check out th rooms."

"Roger that."

"Roger."

Came some very relieved sounding replies.

That done they remained on the bridge while the operation proceeded. Jack didn't think either of them would be able to relax until it was finished.

Once his men had got Landes' colleagues out of their fighters and stood them down he felt he had to come clean with the woman. He gestured at the tactical officer. That worthy poked at his console and the large wrap around displays that functioned as the bridge's "viewport" blossomed with extra tactical symbols. He turned to Landes.

"A large number of in-system fighters in orbit around this place," Landes observed. She seemed strangely unsurprised. "Guess you were hiding them behind the planet."

"We didn't want to spook you."

"How considerate."

"You seem to be taking it well. You're not at all surprised?"

"Well, Captain Black, that's an awful lot of fighters for a system on the ragged edge of nowhere." She eyed the displays with a trained eye. "Not obviously of SDF or Beyonder construction either. Don't know what they are. Don't know where you could have got those. But it's pretty obvious you weren't being entirely honest with me."

"Not entirely," Jack admitted. "I tried not to tell any outright lies. You and your people are safe. I'll see you get home when the dust settles."

"So who are you? Whose side are you on?"

"Technically I'm exactly who I said I was, an SDF officer assigned to watch this system, who outranks you."

"Really? And what else?"

"I was an NCO tech in the SDF for years, then I was a free trader for a few more, and then I was everybody's dog's body running errands across half the sector while being shot at. Now I'm the CEO of this sector's main shipping company."

"Is that all? What are you doing in this system right now? Whose side are you on?"

"No, it's not all, I'm something different to everybody I make a business deal with, and everyone I make a political deal with, and I have to make political deals if I'm to stay in business across a sector with multiple different jurisdictions and competing factions in everyone of them. Understood?"

"Sucks to be you, Lieutenant Commander."

"So you don't. I don't blame you really I couldn't have understood myself a couple of years ago. Maybe you'll understand this. Despite its many faults I served the Federation as a member of the SDF for decades. Faithfully and to the best of my ability. For longer than you've been alive I suspect Lieutenant Landes."

"And now?"

"And now if I could, if it was the same organization I swore myself to I still would. It's not. As a reward for saving this sector from a pirate take over and then economic chaos they tried to have me assassinated. Sent a team from Earth to do it. When that failed they tried to destroy my shipping company. Epsilon sector needs us or its economy collapses. Despite all that I've tried my damnedest to stay on the fence and be neutral and to do no more than keep my company afloat and not drive my customers out of business."

"That's sounds bad but I'm not sure I believe it even if you do," Landes replied. "So far you've treated me right. I'm willing to believe you want to be the good guy, but it sounds to me like maybe you're making excuses to turn traitor or pirate. All those fighters out there they don't seem very peaceful."

"El Dorado was the intended base for that pirate chief I helped take out. The locals helped because they didn't want to be pirates. They were willing to try out being members of the Federation in good standing. I was supposed to help them with that. Turns out they kept insurance in the form of some pirate arms depots. Turns out they were smart."

"I guess if they just defend this system it's not outright revolt even if not clearly legal. Threatening and hindering SDF forces in the course of them carrying out their duties is not legitimate."

"But my right to determine how the SDF interacts with Federation citizens here in El Dorado is," Jack said.

"Bet you don't want to argue that in front of a court martial."

"You're right I don't trust the SDF command or the Federation generally anymore. Like you I have good reasons for my paranoia," Jack said. He looked Landes right in the eye. "Tell me truthfully Lieutenant do you think St. Armand is going to stop his retreat anywhere short of the Solar System itself?"

Landes sighed and looked away. "No, I'm not an admiral or a logistics expert, but I can't see how there's anyplace the fleet can resupply, let alone get repairs done, anywhere closer."

"Do you think they'll leave the FTL production facilities on Newton intact behind them?"

"It wouldn't make strategic sense for them to let the Beyonders capture them. Federation's biggest strategic asset is its monopoly on FTL drives. It was anyways."

"Was?"

"There were a lot of Beyonder ships and fighters. Far more than we expected. Could be the FTL drives were all smuggled off of Newton or something. There were rumors they'd figured out how to make their own. I don't know. It's hard to figure out what to believe."

"That's very interesting." Jack wasn't entirely surprised. It confirmed what Chang had shown him. All the same it was a valuable indication that the strategic situation wasn't as hopeless as he'd feared. On the other hand whether the Beyonders retained whatever capacity they'd had and their willingness to share were both uncertain.

Jack paused to think it over. Landes would doubtless think he needed the time to absorb her bombshell. But he did need to say something more. "Still hard to imagine the Beyonders being able to fill in for Newton and Luna both, and it would still leave the middle worlds the Federation is abandoning in the lurch," he finally replied.

"I guess it would," Landes admitted. "I can see where you're coming from."

"Thanks."

"It's nothing literally. 'Cause I can see where you're going too. Draft dodging is one thing, directly opposing the Federation is another. Where you're going I'm not following."

"I see, Lieutenant. I'll see you're well taken care of, but I'm not letting you or your men back into your fighters."

"Understood." Landes seemed more resigned than resentful.

9: Plan Meet Enemy

Jack felt good.

It'd been a couple of days since the crisis with Landes' fighters. He'd been busy though and hadn't the time to completely digest what had happened or the news the young lieutenant had brought with her.

They'd sent Landes' men down to the surface. Landes herself he'd had transshipped to Caelum Station. He'd had Jackson take over Cynthia's training duties and brought Cynthia up to debrief Landes. He'd promoted Miller and given him Jackson's former job as head of Jack's security team.

As much as he hated to change horses mid-stream he had no doubt Jackson would not only handle the training well but excel at it. Cynthia and Anna Landes seemed to getting along like gangbusters. Both smart women of action, he guessed. Cynthia had informed him Landes was a font of unexpected and useful information.

Miller seemed to be stepping up to his new duties too. Right now both him and Jack were in one of Caelum Station's limited number of docking bays. They'd had to put the SDF fighters somewhere.

So it'd been a busy almost two days, but it'd all gone smoothly.

More than that, Landes' arrival and Jack's conversation with her had clarified a number of things in his mind. And that felt good.

He'd been sitting on the fence letting himself be pushed around by events. It hadn't felt good. He'd been conflicted about what the right thing to do was. Conflicted about who he could trust too. He'd also not felt like he'd had the resources to do any positive good. None of it had made him very happy.

Hadn't quite made his mind up yet, but even if it cost him his life, even if it was a mistake, he was going to climb down off the fence. More than that, he was going to start taking charge of his own fate. Knowing his long sojourn in limbo was about over made him happy.

"So, sir, you going just stand there all day looking stunned?" Miller asked him with his usual mix of genuine irreverence and faked formal respect. Jack was standing at the top of a maintenance access ladder peering into the opened electronics bay's of one of the fighters that had previously been under Landes command. Miller and Jack's two assigned guards were standing around in the docking bay. The guards were trying to remain alert in absence of any credible threat. Miller was amusing himself watch Jack work.

"So couldn't find anyone else to do this?" Miller stood looking up with his hands on his hips. "Or did you just want to get your hands dirty for a change?"

Jack twisted around and looked down at Miller. "Space fighters aren't ground cars," he said. "You don't grease them and they don't bounce around in dirt. All they require is a little dusting now and again."

"Not an answer." Miller paused. "Sir."

Jack gave an exaggerated sigh. "Yes, Miller, I was the most qualified person to do this inspection. It's perfectly safe. And, yes, it's something of a vacation from paperwork and herding cats." It was true too, Jack had been a fire control man as a junior tech, but he'd been trained in aeronautics and supervised such work as a senior tech. Also, there were exactly zero other trained SD technicians in the system that Jack knew of. Likely there were none at all.

"Just keeping you honest, boss."

"Thanks, Miller, now let me work."

In truth, what Jack was doing wasn't very technical most of it.

He was just powering off various systems and resetting them to factory defaults, doing physical inspections for wear, and checking readings were within parameters. Basically, he just wanted to be sure that the fighters weren't locked down or booby trapped somehow. Also given their long deployment he was checking how well maintained they were. As it happened, they were fully functional.

Too bad Jack didn't have trained pilots for them. The El Doradians were half trained at flying their in-system fighters. They had no combat experience. They had no training or experience flying fighters in FTL either.

Still, from what they'd learned from Landes already Jack thought he was going to need both these FTL fighters and the non-FTL fighters both. They wouldn't be that hard to crate up and carry in a freighter. He would need friendly stations to unpack them in and deploy them from.

It was pretty lame, but it was infinitely better than what he'd thought he'd had.

Good thing, too. Landes arrival and the news she'd brought made it clear that the SDF and Beyonders were both played out. They might rampage through the middle worlds, but they couldn't hope to secure them. There was going to be a power vacuum.

Jack had met all the movers and shakers in Epsilon Sector. Some of them, like the government in Hanshan, the Marxians, and Heinleiners, had system defense forces. The Tian Zhong Guo even some limited multi-system capability. There wasn't one of them capable of securing the whole sector. Not one of them Jack would have wanted to either.

Jack figured he was the best person to fill that gap, with the help of the Newtonians, El Doradians, and Ad Astra of course.

He'd been a passive figurehead, resenting the demands of various interests too long. It was time to step up and take charge. Which meant gathering up all the force he could find and going back to Newton. He'd save what he could there. Ideally the FTL production facilities, but if not that people that could set up new ones and help him in other ways.

He figured he'd have to move fast to beat the SDF and the Beyonders there, but if he managed to beat them there, and protected the assets there, then they'd be gone again soon enough.

Then in the aftermath they could call some sort of

constitutional conference for the sector and the politicians could sort out the mess. Pick another figurehead for whatever solution they came up with.

He'd go back to running his shipping company. Probably one with its own armed ships and a substantial security force this time.

Jack hummed to himself as he picked through the innards of the SDF fighter.

It was a plan.

* * *

Jackson was a great admirer of Dr. Cynthia Dallemagne.

The one-time marine didn't think he was easily impressed. A pretty face, or great body, didn't earn a pass from Jackson. Neither did fancy pieces of paper from ivory towers.

No, Jackson had seen Dallemagne in action. She was good in a fight. She was also smart. She picked her fights, and she fought dirty. Dirty, tricky, or with overwhelming force; she fought to win.

Jackson approved. Mightily.

The woman was smart, and not just when it came to book learning.

She'd done a good job preparing their recruits on Caelum. So far. Based on what she'd known about what would be asked of them.

So here he was standing in the back of a truck, in a wet half over grown field, in the early morning light, about to tell the people she'd been training she'd been doing it all wrong.

"Attention!" yelled his second in command, Yolanda somebody. Damn if Jack hadn't dropped him into this without a chance to prepare.

"Ladies, and gentlemen," Jackson declaimed. "At ease!"

He looked out over them. For a bunch of civilians very few of which had genuine prior military service, they weren't bad. A motivated bunch then. Dallemagne deserved credit for the psychological preparation she'd managed to give them in such a short time. That she as an academic understood the advantages of drill and instinctive discipline was unusual and impressive. Still wasn't enough.

"I'm your new commandant, Lieutenant Colonel Jackson." He paused and watched their reaction.

"I just got a big promotion," he said. "A couple of days ago I was just an ex-sergeant in the Federation marines. You might think I'm totally unprepared for this job. Does anyone here think that?"

A ripple of uneasy body language passed through the assembled troops. Jackson waited. Finally, one gangly young man in the front rank raised his hand.

Jackson pointed at him. "We're not in grade school. Come to attention and address me directly. Loudly and clearly."

"Lieutenant Colonel Jackson, sir! Recruit Fallon, sir! Request permission to speak, sir!"

"Very good, Fallon. One 'sir' will do. Permission to speak."

"It does seem like a big promotion, sir."

"It is, and it was necessary." Jackson inspected the faces before him. They were paying close attention. "We've decided that we're to have to impose a regular military command structure on you. Also, we're going to be expanding the force significantly. Do you know what that means?"

"Promotions, sir?"

"That's correct, Captain Fallon. Congratulations. If you don't perform, I'll demote you as fast as I promoted you."

"Yes, sir!"

"Ladies and gentlemen, in the months to come everyone here who isn't a complete screw up will make at least sergeant. I hope that scares you. It scares me." A mild titter moved through the ranks.

"That's enough."

The ranks stilled. They waited expectantly. They knew there was more to come

. "You probably think Dr. Dallemagne was hard on you," Jackson announced. "She was. She'd been in a few firefights. She knows what it takes, and she was determined to prepare you as best she could. Do you expect I'm going to go any easier on you?"

A muttering of "No, sirs!" came.

"Louder!"

"No, sir!"

"Better. I am going to be harder on you. Much harder. Do you know why?"

"No, sir!"

"No, of course you don't. Our security isn't that bad. Dr. Dallemagne was preparing you to be mostly guards deployed in penny packets. We expected some of you might be attacked and were trying to prepare you for that. Anything more me and some other ex-marines would handle it. Understood?"

"Yes, sir!"

"Good. Unfortunately, like most plans that one didn't work out. Turns out we're going to have to take the fight to the enemy. In a lot of different places. You poor bastards are going to be the ones in the front lines. Do you think you're ready for that?"

Jackson wondered if this was the right tack. Certainly the men and women in front of him weren't sure how to respond. Finally Fallon worked up the nerve to lead the rest in a chorus of "No, sirs!"

Jackson smiled at his troops. "That's right you're not." He looked up at the sky. "Now a lot of unit commanders would have reacted badly to your lack of confidence in yourselves. All they want to hear is 'yes, sir'. Not me. You'll do what you have to because you've been ordered to or because you see it's necessary. I want you to fight because our cause is right, not because you're delusional. Understood?"

"Yes, sir!"

"Excellent. A lot of you are going to die. More of you will be maimed. All because we're not going to be properly prepared. That's too bad. The harder we work, the fewer it will be. So no slacking. Understood?"

"Yes, sir!"

"Great. In the truck beside me you will find piles of booklets with your new course outline. We don't use tablets in the field. They leak and can be hacked. Pick up a booklet when dismissed, eat, return to quarters and master the first module. Get a good nights' sleep. Enjoy it. It'll be the last for a long time. Understood?"

"Yes, sir!"

"Dismissed!"

* * *

Deja vu all over again. Jack had already been in one major firefight on Souk Station. That one had been a close call. Jack would have been happy to have never repeated the experience. That time he'd been supported by the SDF and had been based out of their nearby outpost. That time he'd been on the defensive against terrorists assisted by pirates.

This time he was attacking the SDF in that outpost. In at least some people's news casts and history books he'd be called the terrorist, as well as a pirate.

You can't please everybody.

Jack looked over at Lieutenant Colonel Jackson a few meters down the corridor they were both huddled in. He looked back blandly.

Jackson had protested when informed of his promotion. He'd asserted that he was in no way qualified for the job. Jack had understood exactly how he felt. That's why he'd taken a guilty, but distinct, pleasure in telling him that might be true. But the job needed to be done, and there was no one better for it. So step up, suck it up, and get it done.

Ideally given their new ranks, they'd not be in this corridor with a breaching party. In a properly organized military they wouldn't be somewhere where a stray bullet, blaster bolt, or piece of shrapnel could kill them dealing a major blow to their whole effort. Unfortunately, their organization was still too new and uncertain to allow that. They had to lead, if not from the front, from pretty close to it. They had to set an example.

Ideally too, the people manning the SDF outpost in Al-Alhadeen system would have realized they were cut off and vastly outnumbered and simply surrendered.

Unfortunately, the SDF had no tradition of surrender.

Historically that had made perfect sense.

The SDF had had a complete monopoly of interstellar FTL capable military force. Local governments controlled the planet based militaries. Most stations had at least a militia that nominally answered to the system authorities. Usually those system authorities had some small space based in-system resources available to supplement the SDF presence.

Only the SDF had FTL capability. It could obtain control of the local space in any system anytime it needed to. Having obtained that control, any opposing forces on stations or planetary surfaces were sitting ducks for it.

So all any local SDF outpost under siege had to do was sit tight and wait to be relieved. An option vastly preferable to surrendering. Any hostile group crazy enough to attack the SDF was by definition irrational and ruled by emotion. Surrendering to a mob risked being killed out of hand, or at best being held as hostages. Smarter to sit tight and wait for rescue.

Jack knew that historical truism no longer held. The SDF had lost control of local interstellar space. He wasn't happy about it, but it had happened. He was now stuck trying to fill the subsequent void. He'd failed in convincing the elderly commander of the outpost of that.

He still hoped he'd be able to take the place without anyone getting hurt. Normal access was through a single well fortified connection. That was a death trap and not one he intended to try and force.

They'd managed to get into a less frequented part of the outpost. Gone through space. Snuck through maintenance hatches. A gamble on the SDF defenders being complacent and less than alert, but it'd worked.

It was only a good start. The designers of the outpost had known what they were doing. They hadn't left the command and communications portions of the outpost vulnerable to easy attack from its large lessor used parts. The communication and command stations, as well as the living area, mess, commons, and quarters, were isolated in a defensible sub-section.

Still, Jack's plan of breaching the wall in front of them should result in their emerging behind the outpost's main defenses. They should be within easy reach of the command area. The plan called for taking the main access defenses from the rear, then securing the command and communications posts. That done the remaining off-duty part of the garrison could be called on to surrender. If they didn't Jack's people would still be well situated to mop them up piecemeal.

Jack hoped it wouldn't come to that. He hoped with the command staff caught by surprise under his guns they'd see how hopeless it was and surrender.

The planned distraction at the front door should start soon. They'd see shortly.

The loud thump of a bang that the breaching charges made when they went off managed to startle Jack for all that he'd been expecting it.

The young men and women in the front of the party didn't hesitate as they threw themselves through the hole that'd appeared.

A good thing. An intense hail of fire burst through that same hole split seconds later.

Jack felt blows and tags all down his right side as he rolled to the left.

The fire slackened. Jack hadn't had the same time to train as the people around him, but this scenario they'd expected and he acted without thinking. He gathered himself into a crouch and plunged through the breach. Dove to the deck and rolled into the cover of a side corridor.

Jack had been wearing body armor. His right arm felt bruised but still worked. A thin line of sting along the inside of his forearm was likely just a graze. He'd been lucky. He remembered to breathe and tried to think.

A deep breath. He looked around at several bodies laying in the open immediately in front of the breach. They'd given their lives but had managed to suppress the enemy's fire long enough to let Jack and most of the rest of the breaching party through.

It hurt Jack to think he'd gotten more of Mr. Avarim's fine young people killed once again. That he'd get some of his own killed too before the day was out.

He couldn't think about that. He had a job to do. Not like he was sure he'd make it himself.

The enemy fire died off again for lack of visible targets.

Jack processed what his eyes had seen in the hectic moments plunging through the breach. A few pieces of furniture in front of a corridor on the other side of a small atrium like reception room. They hadn't been expecting any defenders here or obstacles. Still, they must have obtained some sort of surprise. The obstacles were ad hoc and didn't look like they could stop heavy arms fire. There couldn't be many defenders, and there must be fewer now.

There be a lot more soon if the breaching party didn't act quickly.

Jackson, who Jack could see across the fire swept corridor in front of the breach signaled for attention. His hand signals called for everyone to give cover fire on his signal.

"Rocket team!" Jackson yelled. The team was on the other side of the breach, doubtless hugging the deck for their dear lives. They didn't have a line of sight to Jackson.

"Sir, ready, sir!" the rocket men replied long seconds later.

Jackson gave the signal, and they all rolled on the open deck. They opened fire on the pile of furniture across the room. Some poor souls returned it. Rockets trails reached out over their heads and the furniture and the people behind it disappeared in an immense explosion.

Jack's ears rang and otherwise all he could hear was an eerie silence. He sprung up and yelled. Didn't hear that either. Waving his men forward, Jack ran at the debris piled where the enemy had been.

It was anti-climatic after that.

Their follow-up troops poured into the room. Some took care of small parties of the enemy responding piecemeal. The largest group went to attack the defenders of the main entrance in the rear. Some others pushed towards the living quarters to take care of the men and women who'd been off duty.

Jack went with the groups headed towards the nearby command and communications center. They burst in and shot the heavily armed guards. The rest surrendered. The outpost commander, an older overweight woman, was one of them. She'd been lightly wounded and seemed stunned. She agreed to order the rest of the outpost to surrender, and that was that.

Job accomplished. They'd taken the SDF's outpost in Al-Alhadeen system. In the absence of SDF forces, the local government would co-operate.

It was a start. It wasn't like they had to take every SDF base and outpost in the sector to control it.

No, they only needed to secure maybe a half dozen more.

Each time rolling the dice with everything at stake.

* * *

John Malcolm was busy. Nevertheless, he waited patiently at Washington Station's in-system parcel service counter. Patiently behind an elderly lady who was in no hurry.

After all, she had no way of knowing how much more important his time and his mission was than hers. She was sending treats out to a nephew working in the belt. Who was he to say that his business took precedence?

Nobody as long as he stuck to acting in character for his cover. Indeed normally even as a spy he'd not have minded the casual chatty atmosphere in the office. He'd use it to pick up bits of information. Also to establish and nurture his network of friendly contacts. Everybody knew John Malcolm was always ready to exchange a few friendly words about whatever was happening.

That he was happy to listen sympathetically to whatever you wanted to complain about.

So he stood there in that office and that line and idly listened to the ambient conversation, beaming at no one in particular.

Mostly the conversation centered on how it was great that trade with the outward systems had picked up due to Ad Astra, but rather ominous there'd been no traffic at all from the inward ones. Not recently, not for several weeks.

"Just normal," one red faced stout bodied know-it-all declaimed, "huge military deployment like that means they'll be paying top credit for deliveries out to the Frontier. Of course the ship's captains will want to clean up doing that, not coming here for less and that risky to boot."

One pinch faced man muttered something about contracts, but nobody contradicted the red faced man openly. Nobody was hurting in Jefferson system, and it had been calm for over a month. Everybody wanted to enjoy that and not have to speculate about scary reasons why they weren't hearing from New Lustania or Newton, let alone anywhere further in towards the Core. Or out towards the part of the Frontier where there was fighting for that matter.

John unfortunately had a pretty good idea of what the problem likely was. He was also as the SDF's spymaster in Jefferson, responsible for acting to prevent that problem manifesting here. The Federation's hold might be slipping elsewhere, but it was his job to see Jefferson was kept in the fold.

"Hey, Johnny Boy, you're up!"

John was startled from his reflections. "Hey, Chuck, sorry drifted off there."

"Yeah. Sorry about that," Chuck, who was manning the delivery counter, replied. "Old Missus Beasley doesn't get out as much as she should. She likes to chat when she does."

"Don't blame her," John said. "You're running a regular information exchange here. Don't imagine you've heard anything from Newton or anywhere else past New Lustania? Any idea what's up? How are people taking it?"

"Whoa, there," Chuck replied chuckling. "Everybody wants to know what's going on. No idea. Imagine Mr. Arnold over there has as good idea as anyone. Could be Feds just bought up all the shipping."

"Could be. Hope so. Pretty big effort they're making. Wouldn't want it to be Beyonders or pirates running amok or something."

Chuck blew out an exaggerated puff of air. "Wow, you're a cheerful one aren't you? Probably not that bad. Interesting times anyway. Remember how Miss Alcott would tell us stories in history, about the old Earth wars, and how we used to wish we lived back then when things weren't so boring?"

"Yeah," John said. "Half the reason I worked so hard to get into the Academy. Then I found out it was mostly just being a bureaucrat in uniform, far from home and the people I grew up with."

"I hear you," Chuck said, "I've got a wife and kids now too. Don't need any interesting times, thank you very much. Say you've got a parcel from the SDF post out in the belt. Bet they're wondering what's going on."

"Can't be too happy, no," John said.

"Running low on supplies, maybe?"

"I think they're well stocked on necessities," John replied nonchalantly, "but there are always little luxuries that aren't a priority with the quartermaster. We try to help them with that."

"Well sign here, and I'll help that gentleman behind you."

John did so, then with a cheerful "Later, Chuck," hefted his deliveries and started back to his office.

He kept a smile on his face, and tried to look relaxed as he walked along, exchanging the occasional greeting with passers-by.

He'd broken with normal protocol to follow an emergency one just a week ago. He'd reached out to the commander of the local SDF post. Normally the regular uniformed SDF forces in a system were kept completely in the dark about the local intelligence network. Those networks were run directly from SDFHQ and refrained from all contact with local identifiable SDF personnel.

Times weren't normal. He hadn't heard directly from SDFHQ for months.

Worse, he'd got news from the outward systems. It wasn't public yet, but SDF posts were being attacked and taken.

John had a network of barflies working for him. They didn't know that. Barflies are not the most reliable and circumspect of people. But they did. And strangely enough people, spacers at least, will go to bars which are public places full of barflies and get drunk. Being drunk they will talk about things they shouldn't.

Things they were told to keep secret like multiple SDF outposts in places like Al-Alhadeen and Hanshan having been attacked and taken.

Attacks on SDF outposts were so rare as to be almost unheard of. Jack couldn't think of a case where they'd succeeded. Multiple outposts being taken that was unheard of.

So he followed a protocol for a circumstance he'd thought completely improbable but which he'd drilled into his memory nevertheless and reached out to the local SDF commander. A decision made all the easier for the fact they needed to be warned that they were in danger.

He'd told them to prepare to meet a well planned attack spear headed by trained marines. He promised help from his end. He asked in return that they help him counterattack and secure Washington Station.

Practically speaking controlling Washington Station meant controlling Jefferson. He could hope it meant disrupting Ad Astra Ventures too. More and more it appeared they were a front for a rebel coalition. Disrupting them should make it easier for the Federation to retake the overall sector.

It was an ambitious plan.

Getting back to his office, John opened his parcel. The contents didn't look like much to an untrained eye. Some data sticks and some small gadgets made of plastic with unlabeled buttons and a few LEDs showing. The gadgets were advanced demolition devices. They'd be useful. It was the data sticks that were truly important.

John stuck one into his standalone computer, found the readme file, typed in the required passphrase, and opened the contained videogram. The visage of the SDF post commander, a Lieutenant Commander Fraser, appeared on his screen. The man was the very picture of a grim, SDF military bureaucrat. Not all of them were competent. As he listened to the commander speak John realized he'd gotten lucky.

He'd known of the man by reputation. He was considered a tough but fair leader by those under his command. No fanatic, but tried to do his job properly. Earth born but had spent most of his life on the Frontier or mid-worlds and considered more sympathetic to local sensibilities than many senior SDF officers. John hadn't been sure how competent he'd prove to be in an unprecedented emergency. In the event, he was pleasantly surprised.

Not only had the man taken John's warning seriously and gone on high alert, he was fortifying the post, and was calling all the local reservists he knew to be loyal to bolster his forces. Discreetly too, nothing less. John was impressed.

Fraser also promised that if the post managed to hold against a major attack that he'd send several attack shuttles of troops to help John secure Washington Station.

Since John directly controlled half the militia force on the station and could sabotage the efforts of the other half, that ought to be enough.

He had hoped to be given charge of Ad Astra's local security detachment. As an officer in the local militia, with Academy training, but strong local roots he was the most qualified local by far for the job.

He'd actually talked to Moe Libreman about it. Effectively passed the interview for the position. Moe had been apologetic about not giving him the job. Said his boss was paranoid and wanted to put his own command structure in place in person. Moe had said he'd still recommend John for the post but that Jack Black would make the final decision.

Right now the shipping company's security was shambolic. They posted guards, but they weren't well trained or organized. Even better John had managed to insert some of his own people into most shifts and positions. Wasn't like work was hard to find or that being a guard was a great job.

John suspected most of the guards that weren't his own people were agents from other groups like the Sons of the Republic.

In any event it was unlikely any fight would be completely bloodless, but John felt optimistic about the ultimate outcome.

Any attack on the local SDF was going to get a nasty surprise. One that should gut the enemy's best forces. The counter attack would take Washington Station. That would not only secure Jefferson system, but by allowing the capture, or at least destruction, of Ad Astra's HQ, prevent the rebels from dominating the sector.

It was a plan. One John now felt confident would succeed.

10: For a Job Well Done

Jack wandered through the desolate offices of what had been, mere days ago, the main SDF outpost in Hanshan system. Like most SDF outposts, it was located on a desolate piece of rock with a low delta V and a clear path to the system's edge. So the gravity was vaguely flaky. A disturbing place.

He would have like to have been on his way to the system's edge himself. Or better well on the way to the next system. The situation in Jefferson sounded shaky based on the reports he'd been getting. More importantly, he needed to beat St. Armand's retreating Battle Group to Newton. Newton was the key, and he didn't seem to be winning the race to get there.

It had started out well in Hanshan.

The local authorities had had everything prepared to go. They'd only needed him and his men to show up to give their assault on this outpost a patina of plausible deniability.

They were even continuing to pretend that the loose coalition Jack was heading was only another SDF faction, not a collection of rebels. They knew better. Jack knew better, as much as he regretted the fact. However, there were many who wanted to believe otherwise. They couldn't quite bring themselves to believe that the Federation was crumbling. That any remaining role it had in Epsilon Sector was bound to be a purely destructive one.

Jack snorted.

"Something funny?" Miller, now Lieutenant Miller, asked.

"In a way," Jack said, "Doesn't this all seem a bit absurd to you?"

"Not in a funny way," Miller replied. "More like in a hull breach sort of way. Everybody surprised. Some just waking up. Everyone scrambling to make the best of a desperate situation."

"Well put. Only you get to drill for hull breaches. Also, you're too busy to worry about how bad it is."

A cat meowed plaintively.

"Damn, how'd we miss that?" Miller asked.

Jack looked around trying to locate the sound. "Must have hid during all the commotion." Finally he located the sound in an adjacent room coming from under an overturned sofa. "Here, give me a hand turning this over." Miller and one of his pair of guards helped Jack turn the sofa back over. There was a frightened gray cat cowering against the wall. It wailed.

Jack dug in one of the big pockets on the combats he was wearing. He pulled out his lunch, the main part of which was a ham sandwich. Tearing off a bit, he waved it at the cat while saying, "Here kitty, here kitty." He felt like a complete idiot, but what was he supposed to do? He couldn't leave it here, and he didn't want to frighten it more.

After eying him suspiciously for a few moments, the cat deigned to accept the proffered gift. After eating Jack's lunch, it offered itself for petting. Jack scooped the creature up and did that. Added a few scratches behind an ear for good measure. Miller and his guards looked on without comment.

"Hello? Hello, anyone here?" came a tentative female voice. Must be the woman he was here to meet.

"In here," Jack answered.

"Oh, good, you found Misty." The cat abandoned Jack with a leap for a pale young woman framed in the doorway. It hit her hard in the chest, but she grabbed it and hugged it to herself with delight. "Oh, Misty. I thought I'd lost you. Good kitty. Good Misty. Good." All while the cat was excitedly licking the young woman's face, while in turn being held and vigorously petted itself. It was quite the scene.

"Ah, Miss Wong?" Jack asked. "You said you had important

news for me? Something we had to meet face to face about?"

"Oh, yes, sorry, but I'd thought I'd lost Misty." Miss Wong spared a bright smile for Jack. It quite transformed her. "She was the only thing that kept me sane here, I think." She looked sadder with that. Almost heartbreaking. "Now Misty, you be good," she said to the cat before hanging it over one shoulder like some sort of thick animated scarf.

"I understand," Jack said, "but we are pressed for time."

Miss Wong nodded gravely. "Yes, but this is important," she said. "Important it be face to face, too. Also here. This might be the one place in Hanshan system that someone hasn't bugged yet."

Jack could see that. The SDF would have controlled access and swept the place clean periodically. Any internal surveillance would now be nonoperative. He nodded his agreement. "Okay. So what's so important?"

"You're probably not happy about having to spend days here rolling up Kent's network, are you?"

Jack allowed himself a sigh. Ask a question and get a question. One with an obvious answer, too. "No, I'm not happy. Anyone with a clue knows it's vital I get to Newton as quickly as possible. Kent was the spymaster? You know something about him more urgent than my making it to Newton yesterday?"

The young woman looked sick. Pale, thin, and trembling because of illness or her obvious nerves, Jack couldn't tell. Still, she stood her ground. Stood straight with a determined expression. "Yes," she said, "I do. If you want to actually reach Newton or succeed once you get there."

Jack couldn't see it, but she seemed to believe it. It was hard not to feel sorry for her, even suspecting she wanted something from him. He was already here. A few more minutes wouldn hurt. Much. "Okay," he said.

"You're going to have to have some patience," she said. "Some small amount of background is necessary if you're to understand."

"Please go ahead," Jack answered. Mildly and without a sigh. He was rather proud of himself. He was getting better at this sort of thing.

"You know who I worked for?"

"Commander Chu's woman weren't you?" Jack named the former commander of the SDF outpost. He hated to be so blunt.

Looked like it wasn't a relationship she'd chosen or enjoyed. Not one she felt good about, but he didn't have time to dance around the facts either.

"Yes, but first of all one of Kent's kept women." She stated it as simple fact, showing no emotion. "There were many of us. All of us young and pretty, but not striking. All of us addicts whose will had been broken. Some conditioning. The SDF Special Directorate has its tricks it doesn't share."

"That's lurid and ugly," Jack responded. "I'm a sucker for damsels in distress, but logically it doesn't add up. What is the 'Special Directorate' and why would they be sponsoring a pimp in Hanshan?"

Miss Wong gave Jack a humorless and twisted little smile. She ducked her head in apparent apology at being so forward. "SDFHQ's Special Directorate is responsible for the SDF's secret operations, both its information gathering ones and its direct action ones. I believe you've some personal experience as the target of the latter?"

It took Jack a second to realize what she was saying. He looked at Miller.

"Sorry, sir," Miller said. "Above my pay grade. I was on a few quiet escort missions, but who they were and what they were doing I wasn't told and I didn't ask. Jackson might know more. Maybe not, they weren't talkative sorts." He paused and thought for a second. "One thing we never checked in with the local garrisons in a system on those missions. It was straight in, all hush, hush like, and straight out, and no stopping to say hi let alone talk."

Jack digested that. Miss Wong waited patiently. The information raised more questions than it answered. "Kent was a spy for the SDF, but one who had a close working relationship with the commander of the local SDF outpost," he ventured.

"You can't be surprised by that, Captain Black," Miss Wong said. "Not by the fact he was more than a pimp and a drug dealer. Having captured most of his people, even without time to question them closely, it has to be clear to you that his main activity was spying. Spying for the SDF."

"That's true," Jack agreed. "You have something for me I don't know?"

"Kent scattered unobtrusive young women all over. Not all of us directly served customers. Some of us were book keepers, cashiers, bar tenders, etcetera. We eavesdropped on men who tended to relax too much around us forgetting. Not just Kent's targets, but also Kent himself and his friends too. From what I and the other girls heard, Kent was part of something much bigger."

"Okay. What?"

"Kent was greedy. Not a surprising fact in and of itself. Key in that it led him into acting in a manner contrary to established protocol."

"What 'established protocol'?"

"The Special Directorate's. Kent was not supposed to have any contact with the regular uniformed SDF contingent in Hanshan. They were well aware that his network could be compromised that way. As it in fact was when you took this outpost."

Jack nodded. He wasn't sure where this was going, but it was interesting. If nothing else, he was going to get a better idea of how his potential opposition worked out of this. "So what happened? Why were you here?"

"At first Kent's pimping was the incidental byproduct of his spying, and his drug dealing a byproduct of his pimping."

"But he got greedy."

"Indeed he did. From a pure business point of view, pimping is a retail operation that doesn't scale well. You might say Kent franchised his operations by way of expanding his network, but even that was a lot of work for modest profit and required franchisees he could trust."

"So he doubled down on drug dealing?"

Miss Wong smiled at him. "Very good. You might make a good businessman someday."

"Gee, thanks."

"Yes, by dealing drugs wholesale he expanded his profits, his contacts, and his control over them many fold. In fact, given his contact with a shadowy ex-pirate and chemist, I think was working out of Jefferson, he could procure custom designed drugs for any sort of potential customer. It was such drugs that he used on me and the other girls like me. But he could sell students drugs that improved their memory and intelligence and had little or no side effects other than leaving them completely dependent on an ongoing supply of the chemical. Just one example. You can see how powerful that could be."

"A horror story. But how did it lead him to break with protocol?"

"He was greedy. He also branched out into the large volume supply of more traditional recreational drugs from out of system. Originally he contracted to Mr. Foxall of the New Byzantine Trading company to smuggle those in."

"I had some direct personal experience with them."

Miller gave a little grunt in the background. He'd shared some of that experience. It'd been dangerous and kinetic.

"When you brought down New Byzantine Trading, you interrupted Kent's supply lines here." Miss Wong smiled once more but very coldly at Jack. "It could be said my being assigned to Commander Chu was a direct result of your actions. Forgive me if cannot bring myself to express a warm appreciation for that."

Jack hardly thought it was fair to blame him. But. "My apologies, sometimes decisive actions have unexpected side effects," he said.

"You can make it up to me and my friends and a more substantial way if you wish."

"We'll see."

"So Kent had unhappy customers and was under considerable pressure to develop some new supply lines."

"Him and most of the rest of the sector."

"Indeed. In any event, he already knew Commander Chu prior to coming to Hanshan, and once here had had some mildly illicit dealings with him. He had not broken cover, though. He was posing as a young officer who'd been cashiered for dealing in illegal substances."

"That fits."

"Oddly enough, I don't think he started his illegal activities of his own accord. From tidbits I overheard, he was actually an idealistic young man at one time. He used to make jokes at the expense of his younger self. The SDF Special Directorate started him down the criminal path."

"Maybe, but he was a pretty rotten bastard there at the end."

"I'm well aware."

"Sorry."

"In any event, he sent me to Chu as part of a deal to set up a new alternative supply line. In doing so he broke cover."

"I see. I'm not sure what the significance of this is, though. Why did the SDF target Hanshan like this in the first place?"

"I have gleaned more facts about Kent's network in Hanshan than the wider context. In particular, I don't know much about the assassins or saboteurs the SDF employs other than the fact they exist."

"Assassins we knew about. Saboteurs, going to have questions about them."

"I'll share what I know. The key point I learned is that, although Hanshan was of particular interest because of its large industrial base and substantial local military, it was not unique."

Jack felt a chill go down his back. Of course he should have realized. "Go on."

"From things Kent let drop in passing, I'm sure every major system in the Federation has an SDF spy network in place."

"And the only reason we haven't noticed is because they're under deep cover and kept isolated from the regular SDF."

"Exactly."

"Damn," Miller said. Jack glanced his way. "Yeah," he agreed.

"Can't say I'm happy to get this information," Jack said to Miss Wong, who was quietly petting Misty, "but I do owe you for it. What do you want?"

"Myself and the other girls like me don't have much of a future in Hanshan. Most of us face reeducation and minor dead end government jobs afterwards, even the few with families that'll take us back face a lifetime of disgrace. At a minimum, we want passage elsewhere."

"Going to have to gather you all up for debriefing anyways," Jack replied. "I can get you berths for other systems. I can probably find most of you minor jobs, depending on qualifications. Maybe not dead end ones, too."

"Thank you," Miss Wong replied. "You hear that, Misty. We're going on a trip," she said to her cat.

* * *

Jack thought he had a pretty good poker face. He'd kept it on after hearing Miss Wong's news. Kept it on all the way back to *The Bird of Profit* and his cabin.

Now, however, he was alone. His guards were outside in the passageway. Miller was off to brief Jackson and Cynthia. They'd be putting in the rest of the day and a long night debriefing Miss

Wong and the rest of the girls like her. That didn't make him happy. They didn't need more delay. It wasn't reassuring they were having to debrief some subjects twice either. They'd missed important facts the first time through. Only Miss Wong's initiative had saved them from that error.

That was, however, only the cherry on top of the outrage Jack was feeling. Jack knew he wasn't the cheeriest guy around. Guess he could be rather grim at times. Bitter, too. Tried to avoid it. It didn't help anything. He figured he was pretty good at being calm and pragmatic most of time. Even in some pretty tight situations.

Outrage was not a familiar feeling. Still a deep sustained burning anger slathered with a generous helping of disgust fit the bill. He was outraged. At multiple targets for several reasons each. His was a pretty comprehensive and all encompassing outrage. Finally he understood the nature of rage that only wanted to destroy, that had no positive goal. Right now he could burn it all down and stand in the ashes and wreckage and be grimly satisfied.

Probably best not to give into that emotion. He sighed.

He didn't smash anything, cry or howl, he simply sat at his computer and started it up. He had a plan to make, and he had to clear his head to do that.

So outrage, anger mixed with moral indignation, directed at what?

The Federation, and the SDF in particular, to start. Most local governments too, Newton's might be a partial exception, for creating the situation. In retrospect, it was obvious the Federation should have surrendered some control of humanity in order to procure the resources they needed to keep the whole thing going. Local governments should have insisted on change. Earth should have surrendered some of its influence. The others should have willing to surrender some local resources and autonomy.

But no, they'd all been too happy with what they had to give anything up. Earth hadn't wanted to share its power over interstellar travel. None of the rest had wanted to pay extra taxes or give up any local autonomy. Instead of letting anything change, they'd fought a secret and morally abhorrent shadow war to suppress any threat to the status quo. An effort that had only ensured it became less and less sustainable.

It was evil and stupid.

It was a system he'd lived his whole life in, and he'd not seen it. In fact, he'd worked pretty hard to keep it going. He was outraged at himself. He wasn't sure if he should feel worse for being so stupid or being morally blind. He should have seen it sooner. He should have done something. He was not impressed with himself.

Finally, he was even less happy with the choices he had in front of him. Maybe more accurately the lack of choices in front of him.

Miss Wong's information meant that there was almost certainly an extensive SDF spy network in Jefferson system. Probably wasn't working to make Ad Astra more successful. In fact, it was likely that exact network he and Jackson had encountered trying to prevent them from setting up the company's HQ there in the first place.

Jack now realized that although they'd cut off one head of the Hydra, they hadn't killed the beast and that it was going to come back and haunt them.

Bottom line, it meant two things, both very problematic.

One, no information shared with anyone in Jefferson, including Ad Astra's HQ, was going to remain secret. Jack's fix on Moe Libreman was that once you got past his outer defenses, he was pretty trusting. Besides which, he was undoubtedly very busy and being forced to trust a lot of people he hadn't known for long. So no secrets in Jefferson.

Two, whoever the SDF spymaster in Jefferson was, they knew he'd been picking off SDF outposts. Too many ships had passed through Al-Alhadeen and Hanshan before going onto Jefferson. Spacers get drunk and talk too much. The SDF spymaster in Jefferson would be taking countermeasures.

Miss Wong's insights had been limited, but it looked like a system's spymaster might in such a situation abandon normal operating protocols and directly contact the regular SDF garrison to warn them of the threat.

Normally he'd have gathered local resources and information in system before launching a systematic assault on the SDF outpost there.

That wouldn't work now, plus he had to face the fact that just holding Washington Station where Ad Astra's HQ was located might be a problem.

He was going to have to make simultaneous surprise attacks on both the SDF outpost and Washington in Jefferson system. He'd have only out of system resources for it. He wouldn't be able to give any warning to the SDF outpost's command or even his own people in system.

The tactical logic was indisputable.

Morally it was abhorrent.

He didn't like attacking people without even giving them a chance to surrender. He'd been one of those people. He'd been in the SDF a few short years ago himself. They weren't all good people, but mostly they weren't bad people either. They were just people doing a job. They didn't deserve to be woken in the middle of the night and maybe killed for it.

But it was their fates in the balance against billions in the rest of the sector.

Leaving his own people on Washington Station out of the loop was even more problematic. At least he wasn't going to have to work with the people manning the SDF outpost in the future. Still, he needed people he knew were trustworthy in control of Washington Station. He didn't know most of the people Moe had hired there. He hadn't vetted them. They were locals, the spymaster they knew was present would have had a chance to compromise them.

No, he could hope that the Washington Station operation was bloodless, but he had no choice but to put his own people in control. Unilaterally, with the threat of force, without asking, or even giving a warning, in advance.

So he had the outline of what his plan had to be. Needed details.

He didn't have to like any of it.

Which was just as well as he certainly didn't.

But it needed to be done. It needed to be done quickly. Then he needed to get on through New Lustania and on to Newton with the maximum of force and minimum of fuss possible. It might be too late already.

Be a pity to have a black stain on his soul for nothing.

***

Dr. "Ted" Smith had spent his career gathering information and manipulating ideas. Managing physical resources not so much. Until he'd started working with Lieutenant Commander Chidley, he'd never realized just how much Newton, information and high-tech superpower that it was, was lacking in physical resources.

It had just one main physical resource, the factory that made FTL drives. The one his brother, Mike, ran. The one he was now leading a strike force to capture. Oh, and to take his brother prisoner while he was at it.

Private Witkowski kicked the door to his brother's office in.

Ted walked in and leveled an assault rifle at his brother. "Hands on your head, Mike."

His brother, who'd been sitting at his desk working on his computer, turned confusion on his face. Seeing the weapons pointed at him, he slowly placed his hands on his head. "Ted? What is this?" He started to look angry. "Whatever it is you won't you get away with it." Anger morphed to indignation. "You're way out of your depth, little brother."

A voice came from the door. "Sir?"

"Go ahead, Sergeant Higgins," Ted replied, not taking his eyes off of Mike.

"Lieutenant Patel reports all the machinery and personnel targets have been secured, sir."

"Good," Ted said. "Tell him to immediately begin transferring the personnel to their final destinations. He's to keep guards on each piece of vital equipment until we're able to move them."

"Yes, sir." With that Higgins disappeared as quickly as he had appeared.

Mike was staring at Ted with narrowed eyes. "You'll never shoot me," he said. "You wouldn't dare. Mother's going to be furious as it is."

"You don't want to bet your life on that," Ted answered. "But it doesn't matter. If you take your hands off your head or do anything else I don't tell you to, Corporal Anderson here will shoot you. Won't you, Corporal Anderson?"

"Yes, sir," Anderson replied. "Had to shoot friends just doing their jobs the last few months. Not going to hesitate with some snotty stranger."

"Very good, Corporal," Ted said. That was the corporal's job. The tactics Ted had worked out with Chidley used a three man team for each target. One man, Ted in this case, was the "liaison" who gave the target their directions. One man, Private Witkowski in this case, was the "bagman". The bagman did the physical handling of the target, bagging devices, and documents, but was also responsible for securing the target. The last man, Corporal Anderson in this case, was the "gunman". His job was to make sure the target didn't do anything untoward like resisting arrest or destroying documents. He was authorized to use lethal force instantly in such circumstances.

"Mike, you may now very slowly take one hand off your head and give Private Witkowski both your communicator and your pocket computer," Ted said. "You will not open them. You will not do anything else. The Corporal can and will shoot you if you do. Understood?"

"Yes."

"Then do it."

And Mike did just as he was told, much to Ted's relief.

"Now stand up slowly, keeping your hands on your head. Private, move Dr. Smith's chair into that corner. The one with nothing but books."

Again, both men did as they were told. Ted began to come down from an adrenaline high he hadn't realized he was on.

"Mike, hands on your head the whole time you may sit down in the chair again. Private, secure his computer."

That done Ted was able to relax to the point of resting his butt on the edge of Mike's desk. He still faced his brother with his weapon aimed just to one side of him. Wouldn't do to shoot him by mistake.

"A few trained thugs aren't going to save you," Mike snarled. "Just wait until Mother hears and starts pulling strings."

Ted inspected his brother. "I don't know about that. Doesn't matter. She won't hear about it. Nobody is going to hear from you or about what happened to you for months at least. Maybe much longer. It's not up to me."

"So you're just going to stick me in a hole and forget me? You can't do that. There'll be questions in the assembly. We have powerful friends."

"And how many trained soldiers do they have? None. But don't worry we'll keep you busy you're going to be writing a long and complete history of FTL production on Newton for us."

"When hell freezes over. When legitimate forces reassert themselves, and they will soon enough, you'll be the one locked away. If you're lucky. All I have to do is wait. You can't torture whole book out of me."

"I can keep you isolated in a small concrete room with nothing else to do for far longer than you think."

"Admiral St. Armand, and his Battle Group, are not far from here. I don't believe a few thugs with guns are going to help you against him."

All too true, Ted had to admit to himself, but not to Mike. "News from the Frontier has been spotty," he said aloud. "St. Armand does seem to be in play. His Battle Group, even the *Saratoga*, it took quite a beating." Normally he'd not give useful information to a prisoner, but he hoped to convince his brother it was in his best interest to share what he knew. There wasn't anyone else likely to know as much about FTL production on Newton or about its history. Ted had to come to have a deep distrust of the public information on it.

"So they're still largely intact and still on the Frontier? Is that correct?" Mike asked, squinting at Ted.

"Correct on both counts. They lost the cruisers and a destroyer and the *Saratoga* was damaged. Badly it seems. Also, the only reason they're still on the Frontier is to cover the evacuation of their support people and garrisons there. Their supplies are exhausted. Their ships are damaged and can't be properly repaired anywhere closer than the Solar System. Their morale is bad."

"You can't really know about their morale. You're grasping at straws."

"Anderson here, Higgins, you just saw, they were out there. They switched billets with Earth origin SDF members who wanted to go back. They didn't want to. They've told us what happened and how the troops have been taking it. Been several SDF transports pass through with refugees. Talked to them all. They're all discouraged and not stopping short of the Core, more likely Earth. I know what St. Armand's people's morale is like. I know it's very bad."

"Doesn't really matter. Only take one corvette, one destroyer, the Saratoga alone, or just the marine detachment on it. That's all it'll take to put Newton back to the Middle Ages. You've done for us all in your arrogance."

"It could be," Ted admitted. "But you really think they were likely to retreat back to Earth and leave your FTL drive factory intact?"

Mike grimaced. "We did have an evacuation plan back to the Core in place. As a worse case contingency."

"And the hell with the rest of us? I can see how you're arguing from a place of higher principle there, brother."

"I'm a realist, I do the best I can based on facts."

"Which you don't and can't have," Ted said. "You don't know what you don't know, but you arrogantly make plans for all the rest of us."

"It's better when you do it?"

"Yes, and by the way I know that the SDF has a spy network as well as the faction you represent present and that they'll try to sabotage us. Thanks for the warning about that. I'm ready for them and I think I've taken care of your group too, don't you?"

Mike just glared at him.

"Don't worry. It's unlikely the SDF will target the location of your cell. It's a long way away from anything. Actually, it's unlikely they'll target anything here on Newton. They have their own problems, whatever you think. Also, they think Chidley controls Newton on their behalf and will destroy this place on their orders. That's the official reason for this operation."

"You think you're clever don't you?"

"I do, but as many things as there are that can go wrong Mike I think you'd better spill the beans and in detail if you ever want to walk free again. We're shutting you down now, but odds are we'll be wanting to start up FTL production in the future. It'll be easier on us all if you co-operate."

"Imagine I'll have time enough to think about it."

"You will," Ted answered. "Private, bind the prisoner. Corporal, you and Private Witkowski will escort him to his transport."

"Yes, sir."

Ted now had the task of sifting through his brother's office. It'd hadn't been an easy day, but somehow, not entirely to his credit, he felt better for seeing his brother as an arrogant and rather angry man who'd taken too much on. Having secured the most important manufacturing facility in the sector, maybe in human space, felt good too.

He and Chidley had secured Newton. Now they had to hold it. They could probably do that. That was arguably within their power.

They couldn't stop St. Armand if he decided to come for them. They had to hope that between his own problems and their deception he'd pass them by unharmed.

They also didn't know where Jack Black was. They didn't know if he could reach the system and secure the space around Newton it in time.

They just had to hope he would.

The die had been thrown. They'd see how it came up.

* * *

Jack walked into Ad Astra's HQ on Washington Station.

Without any gunfire or other violence being necessary. Which was nice. Best case scenario really. So far so good. He felt profoundly suspicious of this good fortune. He'd hoped it'd work out like this, he hadn't really expected it.

He did meet looks of surprise and shock from the staff. That was something. More like the normal to be expected SNAFU standard he was comfortable with.

"Captain Black, sir?" asked the woman who appeared to be in charge. She was one of the ladies from Newton. He searched his memory for her name.

"Stephanie, could you get Mr. Libreman for me, please?" Jack said.

"Yes, sir," Stephanie replied jumping to her feet and opening a door to a back office. Jack followed with his retinue. In addition to his guards, Miller, and Cynthia he had Anne Hitchborn and a man by the name of John Malcolm with him.

Cynthia was co-ordinating the taking of the station. Miller was guarding Jack himself and acting as a kind of aide.

Anne Hitchborn was either the liaison to the "Sons of the Republic" or their leader. Jack wasn't sure exactly which.

All he knew was that when Cynthia and her troops had stormed off of *The Bird of Profit* on to the docks of Washington Station less than a half hour ago that instead of being greeted by gunfire they'd found Hitchborn's people and the local militia in some sort of befuddled stand off.

They'd been standing around in a pair of gaggles, weapons out but not actually aimed at each other. The militia had had actual uniforms. The Sons of the Republic were making do with red, white, and blue armbands. It'd been a tense three way stand off for some long minutes.

Hitchborn had appeared and convinced the militia to put down their arms and to go into "protective custody". That seemed to amount to waiting around in a nearby break room under very light "guard". She'd managed to convince Cynthia to accept that. She'd also convinced Cynthia to allow some of the Sons to accompany each of Cynthia's strike teams. Jack hadn't realized it was possible to bond over an old print to that degree. He also wondered how Hitchborn had heard of their arrival ahead of time. Despite that he wasn't going to look a gift horse in the mouth.

"Jack! Cynthia! John?" Moe exclaimed as Jack's party filled his inner office. A pair of techs, with communications gear they immediately began to set up, completed the crowding.

"Sorry about the lack of warning," Jack said to Moe. "We got word of a possible compromise in our communications. Didn't dare risk a leak. Jackson should be hitting the SDF outpost right now. Going to be tough enough without their being warned."

"Well forget about surprise because of traitor boy here," Anne Hitchborn said shaking John Malcolm by the arm.

"John?" Moe said. "John's an officer in the local militia."

"And I'm not the traitor either," John said. "I'm loyal to the Federation."

"You're a bloody spy for the SDF is what you are," Hitchborn said.

"Who is this woman?" Moe asked Jack.

Jack looked around and sighed. "Anne Hitchborn. She's with the local Sons of the Republic. She's helping us to get the militia to surrender without fighting. We're setting up a command post here. We'll know soon enough if there's going to be any shooting or not."

"Is it that bad?" Moe asked. He looked like he had a bad stomach ache.

"Afraid so. Had SDF stragglers turn up from the fighting on the Frontier. They got hurt bad. Not before pissing the Beyonders off. Don't think they're stopping anywhere before the Solar System. Don't think the SDF plans to leave anything but scorched earth. Turns out they've got spies and saboteurs everywhere trying to make sure of it." Jack gave John Malcolm a measuring look. John looked back with bland truculence.

"Geeze Louise," Moe said. "Guess better go calm down the

For a Job Well Done

staff. You got it under control right? Here at least?"

"We'll know shortly," Cynthia answered for Jack. "We've got strike teams trying to secure all the important parts of the station. Should hear from Jackson how things went at the outpost in about an hour." Jack nodded agreement.

"You think they'll surrender peacefully too?" Moe asked.

Jack gave his head a shake. "Maybe, but to be honest we're not going to give them much of a chance. Seems your friend John here warned them an attack was imminent, but we're hoping for at least tactical surprise. Odds are there'll be shooting and people are going to get hurt. Hope I'm wrong."

"Sir," one of the comms tech spoke up, "Water treatment secured."

Jack looked at Cynthia. "On it," she responded moving over to field the incoming messages.

"Well I'll go see to the staff," Moe said before vacating his office.

"Good idea," Jack replied to the man's retreating back. So much for inordinate respect.

After that nobody wanted to talk. They sat in quiet discomfort and listened to the incoming messages.

"Traffic control secured. No fighting."

"Household heating and air secured. No fighting."

"Distribution center secured. No fighting."

"Central market warehouse secured. No fighting."

"Fire and emergency response secured. No fighting."

Every message was a burden of worry lifted from Jack. Still, he was tense waiting for their good fortune to turn.

"Central Station communications secured. No fighting."

"Power generation and distribution secured. No fighting."

Finally Cynthia consulted her checklist and announced. "Sir, Washington Station, and Ad Astra's HQ have both been successfully secured. No casualties among our forces, or anybody else's." She paused, smiled tentatively. "I don't think anybody so much as broke a nail."

"Excellent," Jack said. "Broadcast the news to the troops. Inform the civilian population of the situation and why it was necessary to act as we did." He looked over at Anne Hitchborn. She nodded.

The room relaxed and although nobody in it was too cheerful, least of all John Malcolm, they heard cheers coming from the outer office and passageways.

"We should be getting an initial report from Jackson soon," Cynthia commented into the silence.

"Yep," Jack acknowledged. It was silly, but he didn't want to jinx Jackson's operation by openly hoping it'd gone as well as the seizing of Washington Station. If they got off with a few people hurt and nobody killed, it'd be a miracle. Jackson was mainly commanding Hanshan "volunteers" with a small cadre of ex-marines and people recruited in El Dorado and Al-Alhadeen. Jack hadn't got to know them as well as the troops Cynthia had led against Washington Station, but they were still people he was responsible for.

"Sir, they've obtained initial tactical surprise," the comms tech finally reported. Jack nodded that was good.

A few tens of minutes later. "Lieutenant Colonel Jackson reports all initial targets on the outpost have been taken with moderate losses. He's asking the defenders to surrender."

Looking over at John Malcolm Jack saw him look grim at this news. Seemed Malcolm had hoped the outpost would hold out. Jack felt sorry for the man but it was Jack's dearest hope right now that this was it. Malcolm's depression was a good sign in that context.

"Sir, they're being counterattacked on the outpost." The comms tech paused to listen intently to something more.

Jack looked over at Malcolm. He had a small smile of satisfaction on his face.

"Enemy isn't surrendering. They're taking heavy losses." The tech looked grim. "We're taking losses too." A few more minutes passed. "The enemy is falling back, sir."

A sigh of relief went around the room. Malcolm wasn't looking so happy anymore.

The comms tech stiffened. "Sir, I've lost contact." He spoke carefully but in a distracted tone as he tried a variety of fixes with his gear. "Static burst on multiple frequencies. Checking with the transports." Another distracted pause. "*The Bird of Profit* and *Frontier Falcon* are both reporting a devastating explosion at the outpost's location. Probably thermonuclear. Sir, Captain Greyfield says he thinks the SDF self destructed. Says nothing left. He doesn't expect any survivors."

Jack almost asked if Jackson had been with the attack force. He didn't, he knew full well he had been. If Greyfield said Jackson and half their combat troops were gone, then they were gone. He looked at John Malcolm. Strangely he looked as shocked as Jack felt.

Malcolm looked back. "It's hard to believe," he said. "Lieutenant Commander Fraser didn't have a reputation as the sort of man who'd self destruct in a final stand." Fraser had been the commander of the SDF outpost. "He was more dutiful than heroic. He had real compassion for his people. He wouldn't kill them just to make some sort of point."

"My people don't make mistakes like this," Jack said. "If they say the post self-destructed it did."

"Then it wasn't Fraser, and it wasn't me or anyone answering to me," John Malcolm said. "You may not believe it, but I try to act like one of the good guys best as I can. Someone else is in the mix here. Criminals or a special black ops team dispatched by a rogue element in SDFHQ, I don't know who."

"Much chance criminals got enough access to an SDF outpost to set a self-destruct device there?" Jack asked. He didn't bother to sound sarcastic. He figured Malcolm's failure to think his words through indicated his shock was genuine.

"No," Malcolm answered. "No, not much chance of that. Pretty clear I guess that there're factions in SDFHQ. People I used to know wouldn't do this. So there must have been a SDFHQ black ops team working here in Jefferson. One no one bothered to tell me about."

"Seems logical," Jack agreed. "Unfortunate you can't tell us anything about it."

"I consider myself a loyal SDF officer and loyal Federation citizen," Malcolm answered Jack with a calm anger. Not one aimed Jack's way. "Done things would rather not of for the greater good, but nothing like this. Not in favor of a scorched earth policy. I'd like to think I wouldn't have followed orders to implement one. Guess someone figured that out."

"So that means you're willing to fully co-operate with us?" Jack asked.

John Malcolm stared bleakly into the distance for a few moments. "Yes, yes, I'll co-operate fully. Not sure what good it'll do."

Jack wished he didn't agree. Any saboteurs had probably laid their plans long before and likely had them ready to go as soon as some key criteria were met. Before he could formulate further questions for Malcolm the comms tech interrupted.

"Sir, broadcast from a point in space close to the New Lustania jump point."

"Put it on," Jack said. What were the odds this was good news?

"Jack, Jack, I warned you. You should have listened. Watch your back. Maybe if you run far away, you can save yourself. You can't win. We're way ahead of you."

"Who's that?" Cynthia asked.

"A man who got the drop on me the last time I was in Jefferson and warned me to keep Ad Astra neutral," Jack answered. "Called himself 'Bonaparte'."

"Probably the head of a special black ops team SDFHQ sent out to prepare the way for St. Armand's expedition," Malcolm commented.

"And to blow us all to hell if it didn't work out well," Hitchborn commented.

Malcolm just nodded.

"Sir, patrol craft sized jump signature at New Lustania jump point," the comms tech reported.

Malcolm grunted.

Jack looked at him.

"Should have realized. Nobody's actually fought a real interstellar war before, but we did run scenarios at the Academy," Malcolm said. "Stealthed scouts along key points on the flanks of deep thrusts were a standard tactic."

"And you didn't think to mention this?" Jack asked.

"I don't know about you, Captain Black," Malcolm answered, "but I've been somewhat overwhelmed by events. I didn't think of it. This whole mess is a catastrophe beyond anything I ever imagined."

"Plus this fellow Bonaparte was doubtless on that patrol craft," Cynthia put in. "Imagine he'll be preparing us a warm welcome in New Lustania."

Gloomy glances between the command post's occupants met this prognosis. Jack was glad nobody bothered taking Bonaparte's suggestion they flee to save their skins seriously.

"Okay, enough gloom, and doom," Jack said. "We're going to

miss Jackson. We're going to miss all the other people we lost. We control this station and, thanks largely to Anne here nobody here was hurt. It cost us but we're one step closer to Newton. Jefferson is free. We should be happy about that. We should be proud of ourselves. Right?"

A mutter of agreement came from most of the people in the room. Malcolm just nodded.

"Cynthia, Anne," Jack commanded. "Set up a standing watch. Stand the rest of the troops down. Let's all eat, have a drink, and get some good sleep. It'll look better once we're rested and we can plan our next steps."

They'd always known it'd be a series of gambles first getting back to Newton and then trying to save the situation there.

Now they had a better idea of the odds.

Not as good as they'd hoped as it turned out.

11: Trying

Jack was feeling battered.

That despite a solid eight hours of sleep and two good meals.

Losing Jackson and half of his security force had been that hard of a blow. Still, if it'd been only him he'd already be in jump space bound for New Lustania. It wasn't and his people needed a rest just as much as he did. Crammed into transports bound for a battle against unknown odds with only a quickly improvised plan didn't cut the mustard in that regard.

Time was precious and Jack couldn't afford analysis paralysis.

A short pause for his people to recover both physically and psychologically, to gather information, to plan, and to get his command group on board with that plan. That was justifiable. Wise, probably. Events would tell. Jack wished it was possible to tell ahead of time. It wasn't.

Hell, he wasn't even sure it was a good idea to continue his advance on Newton. Not in the light of the new information they had.

It was 0738 station time by his clock. He'd called a command group meeting for 0800. It'd take five or ten minutes to reach the conference room it was being held in from his cabin on board of *The Bird of Profit*. He'd be soliciting input from his people,

Hitchborn, and even Malcolm, but he needed to have some idea of what to do ahead of time. He had maybe ten minutes to figure it out.

No pressure.

Alone, he allowed himself a sigh.

Pros and cons.

His default plan was a direct move against Slovo Station in New Lustania with minimal planning. Having secured the station, he could muster his forces for a properly prepared attack on the local SDF outpost in the system's belt. This time maybe he'd be able to get his in-system fighters out of the holds of his transports and manned to assist in the attack. Or maybe not. He had no real idea of the situation in New Lustania. His default plan was to wing it. He'd phrase it differently for the benefit of the command group.

So points against that idea.

He knew the SDF forces now knew he was coming. There'd be no strategic, or operational surprise, and not much chance of tactical surprise. Not if he committed to taking Slovo Station first.

He now knew New Lustania had almost certainly had a sleeper SDF intelligence network for years. He could guess Bonaparte and whatever resources he commanded were in system waiting for him too. He wouldn't be able to keep many secrets and he could expect covert attacks. The evidence suggested Bonaparte was willing to destroy entire stations full of innocent people to achieve his ends.

If that wasn't enough he also knew the SDF's frontier garrisons and the Saratoga Battle Group were going to be transiting New Lustania at some point. It was possible if they'd retreated without any pauses that they'd already done so. Odds were they had paused briefly on occasion and that they were either now in system or about to arrive there. If so Jack's force of a few transports and a trio of FTL fighters manned by unqualified pilots stood no chance. They'd have to tuck their tails in and run back to Jefferson. Count themselves lucky if they managed to get away.

No two ways about it, an attack now with the forces he had was bound to be a gamble.

On the other hand, people in New Lustania and Newton were depending on him to try and fight back. He didn't want to disappoint them, just making the effort had some value.

Also, the Sons of the Republic were fresh and eager to take the battle to the Feds. In numbers, they more than made up for the Hanshanian "volunteers" and other troops he'd lost. Their enthusiasm wouldn't increase over time, and he didn't have the time or means to properly train them anyway, so the sooner he took advantage of their current enthusiasm the better.

Regards Bonaparte he'd been here in Newton until yesterday. The less time he was given to prepare in New Lustania the better.

Last and not at all least, possession of Newton intact was vital if the sector was to have a future. They needed its FTL production. Jack and Ad Astra also needed its bank's finances. In a very real sense, it didn't matter how bad the odds were. They had to have Newton, and they had to gamble at whatever odds were available to get it. New Lustania was the necessary stepping stone, which meant they had to roll the dice to take it too. The sooner the better.

So he was going to go to the command group and listen to them carefully. Then he was going to make sure they had a superficially convincing plan.

One that involved them boarding their ships and jumping for New Lustania and Slovo Station as soon as possible.

* * *

Bonaparte was feeling irritable. Annoyed, too.

He'd given up a lot for the Federation at the behest of his masters in SDFHQ's Special Directorate. Right down to a name of his own.

He'd had one at one time. Along with a family, mother, father, and siblings. Along with old friends and the camaraderie of colleagues united in a good cause. Along with, not least, a future for himself, with a good woman he could share his secrets with and children to carry his legacy forward.

But he'd given up the name he'd been born with, along with all hope of the life that came with it. He'd done that to preserve a system that had given billions a good life. Preserve as much as possible at any rate given that system's dire problems. He'd not just sacrificed a great deal to the cause, he'd also worked hard and effectively for it. He'd done his part.

He rarely thought about that, let alone regretted it.

But he was annoyed. He'd done his part, but others had failed.

He wasn't sure of exactly what resources the rebel coalition had. He knew they weren't great. The local powers of the sector were too cowed and too devoted to grinding the axes of their own self interest to contribute much. More than the Federation's hold on all interstellar FTL travel might have frayed, but it was still an obstacle to hostile interests trying to project power across multiple systems. The capacity to do so was too limited.

It was corruption in this sector, and the lackadaisical treatment of Newton, that had allowed some FTL travel capacity to slip out of Federation control here. A severe, annoying, dereliction of duty by some of the Federation's officials.

On the other hand, that capacity had ended almost entirely under the control of Jack Black. Another sign of the local challengers of the Federation inability to agree among themselves.

He had hoped that the man's residual loyalty to the Federation, and a risk adverse nature well attested to by his service record, would keep that capacity neutralized. That was on his head. He'd been wrong. He'd thought he could intimidate Black.

The man had proved more determined than expected. He'd also proved more adaptable than anticipated. A vital quality in such fluid circumstances. He was, nevertheless, very new. An unknown, untested quantity to many critical actors. An inexperienced leader and strategist.

They were weaknesses Bonaparte believed he could take advantage of.

He wasn't wasting his time doing so.

He'd made Slovo Station bare hours ago, and he already had two nasty surprises for the rebels approaching completion.

Not knowing their resources and not wanting to be caught, he hadn't lingered in Jefferson. He'd departed Jefferson system before the event horizon with all the information about the rebel assault on the system had reached him.

He knew however that the SDF outpost there had self destructed while Washington Station had fallen without significant fighting.

Since the rebel leaders had to lead from the front the explosion of the outpost must have killed some of them.

The easy fall of Washington Station meant others, probably including Black, had survived. That the embedded SDF covert forces there had failed so was an additional source of annoyance. He had to admit they'd had a bad couple of years in a difficult situation, but it still annoyed. That aside the thinness of the rebel leadership cadre was their critical weakness.

He'd already hit them in that weak spot. He'd hit them there again.

His objectives were multi-layered. He had to hold New Lustania system open for the SDF forces retreating from the Frontier. He only had to do that for a few more days. Ideally even if New Lustania fell, he'd be able to deny them Newton. Failing even that much denying them the use of the resources there, the FTL production facility above all, was strategically enough.

In theory the regular forces, if not pressed too hard, ought to have no problem taking out those facilities, but he wasn't going to count on that.

What it meant critically, was that he was going to have multiple chances to oppose the rebels. Each time he did he'd have surprises, ambushes, and booby traps waiting for them. Ones aimed at their leadership.

Killing Black would cause their coalition to collapse. Killing any of his lieutenants would cripple it. He only needed to get lucky once or twice. They were going to need to be lucky every time.

Yes, Bonaparte was annoyed by the way the crisis had developed so far, but he was confident of the final outcome.

The rebel coalition was going to be decapitated. Then it would fall apart.

The Federation would regroup in the Core worlds.

When it returned, to reestablish itself on the key colony worlds actually worth something, there would be little to nothing to oppose it.

He'd have done his job.

* * *

Cynthia was tired. She wasn't feeling too optimistic.

A full night in bed hadn't helped with the first. The just completed O-group with Jack and the rest hadn't helped with the second.

She'd been at pains not to show either feeling to Jack.

He needed to be positive, and he needed to project an active, decisive, confident attitude for the rest of their rag-tag team.

A team now short its most militarily competent member. Jackson was going to be missed.

Particularly by her. She was now going to have to fill his rather over sized boots.

As for the man himself. He'd saved her life a couple of times. He'd always been there, dependable and like the military liked to say, always copacetic. He'd always managed to cope somehow despite whatever life the SDF and then Jack threw at him. Until he didn't finally.

Yes, she hadn't spent the time in his company Jack had, but she was going to miss the man. Now it was time to honor his memory by getting on with it.

"Penny for your thoughts," Anne Hitchborn said. She must have picked on Cynthia's thoughts coming back to Earth somehow. Funny expression that in context. They were a couple of hundred light years from Earth in Jefferson, on a space station, Washington Station. Yet somehow because it was where they lived it was an honorary "Earth" and the expression lived on.

"Your wandering thoughts," Anne said. "I know it's hard, but you've got to get your head back into the game."

Cynthia looked at her and nodded. "So we've got until noon get as many people together and loaded on the ships as possible?"

"That's right," Anne replied. "You heard Captain Black. Good of you to not complain in there."

"Yeah, thanks." Cynthia looked around the corridor they were in, trying to get her bearings. They were just outside the conference room the O-group had been held in and without a map Cynthia was the next thing to lost. She knew roughly where they were in the station, but where things were and how to get to them not so much. "You're going to have to take the lead. I'll stand around look like I know what I'm doing and second whatever you say. Okay?"

"Good. Let's go." Anne strode off down the corridor.

Cynthia followed. She had a rough idea what they were doing. They were going to recruit people, couldn't really call most of them troops or soldiers, from among Anne's followers, the Sons of the Republic, and the station militia, and load them on their waiting ships all in less than three hours. It was a crazy plan to implement in an insanely short amount of time. She didn't say that. She said, "So we talk to your team leads and the militia NCOs and they'll gather who they can?"

"Yep, not enough time to twist everyone's arm individually," Anne replied, not breaking stride. "Plus this'll keep the majority isolated from the naysayers. Always a few. Have some good points too, but we don't have time for it right now."

"I'll distribute my cadre among the ships and let them establish a command structure," Cynthia continued. "Wish Jackson was here. He'd have a better idea how to do that."

"Jackson was a soldier," Anne replied. They fetched up against of a bank of elevators and she pushed a button. "Our people here, even the ones in the militia, they're still civilians really. You and your people are going to relate to them better than Jackson and his marines would have."

"You think so?" Cynthia was disproportionately cheered by this bright spot amongst all the gloom.

"I do. More, they'll relate better to the civilians on the other side too." Their elevator came and Anne got on board.

Cynthia trailed her in. "Still might have to fight," she said. "I do wish we had combat simulators like the SDF does, or those video wargames you see on vids from before the Times of Trouble. It's not going to be possible to do anything resembling actual training stuffed on board transports for a few days."

"Going to have to make do with role-playing and paper exercises," Anne replied as she speared a button on the elevator's control panel. "You can start thinking about those now."

"Map exercises Jackson used to call them," Cynthia said. "It'll help our people to get to know each other and learn a little about what to expect."

"Exactly," Anne agreed, practically vibrating in place, obviously impatient with the enforced inactivity of the elevator ride. She'd worked herself up the better to convince her followers, Cynthia supposed. "You're going to have a couple of hours to work up a set of training exercises before we make jump. Just be sure to leave time to communicate them to the rest of us. Once we're in jump, it'll be too late." Anne grinned at Cynthia. She knew full well how nuts what she was asking was.

Cynthia looked back at her exasperated. "You do know if our disorganized, untrained mob hits any real organized resistance we'll be massacred, don't you?"

The elevator stopped and Anne stepped out. She turned to Cynthia, who followed her out into the concourse. "Probably. It's mostly a bluff, you understand? That and we'll need people we can trust to be guards and establish a presence even if we're not opposed. If we are opposed odds are our opposition will be just as disorganized, untrained, and plain scared as we are."

Cynthia thought she understood. "Jackson had a quote when we started out. He'd say 'You go to war with the army you have not the one you want'."

"Pretty obvious."

"Also to remember that the enemy aren't ten foot tall bogeymen."

"Yeah, don't worry, we'll get this done."

"Or die trying."

"Or that."

***

Jack was sitting in *The Bird of Profit*'s mess, reading over Cynthia's training plans. As serious as the topic was it was downright relaxing given how busy the day had been so far.

He felt like he was on some sort of insane package tour. Today we'll take Jefferson. Tomorrow we're off to take New Lustania. He'd got a full night's sleep last night at least. He'd then started the day convincing his allies and immediate subordinates to adopt a cobbled together plan for taking New Lustania. One that featured starting immediately before they were even organized. Organizing on the way. "Training" on the way. Making an actual plan for the attack on the way too.

They'd recruited ad hoc in the morning, had everyone loaded by noon and taken off for jump. He'd split his command group. He'd gone on *The Bird of Profit*. Cynthia had had to move to the *Frontier Falcon*. He'd given Anne Hitchborn *Prosperity's Child*. He'd kept Miller and a six man guard of ex-marines for himself, otherwise he'd split Ad Astra's former security forces evenly between the three ships to provide a command cadre and leavening for the recruits they'd picked up on Jefferson.

Anne had mostly recruits from the Sons of the Republic to provide her rank and file. Cynthia had mostly ex-militiamen. Jack himself got a mixture of recruits from the Sons of the Republic and ex-militia men. Oddly enough, Anne and John Malcolm had collaborated amicably in selecting him people they thought would get along in the mixed units.

In a brief moment alone, Anne had commented on him to Jack. "Think he's a good man at heart and regretting who he trusted and what he did for them," she'd said. Jack had said he just wasn't sure it was safe to trust him. "Didn't say trust him. Use him. He went to the Academy. I know he knows a lot about the militia and Jefferson. Bet he knows a lot more about what the SDF has been up to in the sector. New Lustania specially. Don't have to trust him. Be dumb not to use him."

Jack had accepted that which was why John Malcolm was sitting across from him watching him read right now.

They'd spent the hours boosting out to the jump point, getting some organization established among the troops on *The Bird of Profit*. Appointing leaders and then giving them some simple training exercises to put their new units through. More to get everybody used to each other than to teach most of them anything new. Malcolm had been very helpful throughout the process. Jack was still wary, but he was willing to use whoever came to hand. So far Malcolm was proving both useful and easy to deal with.

"Take a look at these," Jack told Malcolm, passing him the papers he'd been reading. "I'll go get us supper. What do you want chicken or meatloaf?"

"Right. Chicken's fine," Malcolm replied, taking the papers and beginning to read them with no further ado.

He kept reading them even after Jack came back with their food. Jack was half way through his food before Malcolm finished reading them.

Malcolm looked up. "She's pretty good for someone who never attended the Academy."

"Doctorate from the University of Newton?"

"Sure," Malcolm answered, "but I wasn't aware they had courses in military organization and tactics."

"On-the-job training," Jack said, waving a fork. "Woman finished her formal training early. She might be a bona fide genius. She's certainly really smart and a really fast study. She had Jackson, an ex-marine, and Captain Taylor of the *Rudolf Ferguson* to learn from. She's pretty good at independent research. Never does to underestimate Doctor Cynthia

Dallemagne."

"Okay," Malcolm said. "In any case there's not much you can do with them crammed on board transports and in just a couple of days. This is not perfect, but probably as good as you can reasonably hope to do."

Jack continued to eat while assessing that. He was tempted to ask for suggestions, but he imagined if Malcolm had any he would have volunteered them.

Malcolm accepted Jack's silence and started to efficiently eat his own meal. Tired himself, Jack figured. Tired and bewildered and trying to figure out his new situation and where he was going from here. Jack hadn't appreciated the results of the former SDF spymaster's efforts, not at all, but he could almost sympathize with him.

Finishing his own meal, Jack waited for Malcolm to finish his own before asking, "Any thoughts on we can expect in New Lustania?"

Malcolm paused and took a deep breath. They both knew this was the Rubicon for him. If he answered the question, he would have gone beyond being a model prisoner to co-operating with the enemy. "Thoughts, yes," he said. "The Special Directorate tries to maintain as much compartmentalization between its agents as possible, but I know the situation, and I know what our training calls for given that."

"So no solid facts, but some educated guesses?"

"That's right. First point is that despite what you saw in Jefferson neither the regular force outpost nor the spy network I assume to be embedded in the system is likely to be much of a problem for you."

Jack blinked. "That's odd. Explain."

"Compartmentalization again. Specialization too. Special Directorate wants to keep everything controlled centrally, that's the point. Plus, they have genuine security concerns. So the regulars don't talk to the spies and vice versa. The special ops people like Bonaparte, they mostly don't talk to anyone. Everyone wants to pretend they don't even exist."

"Something of an emergency going on. You did manage to talk in Jefferson."

"That's where the specialization angle comes in. Jefferson was a special case even before all the problems of the last couple of years. Populous planet where the founders were known to be hostile to the Federation on principle. Our whole job there was to keep an eye on the locals and nip any problems in the bud."

"So New Lustania is different?"

"It is. The people there like their independence but they're so balkanized, literally they've imported century old animosities from Earth's Eastern Europe and the Balkans, that there's no chance they'd ever get together to challenge the Federation."

"So what are the Federation spies and the SDF doing there?"

Malcolm gave Jack a thin smile. "Think you know full well New Lustania's position on the main route to the Frontier makes it a place to be watched. Mainly I suspect that's all the spies there do. The outpost is kept pretty busy just providing maintenance and emergency support to transiting ships. Been a lot more busy than usual lately, I'd think. Also the office on Slovo Station, but that's to help the odd SDF spacer who gets into trouble of some sort really. Just a few office personnel. Nothing serious."

"So what; we're going to be able to just walk into the system and they'll just fold?"

"Maybe." Malcolm said, folding his hands, spreading them and shrugging. "Maybe not. Don't forget Bonaparte. Probably won't oppose you directly, but be ready for some potshots from out of the dark. The spies will stay hidden likely, a problem for later. The outpost will likely evacuate after the last ship from the Frontier passes through. Likely already down to a skeleton crew if what you've told me is true. We weren't getting much news about how the campaign in Jefferson. Which I guess was enough to tell everyone it wasn't going well for the Federation."

"Evacuate?"

"Yeah, there's the big issue. Did you want to get to New Lustania before or after St. Armand's Battle Group? Pretty sure you don't want to get there at the same time. No offense, but even badly hurt they'd eat you for lunch."

"You too."

"Just collateral damage. I'm guessing you've no idea about the exact timing on that. For what it's worth, I don't think they'll linger in New Lustania for long. Maybe Newton. That's one of two pieces of good advice I can give you. First thing above all, be careful there are no capital ships in system. If there are just run as fast as you can. Second thing, Bonaparte, there'll be traps. Be careful and watch for them."

"Sent some captured Battlehawks ahead. Going to do a non-standard entry. As will we," Jack said. "If there's a big force waiting right on the jump point we're in trouble. Anything less we stand a good chance of at least dodging."

"Smart," Malcolm said. "Also smart not to tell me until we were in jump. I don't think I'm going back to Earth. Even if I wanted to, I think my career with the SDF is over. Not expecting any pension."

"Well I've been double dipping in theory but somehow my paychecks never caught up with me," Jack said with a smile.

"Yeah, should have gone early and asked for the lump sum, damn," Malcolm replied with a smile of his own.

"Anything else?"

"Have some codes might help on the station. I'll look at your assault plans once you have them. You seem to have managed so far."

"Cynthia again."

"Do wonder what they've been up to on Newton. No, guess that's it."

12: Some Confrontation

Ted had done his best to do the right thing at every turn.

Still felt tremendously guilty. He'd imprisoned his brother, and he was lying to his mother about that and a host of other things.

For perfectly sound logical and morally superior reasons, and he still felt as guilty as hell.

For the first time, he truly understood some of the pressure he'd been placing on his field agents. He felt guilty about that, too. Well, he didn't have time to wallow in it. He was already one of the last people left on the University of Newton's New Cambridge campus.

That'd been in large part his doing too. With Chidley's help, he'd been able to convince the planetary authorities that it was essential to evacuate all major population centers. New Cambridge was now a ghost town. The University, the port, and its high-tech factories made it too much of a target.

There were only skeleton crews keeping the University and city going now.

Rural farmsteads and small towns all over the planet were overflowing with unexpected guests. Tent cities and new barrack blocks were springing up in widely dispersed locations. Whatever happened, most of Newton's population should survive it.

As should the people and machinery necessary to manufacturing FTL drives. They were now widely dispersed too.

Chidley had assured Ted that the SDF was very unlikely to linger long enough to either render the planet uninhabitable or to land marines to search for the disassembled FTL factory.

Ideally, of course, St. Armand would take Chidley's assurances he had it all under control at face value and not see through the deception.

Ideally.

As he tried to decide which of his paper books and precious heirlooms, he could jam into his large, but not large enough, knapsack Ted thought of all the other Newtonians who'd faced similar decisions. It was less than ideal.

Could be worse. He could be at a dinner party lying to his mother.

He grabbed a couple of books roughly and chucked them into the knapsack. Time to go. He'd procrastinated long enough.

The lead destroyer of St. Armand's Battle Group had jumped in hours ago. The *Saratoga* would be following soon.

He ought to be at Chidley's HQ for that.

They'd know soon enough how this was going to work out.

* * *

Bonaparte paced the bridge of the destroyer *Slan* behind Captain Warner's command chair. No doubt to that worthy's chagrin. Not something Bonaparte much cared about. In his mind Warner had proved himself a useless wet noodle.

They were lingering in New Lustania on the approaches to the jump point for Newton.

"Patience is a virtue, Mr. Bonaparte," the Captain said, turning to him.

"Patience be damned, I want to kill something," Bonaparte replied. "We've got a perfect opportunity to catch the rebels here and decapitate them."

"That is not the priority I've been given in my orders," the Captain said. "I strongly suspect it's not the top priority in yours either. Our job is to finish evacuating New Lustania and to guard the rear of Battle Group Saratoga. If we can manage to give the rebels or the Beyonders a bloody nose in the process, that's great. It's not our main objective. Our main objective is to preserve our own forces intact as a force in being."

"I don't like it. I don't like running away."

"Nobody on this ship likes it, but we have our orders. We follow them."

"As do we all but a certain amount of initiative and discretion is allowed within their bounds."

"Perhaps more for you than the rest of us," Captain Warner observed sourly. "Admiral St. Armand is somewhat closer than SDFHQ and a stickler for his instructions being carried out precisely. That said if an opportunity to deal the enemy a blow without undue risk appears I assure you I'll avail myself of it."

"I guess I can accept that."

"I imagine you must."

The worst of it in Bonaparte's mind was that the Captain was, in fact, correct. The *Slan* had been ordered to act as rearguard in New Lustania and avoid any unnecessary engagements. He could hope to persuade the Captain to exercise discretion and stretch that word "unnecessary" as far as possible, but the spirit of the Captain's orders was clear.

The Captain was also right about Bonaparte's orders. They'd been waiting for him when he'd reestablished contact with the SDF in New Lustania. They'd been dispatched from Earth months ago when the first news of setbacks on the Frontier had arrived there. They were quite clear his top priority was to ensure St. Armand's ships got back to the Core as intact as possible. Anything else was secondary to that overriding goal. The destruction of the FTL production facilities on Newton was a secondary goal. They'd been explicit about that.

Bonaparte found it hard to believe that ships could be that hard to re-build as costly as it might be. He thought he detected political cowardice. Certainly the analysts back on Earth were living in some out-of-date information bubble as regards the rest of the Federation. They seemed to think the colony worlds were like spoiled but dependent children that would beg the Federation to return once it had left.

That might have been true a century or more ago, but it didn't reflect what Bonaparte had seen recently. No, he suspected if they gave the colony worlds time to organize that it'd be difficult to impossible for the Federation to return. All the more so if they left Newton's ability to build FTL drives intact. It'd mean an ongoing threat to Earth they couldn't remove. Life on planetary surfaces was wide open to attack from space.

He didn't think it made any sense to spare any effort in protecting Earth from that threat. On the other hand, both his political masters and Captain Warner did have reason to believe they'd taken care of the problem. They had no less than three plans to destroy the Newtonian factories. The forces occupying Newton alone ought to be enough. Failing that, *Saratoga*'s still sizable marine contingent could be landed to do the job. If the marines uncharacteristically failed, then there was still bombardment from space.

He could see how they thought it was enough.

He couldn't even claim they hadn't made an effort to hand the rebels a solid drubbing here in New Lustania. He'd prepared three different surprises for them. Each of those surprises on its own had the potential to take out most of their forces. Given their propensity for leading from the front, most of or all of their leadership too. It wasn't unreasonable to expect at least one of them to succeed. If they did the fragile rebel coalition would almost certainly collapse. The rebels weren't as weak as the desk jockeys on Earth thought, but they were most definitely fragmented and disorganized. Most of all they lacked potential leaders all of their factions were willing to trust.

His little surprises should do.

And if any opportunities to gild the lily arose, he'd be here to goad the Captain into taking advantage of them.

* * *

"Jump emergence, now," *The Bird of Profit*'s navigator announced and with that, and a sickening lurch, the ship found herself in the New Lustania system.

Jack waited for something to happen. For an alarm to sound or the sensor officer to announce an imminent threat. Neither happened.

"Initiating evasive action," the navigator said. That had been pre-planned and was no surprise. They had anticipated someone or something might be waiting for them on emergence in New Lustania and had instituted some countermeasures.

Not keeping precisely the same course, velocity, or acceleration, evasive action, ought to complicate things for anybody firing at them from a distance. They'd not likely be exactly where predicted at the time a far off weapon was fired. Even light took time to cross the distances found in space.

Not emerging right at the usual spot for emergences in the system had been another precaution. The normal exit point was the most efficient, but it was possible to vary it a little by sacrificing some of that efficiency. They had done so. So had their sister ships. Even if one of them was unlucky, it wasn't likely they'd all be.

Finally, the sensor officer spoke up. "We have emergences. Nominal for both *Frontier Falcon* and *Prosperity's Child*. We have pings on objects at the normal exit point. Large rocks likely." He paused and spoke somewhat more urgently. "Sir, weapons fire from a location near the normal exit point."

"Weapons?" Captain Joshua Greyfields asked. Jack thought of him as simply Captain Joshua. There were too many Greyfields starting with Captain Ebenezer Greyfields of the *Frontier Falcon*.

"Sir, fire highly attenuated at this distance. Not likely to hit either if we don't give them a simple solution. Firing precautionary chaff," the weapons officer responded.

"Very well, Weapons," Captain Joshua replied.

"Sir, fighter group reporting," the comms officer announced. "They confirm defenses at normal exit point. They say weapons platform appears to be static. They weren't interested in getting too close to check on that."

Long minutes passed as they waited to clear the danger zone and hoped their good fortune continued to hold.

"Sir," the sensor officer reported. "Source of weapons fire remaining static."

Good, some sort of fort or improvised active mine. Not surprising, but not something they would have dared assume either.

"Commencing system survey," the sensor officer added.

More minutes passed and everyone on the bridge began to relax as they and their sister ships moved further and further out of the danger zone.

"Sir!" the sensor officer spoke urgently. "We have what appears to be an SDF destroyer loitering several light seconds inward of the Newton jump point."

And things had been going so well. Jack remembered what

John Malcolm had said to him, "*First thing above all, be careful there are no capital ships in system. If there are, just run as fast as you can.*"

Sadly, he didn't think he was going to be able to take that advice. It was good advice as far as it went. That destroyer was faster than they were and if it caught them in system they'd be annihilated.

Unfortunately, they had to win here, and they had to win at Newton. Without Newton the whole rebel coalition would fall apart. It was perhaps the only source of FTL drives for the sector. For a fact, the only one not under the control of outsiders. Without those FTL drives, the systems of the sector would fall back to being isolated islands in the great dark.

So, however poor the odds might be, and, however high the stakes, it was a wager Jack had no choice but to make. His life and lives of the people following him didn't weigh much against those of the billions of other people in the sector.

"Comms, forward our scans data to the other ships. Tell them our plan for the attack on Slovo Station remains in force. I repeat the attack remains a go."

"Yes, sir," the comms officer replied. Joshua Greyfields just looked at Jack and briefly nodded. That was a relief. He wouldn't have blamed the man if he'd objected.

It was do or die. That and hoping for a miracle.

13: A Fleet In Being

Jack wished he had John Malcolm's Academy education.

The Bird of Profit and her companion ships were inbound to Slovo Station. The station being the key to the New Lustania system. Or at least the key under normal circumstances. Normal circumstances meaning the absence of capital ships like the destroyer currently hanging off the Newton jump point.

In theory, an unopposed capital ship was considered to control any system it was in. In theory, if you wanted to dispute that control you found more or bigger capital ships to do so.

It was all theory. There'd never been a real fight in space between capital ships. Only the SDF had ever built and operated large purpose-built fighting ships. They'd never fought each other. On very rare occasions they'd been used to track down and destroy merchant ships that had been armed and used for piracy.

It'd been proven pretty conclusively that even the smallest capital ship, a corvette, was more than a match for a pirate. Destroyers had shown themselves easily able to deal with even large groups of well-armed pirates. The weaponry, durability, fire control, and communications of a purpose-built ship were just too much better than anything possible with a civilian conversion. And that was before factoring in their better trained crews and officers.

Jack didn't consider himself a pirate, but that was a moral judgment. For practical purposes, he wasn't any more than a pirate as regards combat power. Less even as his ships hadn't been converted for that purpose. They were working freighters with some weapons attached as a deterrent to actual pirates.

So Jack considered himself lucky to have John Malcolm available. The Academy was the only place the theory of space warfare was taught, and Malcolm had attended it. Jack himself was only a jacked up NCO who was winging it.

He was also the man responsible for the current expedition. Responsible for the lives of its people. Responsible for its outcome. Which was why he'd felt free to make the decision, against Malcolm's earlier advice, to proceed in system despite that destroyer sitting near the Newton jump point.

That didn't mean he didn't want the man's advice in the rather dicey situation he'd thrust them into. So he'd had him called to the bridge right after making it. Something he was now paying the price for in additional aggravation.

"You do understand, don't you, that," Malcolm was saying, "without a long clear lead to a jump point that ship can bring you into weapons range?"

"I do," Jack replied. The bridge crew and Captain Joshua were studiously ignoring the conversation, he noted. "I think I have a working feel for the problem. I'm hoping you'll help with precise distances and closing speeds."

"And you understand that if we come within weapons range of her we're, to use a technical term, *toast*? That we can't hurt her, but she can pick us apart?"

"If I hadn't already been clear on that point, John, your long, detailed, and colorful explanation would have gotten it across. Thank you."

Malcolm snorted. "And you thought it was a good idea not to withdraw anyways?"

Jack would have felt better not having this conversation on the open bridge. However, he'd committed himself to an open command style, and he needed to be here to keep a close tab on the pulse of the operation anyways. "Good idea or not. It's what we had to do. This is not a live to fight another day situation. There's not going to be some other day where we'll get better odds. This is a we have to fight today day and we either lose or win. A retreat would be losing."

"At least we'd living losers."

"For a while. Look, this is not up for debate. I'd like your help. That destroyer is going to be getting the news of our arrival soon. I want to set us up as best as we can prior to their getting that news. I want your opinion on whatever they do once they know we're here. Understood?"

Malcolm looked around and grimaced. "Be easier if we had proper tactical displays. Yes, I understand. I'll help as much as I can. Okay?"

"Okay. Good."

"The event horizon with our emergence should be reaching them in about forty minutes. You're on a minimum time course to Slovo Station, short of running for the exits, that's your best move. Factoring in reaction time we'll almost certainly reach the station before they have us in weapons range. They might fire on ships that they can plausibly call pirates, but I don't think there's much chance they'll risk firing on a civilian station. Can't see much you can change at this point." Malcolm was all professional detachment now.

"Thanks." Jack mulled it over. "Comms Officer, orders for the fighter group. They're to proceed at full tactical acceleration to stand off range from the destroyer near the Newton jump point. They are not to engage without explicit orders."

"Yes, sir," the comms officer answered.

Malcolm studied Jack quizzically. "You realize that they've got no missiles, let alone any stand off shipkillers."

"Yep."

"That their guns can't more than scratch the armor on that thing. That if they get close enough to use their guns, they'll be blown out of the sky."

"Wasn't sure of the details, but didn't figure it be a fair fight."

"So you're bluffing?"

"Yep."

"Guess there isn't much to do but wait and see they do," Malcolm answered.

"Well," Jack replied, "that and keep an eye on what's going on at the outpost. I figure we'll run if they start moving our way. You can help with the timing."

"Run for which jump point?"

"No jump points. If we hit jump we're stuck in it for days, and then it's more days to get back. Maybe we can't get close to that thing, but we can keep it engaged. We'll split up and run fo interstellar space. A stern chase is a long chase. How far do you think they'll be willing to chase us?"

Malcolm had no quick answer for that. "I don't know wha their orders are," he said after a while. "From where they're sitting I can guess they're supposed to be guarding the rear of St. Armand's Battle Group. So just guessing they're expected to be leaving for Newton within a day or two at most."

"So even if they're lucky they might catch just one of us before they have to give it up and boost back to the Newton jump point."

"Logically, but that's cold and there's no saying how it'll actually work out."

"And what would they get if they did chase us?"

"Maybe they'd get a kill. They'd certainly delay our taking of Slovo Station and the outpost. They'd buy time before we'd be able to jump to Newton."

"Might be worth it to them," Jack opined. "But it's a lot of extra stress on the ship and its crew. It means they'd be further separated from the main part of the Battle Group too."

"I think it depends a lot on who's captain over there," Malcolm said.

"Guess we'll just have to wait on them."

The remaining half hour had almost gone before Jack had a belated realization. "Comms, contact the *Frontier Falcon* and *Prosperity's Child*, tell them to conform to any of our movements."

The comms officer acknowledged his orders. Short minutes later he spoke again. "Sir, both *Frontier Falcon,* and *Prosperity's Child* reply that they will conform to our movements."

Not much later, the sensor officer reported. "Our event front should be reaching the destroyer about now, sir. So far, no reaction."

The whole bridge quieted. Everybody still waiting for news of what their enemy would do.

Nothing at first, as it turned out.

Jack looked at Malcolm. The former SDF officer, turned former spy, now Jack didn't know what, just gave a small shrug.

It was over twenty minutes by the bridge's chronometer before anything more happened.

"Sir, the destroyer has started to accelerate in roughly our direction," the sensor officer reported.

Sharp breaths, tempered with a puzzled air, broke the silence. This was what they'd been waiting for, but why had it taken so long?

"Sir, need more data but it doesn't look like they're accelerating as hard as they could be," the sensor officer reported. He echoed his readings to the bridge's main screens.

"Looks like standard patrol acceleration," Malcolm commented.

"So that took a while. Is that normal?"

"No. I don't think any single officer given command of an SDF ship would be so slow to make a decision. They'd not piss about with less than full safe acceleration either."

"So what? They're having debates on the command bridge?"

Malcolm sighed. "No doubt they've had to evacuate civilian officials the poor man in charge of that ship can't ignore without peril to his career."

"Interesting. Navigator, can they reach weapons range before we reach Slovo Station?"

"Just a second, Sir." Jack looked at Malcolm who gave a tiny shake of his head.

"We'll just make it, Sir," the navigator announced.

"Good, continue on course." Jack could practically hear the tense bodies around him relaxing.

Malcolm to his side was shaking his head.

"What? Nobody following the script?"

"It's painful to see. If he'd acted faster or just stayed further in system, he'd have had you. You're not quite home free yet, but you threw away the book, and it looks like you're going to get away with it."

"Sorry about that," Jack said with a grin.

It was not that nothing happened on the rest of their trip in, but it was all rather anti-climatic after the initial period of tension.

The destroyer reversed course after it became apparent they'd not be scared off. Multiple shuttles detached from the outpost out in the belt and boosted to intercept it.

There was a little excitement. They overheard the transmissions of scavengers eager to loot the now doubtless abandoned outpost of anything that might have been left behind. Those transmissions ended in a burst of static as the outpost self destructed.

Jack felt guilty at how pleased he was by that. Those scavengers likely hadn't been the most honest or decent of men, but they'd had mothers and maybe families of their own. Still, the booby traps they'd triggered had no doubt been intended for Jack and his people. Better them than some of Jack's own.

Twenty minutes out of Slovo Station traffic control welcomed them, professed its neutrality and claimed that the station wouldn't resist. Jack scrambled to issue rules of engagement. Mostly don't fire unless fired on. Or unless armed individuals refused to keep their distance. It was the best he could think of on short order.

It might be tricky taking control of Slovo Station. Likely nobody was really in control, which meant the odd wingnut could do what he pleased. They really had to stay alert and at the top of their game.

It was hard though. They'd beat the odds, and the worst threats were past. Everybody on the bridge was trying to be professional, but the exhilaration at what they'd achieved, and the consequent tendency to relax were hard to resist.

Jack spared a smile for John Malcolm.

"It's not all over yet, Captain Black."

"No, but mostly, the worst of it."

"True, but often it's the last mile of a long journey that's the most dangerous."

"Hadn't heard that, but I'll keep it mind."

* * *

Bonaparte was grateful for years of practice at keeping a poker face.

He was utterly furious. It wouldn't do to share that fury with his fellow officers on the bridge of the SDF destroyer *Slan*. Not that the lot of them didn't deserve to be flayed alive and dipped in boiling oil. Cowardly incompetents.

What they deserved, and what he would like, were equally unimportant. What was important was playing the cards he'd been dealt in the way best calculated to achieve the goals he'd been assigned. Neither murdering, nor even alienating, his fellow SDF officers were the best means to that end.

"Captain Warner, I trust we will remain in system long enough to observe events at Slovo Station," he said with the utmost civility.

Warner turned a blank face to him. "Of course, Mr. Bonaparte, I'm sure Admiral St. Armand will want to know if you finally get lucky."

Bonaparte reminded himself that if the onboard dentist was up to the standard of the rest of this ship that he didn't want to break a tooth. He smiled, showing his teeth rather than grinding them. "Thank you, Captain."

It wasn't that Bonaparte didn't believe in luck. He did, the world was too complicated for it to not surprise. He even believed in some people being luckier than others. After all, some people were going to be better at spotting such surprises and dealing with them. Jack Black was such an individual, but so was Bonaparte. So Bonaparte didn't think it was his bad luck, and he certainly didn't think it was incompetence on his part, that Black had escaped his first two traps. It galled him that the Captain would suggest such a thing.

The static defenses at the Jefferson jump point had been a good idea. Unfortunately although static defenses could devastate the unprepared that stumbled into them anyone who expected them and prepared properly could find their way through. He could have hoped that a collection of amateurs in a hurry would have come in blind and dumb and paid the price. They hadn't. They'd been clever, and maybe a little lucky, and escaped unscathed. That was because they were smart and not because Bonaparte was stupid.

The fiasco at the outpost had been even more irritating. He'd known, given New Lustania's plentiful supply of entrepreneurs with a pragmatic attitude towards the law, that scavengers were likely to swoop in as soon as the place was abandoned. He'd left plentiful automated defenses in the outer parts of the base. Ones not connected to the self-destruct. It should have taken a properly prepared military force a sustained operation to penetrate to the post's core where the self-destruct and its trigger were located. The New Lustanians had proved unexpectedly innovative. They'd used a mining laser to drill through the outer shell of the outpost's asteroid and thereby by-passed the outer defenses.

In both cases not having actual, mobile, intelligently directed forces to cover the static forces meant that the attackers could use ingenuity to by pass them. The error was in relying on purely static defensives to try and defeat a capable foe. That error was not Bonaparte's. It'd been forced upon him by the very man that was ridiculing him.

Warner looked back at Bonaparte and smirked. So the man wasn't stupid, he just seemed that way. Too bad he wouldn't use his ability to forward their joint mission.

At least the reception he'd prepared on Slovo Station wasn't completely static. Sooner or later Black's luck was going to run out.

Together they watched the grainy dots of Black's ships merge with the bigger splotch that was Slovo Station. The place was far away, even for large telescopes. They listened to traffic control and its treasonous assertions of neutrality.

Then they waited for more news.

None came.

Captain Warner turned to Bonaparte and shrugged a shoulder. "Well, maybe you got him and they just haven't broadcast it. Can't tell. Time for us to leave." With that, he ordered preparations for the jump to Newton to begin.

Bonaparte left the bridge without replying.

He needed to make plans for Newton. Better ones than he'd been able to make here.

He'd have more resources in Newton.

* * *

Jack didn't want to get overconfident, but so far so good.

Slovo Station Traffic Control had fallen all over itself to accommodate them. Usually traffic control would have assigned them whatever docking bays were most convenient for the station. There were fewer ships docked than normal though, and they'd given Jack the choice of what docking bays he'd wanted.

If this had been an assault as he'd originally planned he would have dispersed them in an effort to get teams to every key target in the minimum time possible. Also in the hope that failure on one axis of attack would be made up by success elsewhere.

Apparently, however, Slovo Station was trying to surrender to him. Not just traffic control, but the station administration and the police had promised him their full co-operation.

The police chief had gone so far as to assure him there was no "large organized" opposition that "he knew of". More usefully, he'd assured Jack that the docks were undefended. The SDF had had only a few staff manning a liaison office on the station, and they'd evacuated the day before. The station militia were a moribund organization. The police chief had talked around that point, but finally gotten to it. In any event, they hadn't been mobilized.

So it looked like the station was wide for them to walk in and take it over without any fighting. So Jack had decided to keep his forces together and dock his three freighters right next to each other on the same docks. He had the fighters hang off to guard against EVA sneak attacks.

Right now he was trying to get all his troops off their ships and formed up out in the docking bay. Once he had everybody organized and formed up in their teams, he'd detail them off to take control of various parts of the station.

Most of his people hadn't had much training. Their leaders had literally only been in their jobs for a few days. Jack wanted to make it simple for them. He wanted to keep them disciplined. Most of all, he didn't want anyone to panic and start shooting the station up at random. So a little parade and giving them orders directly looked like a good idea.

Neither Miller nor Malcolm had been thrilled about this approach when he'd discussed it with them. Both admitted it was likely a good idea given that their forces were not made up of well trained, instinctively disciplined marines.

They had both insisted that Jack was not going to lead *The Bird of Profit*'s troop contingent in person. They'd also both agreed that in an ideal world Miller would have taken that role. On the other hand, Miller was extremely reluctant to let Jack wander about on his own. He'd observed Jack's tendency to bully his guards into letting him do what he wanted, even when it wasn't safe.

In addition, it happened that all their team leaders, coming from Jefferson, knew John Malcolm better than they did either Jack or Miller. Weirdly enough, Malcolm, who'd been their opposition only days before, was now the best candidate for actually leading *The Bird of Profit*'s troops into Slovo Station.

Their command structure was that thinly spread.

So Jack had followed the logic and given Malcolm the job. The man had shook his head wearily once again, straightened up, and got on with it. Jack figured if Malcolm worked out peacefully occupying Slovo Station then he'd be able to use him on Newton where it was unlikely things be so peaceful given the stakes.

Right now, through no fault of his own, most of the troops Malcolm was commanding were stuck in the docking bay of *The Bird of Profit* and backed up into its passageways, while they waited for the troops off of the *Frontier Falcon* and *Prosperity's Child* to stop milling around on the docks and get organized.

It was a Charlie Foxtrot. Jack's fault, too. Miller had him tucked away just inside *The Bird of Profit*'s open cargo hatch. He couldn't see everything out on the docks, but he could see enough to realize it was an unholy mess. Leaning over and peering out he could see Cynthia and Anne in the middle of the docks having an animated conversation while their people stood about in clumps, apparently uncertain about what to do now.

Miller grabbed his arm. "That dock is not secured. They're not organized well enough for that. Just because no one's shooting at anyone right now doesn't make it safe."

"It's my fault I failed to give them clear orders," Jack said. "I should get out there and clean my mess up."

Miller and Malcolm looked at each other. Malcolm gave another of his signature little head shakes of acceptance.

"That's what you got John here for," Miller said. "Tell him he's got permission to give Hitchborn and Dallemagne orders and send him out to sort it out. He's better qualified for the job anyways."

Jack didn't waste time being offended. Miller was right. Malcolm was best qualified. Anne and Cynthia would not be thrilled about taking orders from someone who'd been a POW the last time they'd seen him, but they would. Surreally although they'd failed to establish a tactical communications network of their own, he could text them an order via the stations network. Having a clear line of sight from the hatch to them, he or Miller could confirm the messages visually. What a horrible mess.

"Malcolm," Jack said, "would you please go sort this out. I want the troops formed up and ready to be assigned their missions ASAP."

"Yes, sir," Malcolm replied without apparent sarcasm. He trotted off towards Cynthia and Anne.

Jack busied himself sending a quick message to them. *"Need to form up and give orders. Follow John Malcolm's orders. Jack."*

He stood up and looked out at them. This got Miller's unhappy attention. Jack ignored him. He watched the women get his message and look his way. He waved. Miller pulled him back out of the open cargo hatch.

"Jack, sir," Miller said not at all his normal laid back self. "I repeat, it is not safe. Kapeche?"

"Really, Miller, I think the responsibility is getting to you," Jack said trying to be reasonable. "I know it's your job to keep me safe, but I've got a job to do too."

"Yes, sir," Miller replied, "but you have to be alive to do it."

"Tell you what," Jack said. "How about you tell me what's happening?"

Miller took a step and looked out the cargo hatch. "Well, Dr. Dallemagne and Missus Hitchborn are having quite the talk with John. Arms waving, heads shaking, some pointing."

Jack stuck his head out to see for himself. "Damn. It was looking like he'd have to sort it out himself after all."

Shots rang out. Miller stepped back. "Take cover! Take cover!"

Jack saw Malcolm's head explode with a spray of gore. Anne was spun around and fell to the deck. Cynthia was already there. Jack hadn't seen her fall. He didn't know if she was hit or not. He had just time enough to see all that before he was yanked back under cover.

It was Miller. He had a solid grip on Jack.

Bedlam broke out. Wild shooting nearby. Had to be Jack's own people returning fire. Some of it at least. Under the deafening clatter he could make out shouting and the sounds of running.

"Stand clear!" Miller yelled. He whacked the emergency close button that was set on the bulkhead nearby. He grabbed Jack and held him in place. After a slow groaning start, the hatch ramp lifted and slammed into place. Miraculously, nobody was caught in it.

"What's happening?" Jack yelled. "We have to do something."

"Jack, we can't do anything useful from here," Miller said.

"Probably just a few snipers or they'd never have let any of us off the ships, but it's not safe for you out there."

"It's not safe out there for anyone. Malcolm's dead. I don't know about Cynthia. Or Anne."

"We can't lose you too."

14: Pushing It Home

Jack was bitterly unhappy.

His incompetence and lack of basic military skills had gotten John Malcolm killed. Ironically, removing the only one of them who actually had real military training at the level they needed. Anne Hitchborn had been wounded. She'd been wearing light body armor. It'd been enough to save her life. It could have been worse. She could have easily killed by a head shot like Malcolm. Most of their rank and file were now from Jefferson, and he needed her leadership.

Personally, he couldn't help feeling relieved Cynthia was unhurt. Having been shot at in the past had left her with hair trigger reflexes.

What really bothered him was that as bad as it had been, he knew they'd been extraordinarily lucky.

He'd taken big chances with all of their lives and managed to bumble through.

A few more mines or rocks at the exit point, or just plain bad luck, and they could have easily lost a ship, or two, or even all three, with everybody on it.

If they'd launched an attack on the outpost first, or simultaneously like at Jefferson, they would have walked into the booby trap the scavengers had. Hell, if the scavengers hadn't been so quick he could be leading his people into that trap right now.

That was to say nothing about that destroyer. If its captain had been a bit more adventurous, or shown a bit more foresight, he could have taken them all easily.

Jack looked around his cabin. They were all taking an hour to clean up and get a little food and drink.

It'd turned out that there'd only been a small team of left behind mercenaries at the docks. At least that's what they thought. There hadn't been much left to interrogate after the massive storm of return fire their attack had resulted in. The docks were a torn up mess. Most of the dozens of casualities they'd taken had been "friendly" fire. Ricochets mostly. Ugly, but "only" a couple of additional fatalities.

Miller seemed to think the sniper's main target had been Jack himself. Said he suspected Jack's death was worth a fortune to who ever managed to deliver it. He thought they'd mistaken Malcolm for Jack because he appeared to be giving orders to Cynthia and Anne, who themselves were obviously officers. He'd seemed like he wanted to say more about behavior in the field, but had bitten his tongue.

Jack appreciated that. He had a long enough laundry list of mistakes that he and his lieutenants had made. He didn't need to add to it.

Long story short, Jack's take away was he'd been lucky yet again.

If this was good luck, he'd hate to see bad luck or even only average luck.

Too bad they had no choice but to carry on to Newton against even greater odds.

They'd be lucky if St. Armand didn't blow them out of the sky. The only thing they had going for them was bluff, and the fact the Battle Group was mainly focused on getting back to the Core. If they could be bothered, they could swat Jack and his ships like flies.

Then they'd have to fight whatever SDF occupation force had been left behind on Newton. It was a safe bet if the SDF hadn't already destroyed everything valuable on Newton that they'd left an occupation force behind.

That force would almost certainly consist in part of trained marines. They would have without doubt rigged a self-destruct to take care of the factory that Jack wanted to capture intact.

Jack didn't know how he was going to deal with any of those problems. He only knew he had to try. Somehow trying as hard as he could, he couldn't believe there was enough luck in the world to see him through this time.

Be that as it may, in a few minutes he had to go out and address his people. He had to tell them what a fine job they'd done today.

He had to tell them he had more work for them in Newton.

He had to sound upbeat about it.

He had made it sound like they could succeed. He couldn't tell them it'd likely get them all killed to no purpose.

Despite whatever he believed himself.

* * *

Bonaparte had had to break cover and make threats. Veiled threats, but still threats, and threatening politically well-connected admirals was not something he liked to do.

At least Captain Warner and the other officers of the destroyer *Slan* were according him a bit more respect. Somebody that could threaten an admiral, their own boss in fact, and get away with it was somebody they didn't want to trifle with.

And they'd been doing that.

They'd been giving him the minimum of co-operation. They'd not only shown no respect, but in fact ridiculed him, albeit in a superficially polite manner. They'd had no idea of the risks they'd been running. They must've felt as if they'd been playing with a grass snake only to discover it was in fact a deadly viper.

Bonaparte was disappointed in himself. Disappointed that he enjoyed the change in attitude as much as he did. It was his job to appear innocuous until he struck with decisive effect. Intimidation of the sort he'd employed with Captain Black was not part of his normal methodology.

Regrettable as his partial unmasking was it was going to make his task here in Newton easier. More importantly, it was going to make his success much more likely.

Left to his own devices, St. Armand would have taken Lieutenant Commander Chidley at face value. St. Armand would have believed Chidley's claim that he'd already destroyed Newton's FTL drive factory.

He'd have left the *Slan* at the coreward jump point to act as his rearguard and buggered off. Buggered off taking his all important marine contingent with him.

Well, he'd still bailed out with the bulk of his Battle Group. An act of rank cowardice in Bonaparte's mind. St. Armand, however, had been insistent he'd dare not allow himself to be caught by the pursuing Beyonders. He was convinced they were mere days behind him.

Bonaparte had no idea where the Beyonders were himself. He'd not fought them and had no idea how much of a threat they were to St. Armand's ships either.

What he did know is that they'd never shown any interest in trying to absorb the large planetary populations of the Federation's colony worlds. They weren't genocidal either according to all the reports he'd seen. So whatever threat they might pose to St. Armand's Battle Group, they didn't pose much of one with regards to the goal Bonaparte had been assigned. His job was to make sure the colony worlds were not a threat to Earth. That they'd be easy to reconquer once the politicians back on the home planet got their shit together.

All rather unfortunate when it came to convincing St. Armand. He couldn't reassure him about the threat his ships faced. It was useless trying to suggest those ships were less important than neutralizing Newton. An admiral was nothing without ships to command. St. Armand wasn't going to risk them, no matter how important the strategic goal.

By the time it'd become clear that Chidley wasn't playing fair ball, St. Armand had already been most of the way to the exit jump point. He wasn't going to turn around and come back. He did send his marines back. Back loaded in shuttles that included their three remaining assault shuttles. Assault shuttles guaranteed to spoil the day of anyone who argued with them. Back to have a very serious conversation with Chidley regards following orders.

The *Slan* had received orders to support the marines. Not to just to guard St. Armand's rear end at the exit point. The *Slan* had no room for the marines' shuttles or heavy gear. It would be possible to jam the marines themselves into her so that none of them need be left behind. Worse come to worse St. Armand had authorized orbital strikes on Newton. Strikes to demolish the FTL factories. Strikes to obliterate any place that might contribute to Newton's redeveloping FTL capability.

It ought to be enough.

**

Ted was enjoying the view from Lieutenant Commander "Bill" Chidley's headquarters bunker. For some exceedingly sarcastic value of "enjoy".

Said view consisted of a huge wall plastered with a multitude of video displays. Ted hadn't realized there were so many surveillance cameras in New Cambridge. He wondered how many were new. How many Chidley's people had placed and how many had already been present, but which he'd failed to notice before.

Chidley himself wandered up to Ted's side and looked at the screens for a few moments before speaking. "Let me guess," he said, "you're wondering if your city was always under this degree of surveillance."

Ted looked at Chidley with sharp annoyance. The man wasn't playing at being a clown any more. That ought to have been a relief. Given how he kept springing unpleasant surprises on Ted, Ted wasn't feeling it.

Chidley's smile fell short of a smirk. "Thought so. Proving useful right now. Also, if it's any reassurance I had half of these cameras put up since I arrived. The other half were mostly for private security. Before I arrived nobody would have able to override the security codes. The power has always been there. It's very unlikely anybody was abusing it."

"It's good to hear that," Ted admitted. "Have to confess I still find it disconcerting."

"Because it's a blow to your pride that you missed the existence of an omnipresent surveillance network in your own backyard?" Chidley asked. "Or because it's showing us a lot of ugly, heavily armed marines tearing your hometown apart looking for you."

Ted sighed. He could see why Chidley played the clown. Man was scary when he let the mask down. "Both," he admitted, "but we both know they're not only looking for me. They're looking for anyone connected to FTL production and the actual machinery too."

"Maybe," Chidley replied. "They haven't actually checked out the factory yet. It's a ways out of town. I don't think they've got much in the way of intelligence on the situation here. They didn't get any from me. I'd have had thought there was an SDF spy network here, but if so I guess their reports didn't get shared with those boys there."

"You think they're afraid of spreading out?"

"I think they're exercising good tactical judgment in keeping their search teams within supporting distance of each other and their main body," Chidley said.

Ted looked at one heavily armed marine squad breaking down a door. He was incredulous. "They're afraid we'll attack them?" he asked to clarify.

"Yes they are," Chidley confirmed. "And they should be. Me and you, we know how weak we are. We know the few troops we have aren't as well trained or armed as those marines. The marines don't know that. They have no idea what they're facing. It's only basic prudence to assume the worst."

"Makes for slow progress."

"But sure."

"St. Armand's main body has already left the system."

"True. Thought you'd be happier about that."

"I think these marines and that destroyer lingering between here and the coreward jump point are likely enough to do for us. At least given time. How long do you think they intend to spend here?"

"St. Armand likely thought the same. He likely ordered them to stay long enough to finish the job."

"That's cold. If St. Armand didn't think the Beyonders were close behind him he'd not have left in the first place. They'll follow orders like that?"

"The marines will. The destroyer's commander I think he'll try to look like he's followed orders."

Ted mulled that. "They'll continue to search even if stranded? Do the Beyonder's have troops they can land to fight them?"

"Yes, and no. Marines follow orders. Do or die. Hurrah. The Beyonders are spacers and stationers and mostly civilians. Probably didn't have many troops to start with. After the campaign just passed, probably don't have any."

"So somehow we have to defeat those marines ourselves?"

"Well, I'm kind of hoping your boy Jack Black will turn up in time with enough to bail us out."

Ted bit his lip and looked at a screen showing a dispersed formation of marines walking down an empty street. "Captain Black is more an ally than an employee. Last we talked, our main concern was to keep the FTL transports in this sector intact. Haven't heard anything for months. Even if he figured out we needed help here, I'm not sure how he could. He'd need to raise troops and somehow transport them here, despite both the Beyonders and the SDF."

"Maybe. I suspect between them your Dr. Dallemagne and Captain Black have a bit more strategic insight than you're giving them credit for. I think if they can they'll come."

"I don't even know if they're still alive," Ted said bleakly. He'd always been fond of Cynthia, and even Black had started to grow on him. "Your former employer's already tried to assassinate Black once."

"It's an uncertain world."

"So we just hang on and hope for a miracle?"

"Sure. The unexpected happens all the time. All we can do hang in and give Lady Luck a chance to favor us."

"Maybe it's time to develop religion."

Chidley chuckled.

15: Death Ground

They came over the horizon, flying lower than any spaceship in an atmosphere had a right to. Just in time to see the last of a series of large explosions. Pillars of smoke and even flame had started to climb to the sky along a line of locations. The locations formerly occupied by what had been the SDF marines' shuttles.

"They had them lined up right next to each other in pretty lines like on a parade ground," came Miller's voice in his earphones. "Must have been worried more about saboteurs than an air strike."

Jack just nodded. Miller was crouched right next to him in the open cargo bay door of *The Bird of Profit*. He could see the *Frontier Falcon* no more than a hundred meters from them on a parallel course. A figure in its open cargo hatch waved at them. Damn Cynthia, was she enjoying this?

Jack loved Cynthia, he couldn't deny that any longer, but right now he was missing Anne Hitchborn. Anne and the *Prosperity's Child*, both of whom had died in a ball of light on entry into Newton system. Died along with her troops and a crew he'd known and been fond of.

Their luck had failed them for once.

Fortunately, the "prudence" of who ever was commanding St.

Armand's rearguard destroyer was proving more reliable. If that destroyer had been supporting the marines occupying New Cambridge the way it should have Jack's three starfighters would never had been allowed to make the strike they had just now. Even less would have Jack with his two freighters full of troops been allowed anywhere near the place. But it'd kept loitering half way out to the coreward jump point and declined to interfere.

Jack's ships plunged down towards the smoke. They needed to get down and get their troops out and under cover. They needed to do that before the marines got over their momentary surprise. Reacted and brought whatever heavy weapons they had left to bear.

They could hope the starfighter strike had taken out all those weapons, but realistically nobody's luck was that good.

Frontier Falcon got down a fraction faster. Closer to the shuttle wreckage and the utility buildings the enemy were occupying too. His heart in his mouth, Jack watched Cynthia leap out even before the ship was fully down and her troops follow in a torrent.

Good, they needed to do this quick. Before any remaining heavy weapons opened up and above all before the dispersed marine search teams were able to return to defend their base. They'd got that much intelligence from Ted Smith at Chidley's HQ as they'd approached Newton. It'd given them the opening for this plan they were following. They'd not much chance of taking on the entire marine contingent at one-to-one odds. Instead, they'd take them piecemeal. Strike straight at their heart. Overwhelm the guard detachment at their base. Deal with the remaining scattered units in detail. But timing was everything. They had to be quick.

And *The Bird of Profit* grounded just behind and to the side of the *Frontier Falcon*. They were going to having a longer run for cover. Jack's leading team swung out into the cargo hatch and started to jump out. They'd removed the ramps for speed of egress. Blindingly bright blaster bolts greeted them.

Men ignited and fell in smoking heaps.

The charge faltered.

Jack started to move. He had to get out there and rally them.

Somebody grabbed him and yanked off of his feet. A bolt passed close by. It blinded him briefly. He saw stars and spots as he lay in the protection of the ship's hull at the hatch's edge. His face where it wasn't covered by his goggles felt sun burned. What'd happened?

"Sorry, Sir," Miller said. Apparently it was Miller who'd pulled him back out of the blaster fire still streaming in the open cargo hatch. "But I'd rather you didn't commit suicide right now."

"We can't stay here."

"That's a crew operated medium anti-personnel blaster cannon. It can stop any number of charging light infantry," Miller replied. "Given access to city power to charge their energy packs they can fire all day and all night. Charge into that and you're committing suicide. You and anyone dumb enough to follow you."

"We're pinned down?"

"Yes, sir," Miller answered. "Until you figure out a better plan."

"Damn."

"Yes, sir."

* * *

They were pinned down.

Cynthia had designated Kathy Collins as her "radio person". In the current circumstances, that meant Kathy was using Cynthia's Newtonian personal communicator via the city network to talk to the ships and Jack. They were both hugging the tarmac of the space port with only a large hunk of shuttle hull for cover as small arms fire and blaster bolts filled the air all around them.

Large as it was the hunk of destroyed shuttle didn't seem large enough for the two of them. Cynthia was just occasionally popping out to fire off quick shots to keep the opposing marines honest. She'd not have been doing that much if not for the need to set an example for the men and women hidden behind bits of wreckage all around her.

It wasn't safe.

She'd seen what they were facing before going to ground.

They were facing not one, but two, crew operated blasters dug into heavy bunkers with only a tiny firing slit vulnerable. Th marines had roofed their bunkers with large slabs of concrete. The starfighters, even if they'd dared a strike this close to their own people, weren't going to be able to destroy or even neutralize those strongpoints from the air.

Given the urgency of the situation she'd have dared a charge straight at one bunker hoping that someone got close enough to chuck a grenade straight through the firing slit. She'd have accepted a good chance of being killed herself and the certainty many of her people would be. It would have been costly, but with a little luck it might have worked.

Against two of the bunkers? No way. It'd be pure suicide.

She'd reported the situation via Kathy to Jack. She needed help.

Jack had replied that he was pinned down too, but that she should hold tight and not do anything rash.

She hoped that meant he had a plan.

Couldn't imagine what it might be.

* * *

"So," Jack asked Miller, "what would the marines do in a bind like this?"

The bind being that they were pinned down unable to exit *The Bird of Profit*, attack, and take out the SDF marine's base in New Cambridge. Before said marines pulled in all their teams dispersed throughout the city and counterattacked. Worse, with Cynthia's unit pinned down on the tarmac itself they could not even pull out and try something else.

"Well," Miller replied, "usually we didn't have to deal with folks that had blaster cannons and knew how to dig them in."

"Surely you must have trained for the possibility?"

"Yeah, but we had enough real problems without worrying about more than ticking off the boxes in the training programs HQ dreamed up."

"Try and remember. Those aren't spitballs flying by and we don't have much time."

"Sorry, sir." Miller was more the perplexed student than the tough marine. He screwed his face up in concentration. "If we hadn't got ourselves stuck so close in and we had a capital ship we'd call in an orbital strike. That was always the easiest and least costly thing to do."

"No capital ship."

"I know. But most normal commanders wouldn't have us on the ground without having secured the space surrounding the planet first."

Jack ignored the implied criticism. "Next idea."

"If we had assault shuttles like a marine unit, some would lay down suppressive fire while others dropped commandos or combat engineers on the top of the bunkers to assault them from close in where the cannon can't bear."

"No assault shuttles. The freighters aren't nimble enough to pretend. We're not commandos or engineers."

"Too bad. We can move this ship, right?"

"*The Bird of Profit* can withdraw. So could the *Falcon*."

"But we'd have to leave Dr. Dallemagne and her people behind," Miller finished Jack's thought.

"They're half our already limited strength. Sacrificing ther wouldn't buy us anything."

"It'd be an improvement if we exited the ship through the hatches on the other side and could form up dispersed under cover."

"That sounds like a good idea."

"Yeah, it'd take longer before we were all killed charging them."

"Is there no way we can take them?"

"Sure get close enough to put grenades through the firing slits. We could do it from here if we had grenade launchers. Only we don't 'cause who needs them on a ship or station."

"Anything else we don't have that'd save the day?"

"If we could run twice as fast, had reflexes twice as good, and could see twice as well, we could just dodge right through their fire." Miller gave Jack a lop-sided grin. It was gallows humor. "And if your Aunt had..."

"Wait!" Jack said. He'd almost forgotten about Dr. Caligari who'd stuck a magic tooth and some other things in his skull not too many kilometers from here. Would it make him fast enough to dodge blaster bolts? Not charging through the cargo hatch they were slumped by. It was too small of an area that the enemy had zeroed in on and were watching. But just maybe if he started from cover somewhere else on the ship. His arm and throwing accuracy should be improved too. Maybe he'd not have to get that close. Too bad there were two of them, but maybe if he managed to take care of one, Miller and Cynthia could manage the other one on their own. Hell, it was a plan.

Jack explained to Miller.

Miller listened with an expression on the grim side of blank. "Helluva plan," he said when Jack finished. "So you'll sneak out the starboard EVA airlock. Me and the rest of the boys we'll exit via the starboard cargo hatch, spread out and wait. You'll go first and we'll follow to take advantage of your distraction. Cynthia's folk will do what they can. Got that right?"

"Yep. Three different sets of targets, one of them fast and hard to see ought to confuse those cannon. Somebody should make it. Most of us with some luck."

"Hope that special sauce is real special, Jack." He paused and stuck out his hand. "Good luck. It's been a pleasure working with you."

They shook. Jack took off through the docking bay airlock down the main passage way forward to the EVA airlock. He opened the hatch and cast his mind back to Dr. Caligari.

What was the trigger? Caligari's face. Not hard to remember. Plus supper. Any supper in particular? He visualized Caligari peering at him over steak and potatoes. A hazy transparent menu appeared in his field of view. Jack thought *"Activate Supercharged State Regular Lead Time."*

Count down numbers appeared. As they diminished, his sight seemed to sharpen. His mood became euphoric. He felt like he'd drank a half dozen cups of coffee and could bench press a cow. He wondered if the stuff was addictive.

Count down finished, he jumped to the tarmac. Paused to get orientated. Oddly, the blaster bolts seemed to be moving more slowly. Freaky.

There were two pairs of bright green numbers with a colon between them counting up in one corner of his vision. Handy indicator of how long before he crashed, he guessed.

No time like now.

Both streams of bolts were sweeping to his left. He sprang out of cover and ran like hell for the right-hand bunker only tens of meters away, but it'd been too far before.

As slow as the blasters bolts were, and as slow as where they were aimed moved, Jack barely made it half way to the nearest bunker before they shifted back towards him. He couldn't tell if the enemy gunners saw him or were just following a pattern. The whole world seemed brighter, the colors more vivid, the edges of things sharper than usual. He wondered what the precise psychological effects of whatever it was he had in his veins were.

In any event, best not be standing up when those blaster bolts came his way. Jack dived for the tarmac, aiming behind a chunk of shuttle hull barely a meter square. It was more like flying than falling. The time dilation was the oddest sensation Jack had ever had. He felt himself plow into the ground as if he was a distant observer. Couldn't help thinking it was going to hurt once he returned to normal.

He tried to glance behind him. It took forever, but his sight coming to bear he could see Miller's men lumbering out from behind *The Bird of Profit*. Some people towards where Cynthia was seemed to be lackadaisically gathering in the view.

Blaster bolts passed over head, missing him by whole tens of centimeters.

He shifted his view back forward towards the bunker slit he was targeting. The closer blaster fire moved to his right. The other fire remained concentrated far to his left. He forced himself up. He dug his feet in and forced himself to run.

By the time the stream of fire coming from his target started to shift back his way, he was already well within ten meters of the firing slit from which it was emerging.

He could see it clearly. It was well defined in his vision. He had no doubt he could slam dunk a grenade into it. He grabbed a grenade from his webbing, pulled the pin and pitched the thing into the slit the same way he'd have tried to strike a batter out as a boy playing baseball. Caligari's crap was strong stuff because he knew this was life and death, yet it felt more like a ballgame on a lazy summer's afternoon.

Better hit the deck before the blaster bolts found him.

He had no idea just how close those bolts came. He couldn't see them. He was facing down as they passed by. He was still in the air and he felt the heat of their passage. Must have been close. Must be more careful.

A flash and he raised his sight to see debris being blown out of the firing slit mere meters in front of him. It stopped producing blaster bolts.

One down, one to go. The numbers in his vision were still only single digits but had turned yellow. Not good.

The marine gunners in the other bunker must have seen him. Their stream of death was moving in his direction. They were depressing their aim. Meant their bolts weren't reaching much beyond Jack. Meant they were tearing up the ground in a cloud of little explosions, moving his way. He'd not be able to hug the ground and let them go over him this time.

He timed it carefully and jumped into the air as the deadly stream passed. Just like skipping rope, except for the little bits of burning hot concrete he was pelted with.

He landed hard and stumbled. It cost time.

A few more meters and he'd have a good shot at the second slit. The blaster fire had already started to shift back his way. They were alert, and he was too close. Didn't think the same stupid jump out of the way trick would work twice. Jack ran a few more meters and realized he was out of time. Still too far, but maybe he could make the shot.

He grabbed and pulled the pin from another grenade.

He jumped towards the slit and threw the grenade all in one motion.

He hit the ground face first, but despite the pain and the danger raised his head to see what had happened. His grenade bounced off the edge of the slit, came to rest just outside it and exploded. A piece of shrapnel whizzed by one ear.

A blaster bolt burned by the other ear before burning along the back of one of his buttocks. Damned, that hurt.

Momentarily the fire was falling to one side. He had to try once more. The numbers on the edge of his vision were turning orange. He wobbled to his feet and tried to run forward.

He tripped on something.

In his mind altered state he had time to watch the ground coming straight at his unprotected face.

Blinding pain, then all went dark.

16: A Battle Fought

Bonaparte watched the bridge's view screens in disgust.

The *Slan* was hundreds of millions of kilometers, many light minutes, away from the planet Newton most of the way to the coreward jump point.

The images they were watching were of events that had happened over a quarter hour ago. Even the *Slan*'s powerful telescopes and corrective optics couldn't make the pictures perfect. They were grainy, at a not great angle, and some atmospheric haze and shift remained to further degrade them. Nevertheless, what they showed was clear.

The shuttles that were supposed to ferry the marine contingent back to the *Slan* once their mission was completed had been destroyed. All that remained of them was wreckage and pillars of smoke rising from the tarmac of New Cambridge's space port.

"Weapons, ready a pair of missiles for a strike on the site of the FTL factory," Captain Warner was saying. "Navigator lay in a best time course to the coreward jump point."

Bonaparte had all sorts of recriminations he could have had made with the Captain, but it was past pointless.

Once the Captain had made it clear he wouldn't support the

marines from orbit for fear of being caught there by pursuing Beyonders he'd realized he had no leverage. The Captain was borderline defying St. Armand himself. He must believe he was covered politically. That or he simply was that afraid.

Bonaparte had objected to the Captain's unwillingness to close with and occupy the attention of the Battlehawks the rebels had somehow obtained. Obtained and just used against the marines. He'd done so most mildly and for the record.

The Captain had asserted they couldn't be sure the Battlehawks weren't carrying ship killers, and that the *Slan* was basically out of anti-missile missiles.

Bonaparte believed he simply wasn't willing to take any chance of being caught too far away from the jump point. He wondered if the Captain would have been willing to meet the marine shuttles part way to Newton if they'd survived. He suspected not.

It did no good to raise the issue.

"Captain," the comms officer said. "We've lost contact with the expeditionary force HQ."

"Copy, comms," Captain Warner answered.

"Did they manage to get positive conformation of the location of the FTL manufacturing machinery before we lost contact?" Bonaparte asked. He knew they hadn't. He wanted it on the record.

"No," Warner replied. "Didn't find any of the personnel either. Not even a janitor, let alone a tech."

Daring of him to admit it. They both knew it suggested th Newtonians had managed to evacuate and that the Captain's long distance missile strike was a pointless act of butt covering vandalism.

Bonaparte suppressed the urge to sigh. This show was all over except for the closing music. He'd remain on the bridge for appearances' sake. Given the likely collapse of interstellar trade with the sector, it could be months or even years before they learned for certain what had happened here. Didn't mean he couldn't guess. Likely they'd failed completely. It was time to move on.

It was time to start thinking about what he'd do once they were back in the Solar System.

Likely a political dogfight of the first order going on. He'd be drawn into that. It was unavoidable.

Better start plotting for contingencies. Better start working on bug out and retirement plans too.

* * *

Jack woke up rather slowly. He was distantly aware that everything hurt. Must be drugs. Seemed everything was there to hurt did hurt. Good. Seemed he was still alive to hurt. Even better.

His nose was stuffed with cotton. He was breathing through his mouth, which had a tube stuck in it. His face felt like it'd had a close encounter with an industrial sized cheese grater. His back felt like a sunburned pincushion. Something had bitten him hard on one half of his butt.

Altogether he didn't feel bad at all for a man that ought to be dead.

The ache in his joints and the soreness in his muscles hardly registered at all.

He was feeling quite amazed and pretty pleased with life.

He opened his eyes to see dust motes dancing in the summer sunshine between them and the ceiling. A hospital ceiling going by the sounds reaching his ears. They still worked, which after all the explosions and other noises they'd been subjected to was a minor miracle.

He couldn't smell anything. Usually he identified hospitals and sick bays by their smell mostly, all that disinfectant and medicine.

"He should be waking up soon," a voice said nearby. He didn't recognize the voice. It had a professional bed side manner tone to it. Another hint he was in a hospital.

He moved his head to look around. The tube in his mouth and the pain in his neck muscles didn't help, but he managed. He saw a young man in hospital scrubs talking to Cynthia and Ted Smith.

He tried to say "hello". It didn't come out that way around the tube. Sounded more like "Ow, ow, oh". Did get their attention.

A nurse moved into view. "Here, love, I'll just remove that breathing tube. You can breathe on your own, right?"

Jack nodded the best he could.

"Okay, just stay still." It stung a bit as she pulled the tape holding the tube off of his face. Apparently he hadn't shaved recently. Tube scraped some as she removed it. It was good to have it gone.

"Hi. What's happening?" he asked Cynthia and Ted, who were now looking his way.

They both moved closer, brushing past the doctor.

"You're okay," Cynthia said. "We'll have you out of here in no time." The doctor behind her nodded, not too happily at that. A story there.

"The Feds are gone. We won. The Beyonders aren't here yet," Ted said. "They hit the FTL drive factory. Flattened that whole section of town. We got all the machinery out and most of the people. Losses were nowhere as bad as they could have been." He glanced at the doctor with that.

The doctor grimaced. "Could have been much worse. We'r still swamped as it is." He looked at Jack. "Going to be sending you home much sooner than I'd have liked. We need your bed."

Cynthia placed a hand on his shoulder. "We'll take good care of him, doctor," she said.

Ted kept his hands in his pockets, but he beamed at Jack. "Yes, Jack's done his bit. He'd going to get a long vacation before we put him back to work."

"Great," the Doctor said, moving around to the other side of Jack's bed and beginning to fiddle with his IV. "He's going back to sleep right now. He needs the rest. Come back tomorrow with a gurney or stretcher and your own nurse and I'll let you keep him."

It was great, Jack thought as he drifted away. He'd changed the universe for the better. He'd survived doing so. Been the biggest adventure of his life. He figured it'd be his last. He was going to sleep now.

He was going to wake up and have a normal life from now on.

He was going to stop risking it.

It was a plan.

**

Cynthia surveyed the interior of the New Cambridge Spaceport warehouse they'd been keeping their SDF marine POWs in.

The marines were dispersed in small groups. They had mostly crates and boxes for furniture to sit on or play cards on or use as tables. Blankets, mattresses, and gym padding constituted their beds. A few of them were lightly wounded. The worse wounded were in hospitals, but there weren't that many of them.

It wasn't ideal, but the Newtonians under Cynthia's direction were doing their best. Cynthia had just come from the hospital

Jack was in. It was crowded, the hallways were full, and many of the more lightly injured were still waiting to be taken care of. The staff was falling over from lack of sleep. Cynthia herself had only had a couple of hours of it last night. She was light headed and just plain slow witted. Her eyeballs were gritty and itchy.

Yesterday had been demanding. She'd been battered badly. Physically, but also emotionally. The pain of losing Anne. Th adrenaline spike of charging into that blaster fire, which had been followed by bleak despair when they'd been pinned down.

Only training and experience had allowed her to move when Jack charged like some sort of humanoid antelope into the face of the fire of those two dug in blasters. She'd been astounded when somehow he'd survived the first salvos. Her body had moved on auto-pilot and her people had followed her just as automatically.

She'd felt elation when the first bunker had been silenced. It'd been a kick in the gut when Jack had fallen in front of the second one.

By that time both hers and Miller's people were within a grenade's throw of that bunker. Nobody would ever know exactly how many of the grenades they'd thrown had made their way through its firing slit. Even less would they know who had thrown them. But some made it, and they finished that second bunker off. She'd found out then just how ugly and satisfying revenge could feel.

It'd been a feeling of retribution well flavored with alarm. Many of the grenades thrown at the second bunker had fallen short and Jack's body had been caught at the edge of the cloud of shrapnel produced.

Turned out hope and relief could be painful. Who'd have thought. She'd almost cried when she'd reached Jack and found him throughly battered but still breathing. She would have if she'd had time for it.

She hadn't. Fortunately, Miller was there to handle the mopping of the marines. She'd taken charge of getting Jack on a makeshift stretcher and to a hospital.

Yes, it had been quite the emotional roller coaster, and it'd left her exhausted in a way she'd yet to recover from. Body and mind, she needed rest.

First things first.

The marines were passive and disciplined.

They were also lacking any officers. They'd been short in the first place. All of those remaining had been at an orders group in their HQ in one of the assault shuttles when it had been blown up.

They didn't feel broken or depressed, though. They didn't feel defeated.

They all knew they didn't have a ride home anymore, but Cynthia would feel a lot better once she managed to disperse them all into small groups and individuals spread across the whole planet.

It was a job the Newtonian volunteers, mostly police and planetary militia, seemed to be performing well. She really hadn't had much to actually do. Damned if she'd go away and sleep until the job was finished though. It was too important to finish neutralizing the threat a body of trained soldiers like this had the potential to be.

Watching her people march small groups off, she knew in a few hours she'd get the sleep she needed. Miller, Ted, and Chidley were handling the other clean up tasks. Ted seemed to be in charge so far, but she sensed he'd try to hand over to Miller or Chidley as soon as he could. Their organization was just too thin.

She expected Ted would try to get her to organize a new armed forces, here on Newton or perhaps as an armed wing of Ad Astra. She didn't know. All she knew was her days of fighting were over. He was going to have to make do with Miller and Chidley or someone else.

She missed Anne Hitchborn and Jackson bitterly. Not just because they should be here handling this, but as people. One made friends fast under stress. She hurt thinking of them and a dozen other people she'd got to know, and love, and then lost over the past months.

No, she had a lot of thinking to do and decisions to make. Best not to make them while tired and stressed out.

But one thing she knew; she'd had enough of combat and being shot at.

An hour or two and she'd go to sleep until tomorrow.

Tomorrow she'd collect Jack and figure out what to do with the rest of her life.

The one she was ever so lucky to have.

17: Amidst the Debris

Ted was taking the time to enjoy a meal for a change. As always, the Faculty Club of the University of Newton at New Cambridge served excellent food. That despite having a skeleton staff that had only recently returned. They were ramping back up after having evacuated the city like all other non-essential personnel. He was having his usual roast beef and baked potato with seasonal greens. It was nice that some things at least remained constant.

It was nice not to be rushed for a change. His former de facto boss, Ted wasn't sure what their current relationship was, Michael Blake shared the meal in silence with him. They had the time to eat and talk later. At least despite all the changes, Michael remained a friend.

Ted knew he had a lot of work to do. He knew that Epsilon Sector's politics and economy were going to be in flux for some time, likely years, many months at the very least. Both the Beyonders and the Federation remained enigmas. He knew he'd continue to be a key figure in Newton's and probably the sector's response to the dramatic events of the last couple of years.

The crisis had passed though. The dust might not settle for years, but Ted's life for one was going to return to something approximating normality. It was an immense relief. They'd not only survived, they'd come out more or less on top and better off. It had cost. It would continue to cost, but Ted felt good about the future. He intended to savor that feeling as long as he could.

"So the storm has passed?" Michael asked.

"Believe so," Ted answered, sipping a little of his strong red wine. "That Beyonder carrier just breezed through the system, barely bothering to message a hello."

"Can they keep the Federation in check?"

"Not sure. They said they were just a reconnaissance in force. I think they're just following St. Armand to see how far he's going to retreat."

"What do you think?"

"I think the St. Armand and the rest of the SDF are going to run all the way back to Earth and then get tied up in politics. Don't know if there'll be open revolution, but I do think there's going to be turmoil for years to come. I think they're going to be much too busy with their own problems to be giving us any for years to come."

"And the Beyonders?"

"Same thing really once they've determined they don't need to worry about the Federation any more. They've got a lot of rebuilding to do."

"So they're not going to try to take charge of our local space?"

"Don't seem to have any plans to. The fellow in charge of their task force said he was sure they'd want to send an ambassador eventually and that they'd like to trade. He also said it could be months or longer before any embassy or trading mission arrived. Seems like they've got a great deal to keep them busy closer to home."

"So a complete economic and power vacuum?"

"Don't think there's much doubt that Jack and Ad Astra are going to filling the economic vacuum and even some of the political and military one further out."

"Black is well disposed to us?"

"He is. Dr. Dallemagne will help keep that so, I believe."

"A bit of a sacrifice?"

"Not at all. She was feeling cramped here. They went through a lot together. There's genuine affection there."

Michael made an amused sound that was not quite a chuckle.

"A happy ending. Who'd have thought after this all?"

"We worked hard for it. People died and bled for our happy ending."

"I understand. Honestly, Ted, I do. I appreciate what you and the others have done for us. So does the rest of Newton's leadership. They were a long time coming to it, but recent events have been an unambiguous wake up call."

"Just doing my job."

"And what a job it was. We asked more than we knew. We still need you. We'll try to be more reasonable in the future. You have my personal promise on that."

"Need me for what?"

"As the head of a new more public much better funded CHSG for one. As our representative on Ad Astra's board and therefore in the sector in general. Just temporarily as head of the reconstruction committee. It's essential we get our FTL production back up and running."

"That's three full-time jobs. By the way we're going to have to start building ships as well as drives despite not having an adequate manufacturing base for it."

"You're absolutely the best person for each of those jobs. You can delegate. You can have whatever resources you need. You have authority to negotiate whatever partnerships you need to with New Lustania and Jefferson to get the needed people and resources."

"That's great," Ted replied. "I'm going to start finding time to spend with my family regardless. Understood?"

"Yes, we understand. We're in this long term. We need you happy and working in a sustainable way."

"Going to bring Chidley in on the FTL production side. You can live with that?"

"We can."

"Mike is not going to be happy. My mother, to put it very mildly, is annoyed."

"We'll have it made clear from all quarters that they need to be supportive."

Ted sighed. "Sounds close to too good to be true."

"Going to be a lot of hard work. You're not afraid of that. It's a new world. Promising one in many ways and you're going to be in on the ground floor of building it. Tell me you're not happy about that."

Ted considered it. "You're right, I'm going to enjoy this."

"Told you so."

***

Things were changing on Newton. Time would tell how and by how much. It didn't really matter to Cynthia. She wouldn't say she didn't care, but it wasn't going to stop her from doing what she wanted to. She didn't expect she'd be spending much time on the planet anyways. When she was she'd hope to visit family and the friends of her youth, but how that went was as much up to them as to her.

She'd fought, made new friends, and seen some of them die, in other places. Her heart and her future lay in places other than Newton now.

She was in New Cambridge. She could have spent the night in her old room in her parent's place. They still kept it open for her. She hadn't. Her family wouldn't have understood her desperate need for sleep. They wouldn't have understood that even while awake she needed down time to absorb the traumatic events she'd been part of. They certainly wouldn't have understood that the cabin she now occupied on the *Frontier Falcon* felt more like home than the place she'd grown up in.

But it did.

Felt far more like her future too.

She was tired, and frankly sick, of being first a spy and then a soldier too. She was done with both.

History retained its interest. Being an academic did not. Less so being one on Newton. She'd didn't doubt they'd learn to be more open minded in the coming years. She doubted they'd become so quickly enough for her taste.

Better to make a clean break.

She'd changed. So had Jack. She'd liked the man well enough when she'd first met. Couldn't accuse him of not stepping up to the plate. She'd felt that way despite knowing her family would never find him suitable. She'd liked him, a lot, despite wondering if she could ever hope to have an interesting conversation with him on the topics dearest to her heart. Frankly, she'd also been concerned for both his life expectancy and his hopes of staying out of bankruptcy.

She rather hated herself for such pragmatic feelings, but she'd had them.

Well the hell with her family. Amusing given that he was now both rich and powerful controlling most of the sector's FTL transports, they might just find it in their snobbish hearts to accept him. Albeit, somewhat grudgingly. No, the hell with them. She'd not have him have to put up with that. He would, but he shouldn't have to. Too bad he was too nice to be condescending right back at them.

Jack himself had surprised her with his willingness to listen to her talk about anything, and the clear common sense he applied to what he heard. He'd never have all the dates she did memorized, and it was too late to expect him to learn much of the math she used in her cliometric studies, but she could share her thoughts with him. Icing on the cake, but a welcome development.

As for getting himself killed, or going bankrupt, he'd done a fine job avoiding the first and the second hardly seemed likely anymore. He'd become a man any woman in the sector be delighted to have.

She had first dibs though, and she intended to call them.

* * *

Jack was standing in his favorite place at his favorite time of day.

He was on the *Meal Ticket*, standing in its open cargo hatch watching the sun come up over New Cambridge's space port. In less than an hour he'd be taking off with Cynthia. They'd be bound for El Dorado.

"I still can't believe we all missed an FTL capable ship," Cynthia said, coming up behind him. She wrapped her arm around him, and he did likewise with her. They snuggled side by side leaning into each other watching the sky mellow from dark blue to a lighter blue tinged with pink. The body warmth felt good in the cool morning air.

Jack replied in good time. "Turns out Moe is quite the hand at legerdemain. Stuck her in a small warehouse under a pile of crates labeled as spare machinery parts waiting to be shipped to Jefferson. Somehow convinced someone to lose the port records. Left with everyone who knew what had happened except for Terry's Dad, who was in charge of the warehouse's security."

"Amazing he found time for all that."

"Scary. This is the man who's basically running Ad Astra for us."

"We can trust him. Practically we've no choice we have to delegate. How did you and Ted manage to forget her?"

"We were kind of busy as you might remember. I'm not sure myself. Didn't really think about it, I imagine I just assumed the SDF must have confiscated her."

"We've left a lot of loose ends just concentrating on what was most urgent, haven't we?"

"Yes, dear, we have, but we're going to have a honeymoon just the same. We wait until we've got free time and it'll never happen."

"So saving the galaxy will just have to go on the backburner?"

Jack grinned at the woman who'd agreed to become his wife. It'd be days, maybe forever, before he came down from the euphoria of Cynthia's having said "yes". "I think saving one galaxy once in one lifetime meets our quota."

"Maybe. You do know they're not going to leave us alone? And Ad Astra is going to be more than just a shipping company. No Feds to protect us, we're going to need our own soldiers and our own fighting ships. Don't think we'll be able to keep a near monopoly either."

"Like you said, we're going to have to delegate, basically just guide strategy and arbitrate between people," Jack answered.

"Well Moe will handle the business ends of things. I think he's got a feel for the local scene on Jefferson now too."

"Going to miss Anne."

"True, and Jackson too, but Miller and the other ex-marines can handle setting up a proper security force."

Jack nodded. "You said you were sick of being a soldier and a spy that you wanted to retire, write history and raise our kids."

"I did. I don't mind helping you, but I don't want the front line responsibility where I don't get time for, or to prioritize, my family," Cynthia answered.

Jack looked towards the horizon the sun had just cleared. "I hear you. Spent my career in a job that wasn't good for family life. I can't help wondering how things are going back on New Idaho, but even if we get to visit sometime, everyone I knew is getting old. They'll have grown up kids I never knew."

"We still have time to build ourselves family here."

"Forgive me, but right now we don't have an intelligence branch of our own. I think it's going to be essential we have one."

"I'll try to get something set up, but it's temporary, Jack," Cynthia replied. "I repeat temporary. You hear me?"

"Loud and clear," Jack confirmed. "It's tricky, but we do have candidates to replace you. Mr. Avarim, Miriam, and Miss Wong all come to mind."

"Anne Landes might be convinced."

"Really," Jack said. "I thought she was set on returning to Federation territory. Anyway if she did sign on with us, wouldn't she be best suited for heading up our armed escort branch?"

"Nobody really even knows if there's actually a Federation to return to. Earth is still there, but Anne was a mid-worlder. Think she'd be good at anything we gave her to do if we can convince her to stay."

"So is this going to be a honeymoon trip or a recruiting trip?"

Cynthia sighed and gripped Jack harder. "A bit of both, but I promise you I'll make you take it easy if you make me take it easy."

Jack laughed. "Deal. I'd better go inspect the old girl for lift off."

"Let's do it together."

If you enjoyed this novel, please leave a review!

To be notified of future releases visit:
http://www.napoleonsims.com/publishing

Printed in Great Britain
by Amazon